MAYHEM

MAYHEM

ESTELLE LAURE

WEDNESDAY BOOKS
NEW YORK

This is a work of fiction. All of the characters, organizations, and events portrayed in this novel are either products of the author's imagination or are used fictitiously.

First published in the United States by Wednesday Books, an imprint of St. Martin's Publishing Group

www.wednesdaybooks.com

Designed by Anna Gorovoy

Library of Congress Cataloging-in-Publication Data

Names: Laure, Estelle, author.
Title: Mayhem / Estelle Laure.
Description: First edition. | New York : Wednesday Books, 2020.
Identifiers: LCCN 2020005578 | ISBN 9781250297938 (hardcover) | ISBN 9781250297952 (ebook)
Subjects: CYAC: Magic—Fiction. | Fate and fatalism—Fiction. | Wife abuse—Fiction. | Family life—California—Fiction. | California—History—20th century—Fiction.
Classification: LCC PZ7.1.L38 May 2020 | DDC [Fic]—dc23
LC record available at https://lccn.loc.gov/2020005578

Our books may be purchased in bulk for promotional, educational, or business use. Please contact your local bookseller or the Macmillan Corporate and Premium Sales Department at 1-800-221-7945, extension 5442, or by email at MacmillanSpecialMarkets@macmillan.com.

First Edition: 2020

10 9 8 7 6 5 4 3 2 1

Some of the thematic material in *Mayhem* hinges on domestic and child abuse, and violence. Additionally, the book includes serial kidnapping, drug use, murder, and a suicide (not depicted). For a more detailed description of sensitive content, please visit estellelaure.com/mayhem.

For my brother Christophe, my truthkeeper, my witness, and my best friend

When I dare to be powerful . . . it becomes less and less important whether I am afraid.

—*Audre Lorde*

PART ONE

Brayburn lady coming for you

ONE
ROXY BRAYBURN AND A BROKEN HEART

1974

Dear Mama,

Losing Lucas has embittered me to the world, to every couple on the beach, Elle, Santa Maria, and even you. You've had twenty years with Daddy. Why didn't I get that with mine? I expected to live with Lucas and Mayhem and maybe a whole bunch of babies for the rest of my life. But then Lucas jumped off the cliffs like he was late for an appointment. You know what that means.

I can't look at Elle after what she did, and if I have to fight this battle, cleanse my Brayburn blood, I have to do it away from here, where I can't hear the water whisper, where I can't feel its pull on my heart, never mind my body. I been thinking, Mama, Santa Maria is just like us, like Brayburns. It seems like a good, safe place for some free love and a party on the beach, but once you peel back the first layer, you realize it's a lie, and what's underneath is rotting and dirty. Spoiled, like meat that's been sitting out too long.

I know what you're thinking: I'll be a Brayburn wherever I go, and so will Mayhem. You're thinking that being born a Brayburn is a gift, that your grandma Julianna blessed us. I wish I had never known anything about it. I wish I was normal, and there was no Millie the cat, no birds, no cave, and most of all, no water. Even more than that, I don't want to see, because that is the worst thing. I want to make myself blind like the rest. I want to be whole, and Brayburns are thorns.

I love you, Mama, and I'm sorry to do this to you. I know how much you and Daddy live for Mayhem, and I know how much you care for me. This will hurt you, but I don't want to be at the mercy of my lineage, and I don't want it for my daughter, either. I want both of us to be free. Since Elle can't have babies, we might be able to end it all if we go away. Don't worry, Santa Maria will survive, like every place on earth. It doesn't need us.

I keep going back there, standing right at the edge of the cliff, looking down. I will fall if I stay. And Mayhem? Well, you've seen how curious she is, how determined she is when she wants something. Fate is umbilical for her.

Don't blame yourself. You did your best for me. I'm going to do the same for Mayhem.

You understand, don't you?

I love you,
Roxy

TWO
TELL THE TRUTH

1987

All I ever do anymore is swim. I like how the world is muffled underwater.

I float.

Last night, I woke up and Lyle was standing over me, darkened and backlit by the hallway, so at first I thought he was a demon, come for me. Roxy tensed, held on to me a little tighter.

This is how it goes.

Since their fight two days ago, he's feeling bad, or maybe he's just smart enough to stay away. That won't last long. Then he'll start giving her stuff and being sweet to me, which will make me want to vomit all the time. Then, after a period of contrition and seduction, he'll get comfortable and drunk and mad and then he'll do it again. Last time, she couldn't walk for days. It used to take a while to come around to the hitting part again, but lately he loops fast.

I've been to the cops.

Well, the station. I haven't gone in yet. I don't know what I would say.

"My stepdad is a creep who's always in a corner, watching." (big dimpled smile)

"My stepdad has an arsenal in the workshed. Might want to check that out." (finger guns)

"My stepdad looks at the odometer when my mom leaves the house. He won't let her shower alone. He won't let her work."

"I think my stepdad is going to kill us someday, maybe soon. Maybe that's why he was in my doorway, watching. Can you do something about that?"

What would they say? They've all seen him at my swim meets, cheering, hugging me when I win. They've seen him show up to chaperone dances where I stand at the side, alone. They don't know the way I recoil when he touches me, that I cringe as he glides across a dance floor, and that at home he never dares come so close.

I don't know how they don't smell the steamy sickness coming off him.

Dear Lyle,

At night, when I'm holding on to my mother because she's trying to get away from you so she can have a few hours of peace, I think about ways you might die. I'd love to stab you, to pull your dreamy blue eyes from *your head. I'd love to hear you scream, to see you beg for your life and then take it from you anyway. You're a plague and a pestilence, and the way you carry your manliness like it's a permission slip from God to act like you rule everything and everyone in your path, like you can do whatever you want—well, I think the guillotine is a good option. I'd love to watch your head roll across the grass.*

I wish you were the kind of drunk that passes out. I wish I had the guts to get your handgun and blow your brains against the wall while you were sleeping. I would never feel sorry a day in my life.

You did that to me. You turned me into a person who hates, one who dreams of ways to die. Roxy is the only thing keeping me here. Protecting her from you. I often wonder who I would be without you. Maybe I would be in love, somewhere beautiful, dreaming about the future, instead of struggling to make it through the day, worrying every time I step out the door to go to school or practice that when I come home, my mother won't be there anymore. She'll have disappeared.

You did this to us. Everything is your fault.

Sincerely and with hate,
Mayhem

Roxy doesn't cry. Neither of us do. We don't talk about it, even to each other, like if we never say it out loud, it will stop. We just lie there, awake, except where our bodies warm each other. And of course I'm always worried about Roxy and her stomach and her achy bones that never go away. The doctor can't find a reason, so she lives like that, taking pills to ease the pain. All the pain.

I always go back to the pool, to swimming. Underwater is the only time I'm safe. Seems like I may never have a person wrap himself around me, care about me the way I think is possible for some.

The water is the closest I get.

THREE
SANTA MARIA

"Trouble," Roxy says. She arches a brow at the kids by the van through the bug-spattered windshield, the ghost of a half-smile rippling across her face.

"You would know," I shoot.

"So would you," she snaps.

Maybe we're a little on edge. We've been in the car so long the pattern on the vinyl seats is tattooed on the back of my thighs.

The kids my mother is talking about, the ones sitting on the white picket fence, look like they slithered up the hill out of the ocean, covered in seaweed, like the carnival music we heard coming from the boardwalk as we were driving into town plays in the air around them at all times. Two crows are on the posts beside them like they're standing guard, and they caw at each other loudly as we come to a stop. I love everything about this place immediately and I think, ridiculously, that I am no longer alone.

The older girl, white but tan, curvaceous, and lean, has her arms around the boy and is lovely with her smudged eye makeup and her ripped clothes. The younger one pops something made of bright colors into her mouth and watches us come up the drive. She is in a military-style jacket with a ton of buttons, her frizzy blond hair reaching in all directions, freckles slapped across her cheeks. And the boy? Thin, brown, hungry-looking. Not hungry in his stomach. Hungry with his eyes. He has a green bandana tied across his forehead and holes in the knees of his jeans. There's an A in a circle drawn in marker across the front of his T-shirt.

Anarchy.

"Look!" Roxy points to the gas gauge. It's just above the *E*. "You owe me five bucks, Cookie. I told you to trust we would make it, and see what happened? You should listen to your mama every once in a while."

"Yeah, well, can I borrow the five bucks to pay you for the bet? I'm fresh out of cash at the moment."

"Very funny."

Roxy cranes out the window and wipes the sweat off her upper lip, careful not to smudge her red lipstick. She's been having real bad aches the last two days, even aside from her bruises, and her appetite's been worse than ever. The only thing she ever wants is sugar. After having been in the car for so long, you'd think we'd be falling all over each other to get out, but we're still sitting in the car. In here we're still us.

She sighs for the thousandth time and clutches at her belly. "I don't know about this, May."

California can't be that different from West Texas.

I watch TV. I know how to say *gag me with a spoon* and *grody to the max*.

I fling open the door.

Roxy gathers her cigarettes and lighter, and drops them inside her purse with a snap.

"Goddammit, Elle," she mutters to herself, eyes flickering toward the kids again. Roxy looks at me over the rims of her sunglasses before shoving them back on her nose. "Mayhem, I'm counting on you to keep your head together here. Those kids are not the usual—"

"I know! You told me they're foster kids."

"No, not that," she says, but doesn't clarify.

"Okay, I guess."

"I mean it. No more of that wild-child business."

"I *will keep my head together*!" I'm so tired of her saying this. I never had any friends, never a boyfriend—all I have is what Grandmother calls my nasty mouth and the hair Lyle always said was ugly and whorish. And once or twice I might've got drunk on the roof, but it's not like I ever did anything. Besides, no kid my age has ever liked me even once. I'm not the wild child in the family.

"Well, all right then." Roxy messes with her hair in the rear-view mirror, then sprays herself with a cloud of Chanel No. 5 and runs her fingers over her gold necklace. It's of a bird, not unlike the ones making a fuss by the house. She's had it as long as I can remember, and over time it's been worn smooth by her worrying fingers. It's like she uses it to calm herself when she's upset about something, and she's been upset the whole way here, practically. Usually, she'd be good and buzzed by this time of day, but since she's had to drive some, she's only nipped from the tiny bottle of wine in her purse a few times and only taken a couple pills since we left Taylor. The withdrawal has turned her into a bit of a she-demon.

I try to look through her eyes, to see what she sees. Roxy hasn't been back here since I was three years old, and in that time, her mother has died, her father has died, and like she said when she got the card with the picture enclosed that her twin sister, Elle, sent last Christmas, *Everybody got old*. After that, she spent a lot of time staring in the mirror, pinching at her neck skin. When I was younger, she passed long nights telling me about Santa Maria and the Brayburn Farm, about how it was good and evil in equal measure, about how it had desires that had to be satisfied.

Brayburns, she would say. *In my town, we were the legends.*

These were the mumbled stories of my childhood, and they made everything about this place loom large. Now that we're here, I realize I expected the house to have a gaping maw filled with spitty, frothy teeth, as much as I figured there would be fairies flitting around with wands granting wishes. I don't want to take her vision away from her, but this place looks pretty normal to me, if run-down compared to our new house in Taylor, where there's no dust anywhere, ever, and Lyle practically keeps the cans of soup in alphabetical order. Maybe what's not so normal is that this place was built by Brayburns, and here Brayburns matter. I know because the whole road is named after us and because flowers and ribbons and baskets of fruit sat at the entrance, gifts from the people in town, Roxy said. They leave offerings. She said it like it's normal to be treated like some kind of low-rent goddess.

Other than the van and the kids, there are trees here, rosebushes, an old black Mercedes, and some bikes leaning against the porch that's attached to the house. It's splashed with fresh white paint that doesn't quite cover up its wrinkles and scars. It's three stories, so it cuts the sunset when I look up, and plants drape down to touch the dirt.

The front door swings open and a woman in bare feet races past the rosebushes toward us. It is those feet and the reckless way they pound against the earth that tells me this is my aunt Elle before her face does. My stomach gallops and there are bumps all over my arms, and I am more awake than I've been since.

I thought Roxy might do a lot of things when she saw her twin sister. Like she might get super quiet or chain-smoke, or maybe even get biting like she can when she's feeling wrong about something. The last thing I would have ever imagined was them running toward each other and colliding in the driveway, Roxy wrapping her legs around Elle's waist, and them twirling like that.

This seems like something I shouldn't be seeing, something wounded and private that fills up my throat. I flip myself around in my seat and start picking through the things we brought and chide myself yet again for the miserable packing job I did. Since I was basically out of my mind trying to get out of the house, I took a whole package of toothbrushes, an armful of books, my River Phoenix poster, plus I emptied out my underwear drawer, but totally forgot to pack any shoes, so all I have are some flip-flops I bought at the truck stop outside of Las Cruces after that man came to the window, slurring, *You got nice legs.* Tap, tap tap. *You got such nice legs.*

My flip-flops are covered in Cheeto dust from a bag that got upended. I slip them on anyway, watching Roxy take her sunglasses off and prop them on her head.

"Son of a bitch!" my aunt says, her voice tinny as she catches sight of Roxy's eye. "Oh my God, that's really bad, Rox. You made it sound like nothing. That's not nothing."

"Ellie," Roxy says, trying to put laughter in her voice. "I'm here now. *We're* here now."

There's a pause.

"You look the same," Elle says. "Except the hair. You went full Marilyn Monroe."

"What about you?" Roxy says, fussing at her platinum waves with her palm. "You go full granola warrior? When's the last time you ate a burger?"

"You know I don't do that. It's no good for us. Definitely no good for the poor cows."

"It's fine for me." Roxy lifts Elle's arm and puckers her nose. "What's going on with your armpits? May not eat meat but you got animals under there, looks like."

"Shaving is subjugation."

"Shaving is a mercy for all mankind."

They erupt into laughter and hug each other again.

"Well, where is she, my little baby niece?" Elle swings the car door open. "Oh, Mayhem." She scoops me out with two strong arms. Right then I realize just how truly tired I am. She seems to know, squeezes extra hard for a second before letting me go. She smells like the sandalwood soap Roxy buys sometimes. "My baby girl," Elle says, "you have no idea how long I've been waiting to see you. How much I've missed you."

Roxy circles her ear with a finger where Elle can't see her. *Crazy,* she mouths.

I almost giggle.

Elle pans back to scan me up and down. She's checking me for signs of a fight, but then her face softens and unspilled tears hover at the edges of her lids. "Roxy," she says, still staring at me, "Mayhem looks like Mama."

I know the mother she's talking about from the picture Roxy keeps in her wallet, the one I've stared at so hard I have memorized every millimeter. Black shoulder-length hair parted in the middle, tall, big glasses, a bottle of Coke and a cigarette in hand, always lipstick on, clothes like in a magazine. That woman is gorgeous, nothing like the wreck I see in the mirror. When I look.

Roxy nods, and now she finds those smokes again and *chk chk chk* she lights one. "Same reproachful stare, too," she says. "Can't escape it." Her jeans are skin-tight, blue blouse straining over her push-up bra, tied at her waist so most of her is covered even though it's hot, brown Candie's that draw so much attention to her legs you can't help but take her in head to toe, yet cloaked so you can't see the beating.

Elle lets her hand run across my cheek. "We used to read together, me and you," she says. "We'd take long walks right over there." She points to an orchard not far off and a bench with its back to us, and then looks at me as though expecting a reaction, or at least hoping for one. "Well, never mind. You're here now and that's all that matters. You really do look like your grandmother. We both loved her so much. But your eyes . . . reproachful stare or not . . . ," she nearly whispers, "those are your father's, right down to the blue flecks."

I let her inspect me because it gives me the chance to inspect her back without her knowing. She's tan, hair shiny, muscles taut, like she spends a lot of time moving around outside. She isn't wearing a bra, and the same bird necklace Roxy has dangles from her neck, though hers still has some details: eyes, feathers, and it's silver instead of gold. She's so different from my mother. I thought twins were supposed to be alike, but if Roxy's air, Elle is earth.

"Can I carry your bag inside?" She tries to pull it from my shoulder.

"No," I say quickly. "Thank you."

A blade runs through me when I think about Lyle violating my room, buzzed, finding my journal, opening its pages. It was the only place I could be honest. And I was. I was so honest. I don't want anyone touching what little I have that's mine, and that's pretty much just this bag.

"Out of the way, Muffin." Roxy nudges me from the passenger side. She looks weak and pale next to Elle, but even with everything that's happened, my mother is still a knockout, as Lyle would say. All curves and heels and painted toes.

Well.

Not everyone is born with a pinched waist and Cupid's-bow lips.

"Come on." Elle swings an arm around my shoulder like we know each other. "You hungry? You must want a shower, something to drink."

What I want is to push her all the way back as much as I want to let her pull me in. I try to make my body soft against her. "Yes, ma'am," I say. "That would be lovely."

"Ma'am?" She lets out a loud laugh. "Oh no, no. You're in California now. Please don't ma'am me. I was at Woodstock, for Christ's sake. I'm not an old lady yet."

"Ma'am" gets everyone's sweet spot in Taylor, Texas. I have a lot to learn about this place. Elle seems to have moved on, though, because she's still talking like crazy.

"We've got so much to show you. The house, the garden, I mean . . . all of it. But first you have to meet my kiddos."

The kids are standing there, watching me, so still they could be wax. All around them more birds are landing, chattering like they're at a cocktail party.

"I don't know if your mom told you, but I'm working on adoption. I'm hoping we can make it work with everyone living here." Elle takes me in again. "I'm sure we will. Brayburns are all about family."

I flash a look at the boy.

And then her. The older girl. Staring at me sharply.

Elle turns her attention to the kids.

"That's Nevie. I call her my soft-boiled egg. All goo on the inside, but first you have to *tap tap tap* on that shell. Jason and Kidd are brother and sister. Jason's almost eighteen, so in some ways it's silly for me to go through the adoption process, but it's important to me to keep them together. People are afraid of teenagers, but I think that's only because kids can see through bullshit. Every revolution and social movement has started with teenagers, right?"

While I'm contemplating that an adult has just sworn in front of a kid with impunity, I pull a Kissing Kooler from my pocket and slather my lips, because something awkward is about to happen.

"Don't be rude!" she calls out to the fence. "Come over here and meet Mayhem."

Grown-ups love to force meetings between teenagers. I let myself get scooted forward as the three of them saunter over.

Neve comes first, the smaller one trailing behind her. I extend a hand and she takes it in hers. A jolt slips through me, like I just touched a bolt of lightning, and I say, "I'm so nervous to be here. It's all so different. I've never had a friend, so maybe you can be one . . . for me."

"Neve!" Elle says, her face suddenly creased. "Let her go."

"Sorry," Neve says. She pulls her hand away.

I feel dazed. "I don't know why I said that."

"It's cool," Neve says, with a little smirk. "It's nice to meet you."

The little girl beside her holds up two of her fingers. "My name is Kidd, and I got two *d*'s in my name."

"I'll remember that," I promise.

She crosses her arms in front of her chest and eyes me stonily.

"Kiddo doesn't talk much, but when she does we all listen." Elle rubs the girl on the head, and Kidd smiles at her.

"What's up?" Jason says. "Welcome to your home, I guess." He doesn't offer to shake my hand or anything, so I hug myself, wishing I could evaporate, except then I wouldn't get to see what's inside that house, and I really, really want to.

"I've told them to treat you like a sister," Elle says. "I'm not big on discipline, and I suspect your mom isn't either. I think kids need to be kids, explore the world, get in touch with their primal drives." She flings her arms open. "Follow their bliss!"

Okay, maybe I didn't know everything about California.

"We'll be like the distorted Brady Bunch," Neve says. "Not to worry, Elle."

"Cool," Jason says.

Kidd laughs.

"This isn't funny," Elle says. "I expect you all to get along and for all of you to welcome Mayhem."

"I'm Roxy, in case anyone cares. *You* care, don't you, birds? Yes, hello, friends," my mother says to the crows, as she gathers up a couple of bags and hands me one. What's in the car is mine. When we got to the Texas border, Roxy threw everything of hers out the window but the clothes on her back, piece by piece, howling like a loon. I wonder where Jason and Neve were when we stopped to call, if they heard Roxy hyperventilating through the phone when she told Elle we were on our way.

I search their eyes for clues but find them opaque.

"Nice to meet you." Neve fidgets. "Can we?" She looks to Elle.

"Go ahead. Thanks for waiting until Mayhem and Roxy got here, honey. It means a lot." Elle assesses me, my blue hair and black lace choker. "You're going to fit right in, May. Friday nights in Santa Maria are all about bonfires and beaches and all the rides on the boardwalk. When you're ready, it's down the road, and it's a great place to celebrate life, to relax, and forget the rest of the world."

Roxy makes an ugly noise.

"You should come with us sometime," Neve says.

"Yeah." Kidd makes spooky fingers. "If you dare."

Neve laughs. Kidd refluffs her hair, then climbs into the van. "Later, Mayhem," she says. "Until next time."

"Oh shit, I left soup on the stove." Elle smacks her own forehead. "I'll be right back."

Roxy gives her a wan smile.

"Thanks for taking us in," I say.

"Thanks for coming home," she says, and then she runs into the house.

I'm distracted by the van door sliding shut, by the music coming on.

The VW bus bounces down the driveway. I contemplate my situation. When I was younger, I used to lie in bed looking at the bunny-shaped water stain on the ceiling and fantasize about living in Santa Maria and having brothers and sisters. Things might still not be perfect, but they would be better, because someone besides me would know how things were and I wouldn't have to spend so much time wondering if I was crazy. And of course, in my fantasies my father, Lucas, is here. There's no Lyle and there never was. Every mile has erased a week of his life, so there's nothing left and he was never born, and those same miles have closed the gap between me and my dad. My father, Lucas, is going to come around the corner of the house any moment, completely legitimately alive, with his arms so far open I won't even have to reach for him at all. I'll just be able to sink and he will catch me.

"You all right, May?" Roxy asks.

"Fine, Roxy," I return.

I stare up at the Gothic roof and its raven weathervane. Inside that house lives the past, my family, remnants of my father. I remind myself why I pulled over at the pay phone and made Roxy call Elle instead of going back to the shelter.

I wanted answers.

"Well, you may be fine, but I need you to hold me up for this one." Roxy threads her arm through mine and leans against me as we approach the house.

I want to ask her again why she left Santa Maria and all of this and why she's so freaked out about being here. But I don't ask her any questions, because with Roxy you can't. You can only wait. I take her arm and steady her as she negotiates her heels across clods of dirt.

And.
My mother is shaking so hard my arm is shaking, too.
And.
Watching her, I'm certain all the answers are in that house.

FOUR
FAMILY

There's weed growing on the porch in little pots along the wall. I know what it looks like from the "drugs are bad" movies they show us at school. Birds are literally everywhere. Real ones, but also depictions of them, on the pots, the pillowcases, the throws. They're carved into the doorway and the legs of the ironwork chairs.

"I guess the birds are a family thing?" I say.

"The tales around here have it that my great-grandmother started feeding them one day and they never left. Brought their babies to nest and have been here for generations."

I glance back. The birds seem to be watching me.

"You'll get used to it," Roxy says.

We step over the threshold.

It's not regular old-house weird, it's . . . I don't know . . . hippie weird; covered in candles, incense burning, crystals of every color everywhere I look. I wander through the rooms, hungry for any evidence of who I am, where I came from, what happened to my parents, and why Roxy took me away from here and dragged me straight to hell with her.

All I find is a lot of pictures of people I can't identify and books about astral projection, herbs, politics, the Vietnam War, cats . . . stuff like that. And of course more black birds in art, on chairs and lamps. It should be too much, but it works somehow.

Roxy plays with another cigarette but doesn't spark it because Elle told her there's no smoking inside. I stop at a painting of a woman with a scarred cheek. I see the traces of my cheekbones and lips, even without looking too closely.

"That's Julianna," Roxy says. "Your great-great-grandmother." She ducks down, smiling at a cat that has appeared on the stairs. "Hello, Millie," she says, in a voice I've never heard before. The cat meows and then purrs loudly. She must be old, but she doesn't look it. Her coat is a silky gray, her paws dipped white, nose a pink gemstone.

Elle opens her arms and then claps her hands together. "Well," she says, "look at that. Reunion."

"It's my Millie," Roxy says into the ball of fluff rubbing at her face. "Millie the Best Cat." She scratches the cat under her chin and another patch of white appears. We were never allowed to have pets in Taylor.

Millie presses into my calves and then sits waiting to be acknowledged. She is so soft.

"Millie and your mother were always inseparable," Elle says. "Millie belongs to all of us, but your mom most of all."

Roxy picks up the cat, and Elle walks ahead of us, skipping the creaky boards, avoiding the protruding nail, rattling on about how we're going to be sleeping in Roxy's old room. The kids are upstairs in the attic, which is huge and half finished, she says. They prefer to treat it like their own little apartment, and I'm welcome to go up there, too, though she'd have to move the boxes out if I wanted to move in. She says I should just let her know what I want to do.

A bunch of kids with their own apartment sounds like some kind of heaven.

Roxy buries her face into Millie's fur again. "May and I stick together."

"Oh?" Elle says. "I just thought since they're all teenagers, well, except for Kidd. I guess I could move all Mother's stuff out of her sewing room. I haven't even touched it."

"We're good is what I mean," Roxy says. "We'll both sleep in here. I like to have May close."

I can't read Elle's look exactly, but it's saying something. "Of course," she says, "that makes sense."

She would probably think it was wrong if I told her the truth—that Roxy slept with me half the time back in Texas, that there's an indentation in her stomach where the base of my spine fits perfectly. That's why Lyle hates me so much and always has. He had her, he married her, but I'm the one who fits her best and I always have been, no matter how much he gave or took.

Roxy's old room is like passing through a time portal into 1974, the year she left. She's told me about how everything she owned when she was little smelled like tanning oil and cherry lip balm. I catch phantom traces of coconut as I walk around, touching everything. Roxy still has her sunglasses on her head, which gives her the air of a movie star, which is her favorite. She settles on the bed and pets the cat, as though focusing on that is keeping her steady.

Elle tells Roxy that she hasn't touched a thing in here since Roxy left, and neither did her mother, though her mom used to come in here and sit sometimes; and of course it's obvious by the patch of gray fur on the bed that Millie has spent plenty of time in here, waiting.

Everything is exactly how Roxy and my dad left it. This seems important to Elle for Roxy to know, but it doesn't matter to us right now. I want to tell Elle we slept one night at a truck stop, with lights and engines and music going all hours, people drinking and making out, and another night in one of those camping spots you can rent for four bucks.

Elle disappears downstairs. Her soup smells like dirt-soaked toes. As soon as she's gone, Roxy opens her bag and throws me a Twinkie.

"I knew we would need provisions. Elle's been on that my-body-is-my-temple crap since we could talk. We're going to have to keep a stash of real food around here."

The sponge cake dissolves into my mouth.

"She doesn't eat meat, doesn't eat dairy either, so prepare yourself to get healthy," Roxy says.

"Or to move into a 7-Eleven."

Roxy helps herself to some Hostess cupcakes, brown with white squiggles on top and cream filling inside, and for a bit it is quiet and good and smells like vanilla and chocolate, the only sound a loud purring.

"We're going to be okay now," Roxy says, after a while.

"You promise?"

She snorts. "What would I do in Taylor now that I've left their hero in the dirt? They already thought I was a Jezebel just because I don't live my life in a polyester robe and orthotics. But now I've gone and left Lyle St. James." She laughs. "I bet he's up to his ass crack in casseroles and church skirt."

We let that sit a minute, envisioning all the flower prints and nude stockings. The ladies in Taylor have a way of wrapping themselves around a man in need. My stomach lurches. Roxy runs a finger around her lips to wipe any crumbs, then searches around in her bag until she finds a jar of blue pills. Valium. Ten milligrams. Her shoulders relax as soon as she has the bottle in hand. She takes one dry, then and there, sinks into the bed, and almost instantly seems to be drifting backward. Some minutes pass in silence.

"Did you love Lyle?" I ask. "I mean, do you?" Her pills make me uneasy, but they also open her up and peel her back.

Sober, this question would produce a slammed door, a face hidden under hands, but now she looks over at me, already blurring at her edges with the promise of the relief to come.

"I had my love. I only ever had one. Two, including you. Lyle wasn't bad to start, and he could dance. And he protected me at first, so all I had to do was be there. He rescued me right out of the welfare office."

I know this story. Us, no place to live, Roxy out of gas and money, too proud to call home to ask for help. The woman at the welfare office gave Roxy Lyle's number for a cheap place to stay, and the rest is history. He danced her into the night and into his nice house and nice car and right over to the nice altar. She said she had cried all day in that welfare office and he seemed like an angel. Said she thought we'd have to sleep in the car instead of that terrible hotel at the edge of town and then who knows what would have become of us. I was only three. Lyle saved us. That's the story. But I think the real story is in the reasons why she wouldn't just call over here, where everyone loved her, where she would be safe; why she didn't let her own family rescue her instead of some smooth-talking prick who took her freedom in the exchange. That's a question she's never answered, not even when she's puttied up.

"But true love, that's another thing entirely." She stretches out. "Brayburn women only ever have true love with a mate once. You remember that. Once is enough, May. Once is damn lucky."

This room is where my parents lived, where they had me and we became a family. This is the bed I was born in, and though I have no real memories of it, it's familiar. I reach out and run my finger over the side of the pine crib, with its crocheted yellow blankets and stuffed animals. A surfboard hangs from the wall. It's beat up on the bottom, blue and white and massive, and I imagine a memory of my father taking it from its hooks and slinging it under his arm, winking at me as he leaves, motioning for me to follow.

I poke around in my mother's closet full of clothes. Some dresses, a couple hats, some things that belonged to my dad. Old T-shirts, bowling shoes, bell-bottom jeans. I run my hands over them and smell them.

"Well, would you look at this?" She shows me a blanket made of satin and silk. "I never thought I'd see this thing again."

"What is it?"

"My mother made it for you."

We don't talk about her mother, because by leaving here and never coming back, Roxy took that grandmother away from me and her mother away from herself. Instead of Grandmother Stitcher with the magic hands and hazel eyes, we got Lyle's mother, a woman so cold she'd give you frostbite. She told me I was a bull in her china shop and then she laughed unnaturally so you could feel all her hate. She told me I didn't sit right, or stand right, or talk right, and then she said it to her friends right in front of me, like she was apologizing for all my ways.

Roxy would flip her off under the table. She'd smoke in her backyard and ash on her precious roses. She even spit in Grandmother's iced tea a time or two, but she never said a word out loud, even when Grandmother was mean to me.

And oh, when I dyed my hair blue . . . I tried to tell Grandmother I wanted hair like water, but that only made her tighten her butt harder. *The good Lord did not make hair blue for a reason. It's not natural. You look like some kind of creature from some kind of lagoon.* I didn't mention that the good Lord didn't make her hair red either, or curly, but I decided to let that fight go. Roxy didn't make me dye it back, even when Lyle said I should join a carnival and make best friends with the bearded lady and the tattooed man.

"We went to Sew Good, the shop in town, Mama and I, and we picked out material together," Roxy goes on, touching the blanket. "She said she wanted your baby blanket to be just right for you. She asked me if I wanted to get pink or maybe red, but I said no, that I wanted a blanket like the ocean. So blue silk in three shades with satin trim is what we got. And it was perfect for you."

I pull it over me, and even though it only covers my top half, it soothes me to just the right temperature.

Roxy opens the window and crosses her arms, looking outside, across the orchards laid out as far as we can see. We didn't come back when her mother, Stitcher, died. Roxy said if we did, Santa Maria wouldn't let us leave again. She said Santa Maria was heartbreak itself. And then later, when she had taken to her bed, she told me it was heaven, it was her bones, it was too powerful for her to touch. Even for her mother, she didn't dare.

After Grandmother Stitcher died, Roxy wore black for months. I would hear her weeping on the phone with Elle late at night, when Lyle was out and she thought I was asleep. A silent house magnifies everything, so that whispered conversations find you in between your own insomniac breaths.

No, she would say, *no, I can't, Ellie. I can never come home.*

And I would wonder what the truth was and how I would ever get to it. And now we're here. Looking at the pictures hanging next to Roxy's bed is like staring into oncoming headlights, but I can't stop. My father on his surfboard, legs in the sea. My mother, pregnant and smiling. Me, a baby. Roxy and Elle and my father, together, arms linked. Was it this she didn't want to look at, that she didn't want to see? My father's warm green eyes with the bursts of blue, Roxy slipped into the crook of his arm, where she looked to fit perfectly, her smile big and free and white inside her tan, brown hair waved over her shoulders.

"He used to stumble over his words sometimes," Roxy says. "His English wasn't as good as he wanted it to be. I didn't care. I didn't want him to change a single thing about himself, not then. And when he spoke Portuguese, it was the sexiest." She wipes at my cheeks, even though they're dry.

This is what I know about my father, Lucas Machado. He came to Santa Maria from a small beach town in Brazil with a surfboard and a few dollars in his pocket. He had broken contact with his family and never wanted to go back. He and Roxy met at a bonfire. He was dancing like he was part of the flames.

My mother loved his accent, the way his words slid into each other, the way he kissed her like he had been waiting for her his whole life, like he couldn't wait one second more. He was her true love. That, she knew from the first night they met, from the way he ran at the ocean like he was picking a fight, squawking and hollering and then going completely still when they were together, watching her so as not to miss a moment. Lucas Machado caught her heart in a net. And then her family's, too. Best of all, he didn't expect my mother to leave Brayburn Farm or to give me any other last name. He contorted himself around her, to be her buffer against the world, to be the world itself.

Then he died. Fell off a cliff. *Jumped* off a cliff. Nobody knew why, or if they did they've never told me. Why he would end his own life and leave me when he was supposedly so happy is something no one has ever been able to answer. Or no one has ever wanted to.

I don't know why my father died, but I do know most of my mother also died that day. I don't know how else to explain what's happened to her since. I've never known her any other way. The only time she's whole is when she lets my father's memory through the cracks of the fortress she's built against him, everything that came before he stepped off the cliffside.

Now, Roxy's lying on the bed, watching the candlelight flicker across the ceiling, Millie on her chest.

Roxy says *obrigado*. She says *amor*.

Whatever ghosts she thought she was escaping all those years ago were here all along, just waiting for her to come back.

FIVE
MOTHER

After my shower, Elle appears in the bedroom doorway with a camera around her neck. Even though she knows we're sharing a room, she seems shocked to find me there, curled around Roxy. Now that I'm clean, I can smell the road trip on her. She should be taking her own shower, but is drifting in and out of consciousness and seems peaceful, so I don't want to bother her.

"You find the bathroom all right?" Elle asks.

My hair is wet, my skin still damp.

Roxy opens up her eyes. "Hey, Ellie," she says.

"Hey." Elle leans against the door, unable to take her sad gaze from Roxy's face. She hesitates, then steps into the room, folds her hands across her chest. "Listen, I know you left Texas with nothing. I know how brave that was, and I want to support you in your decision. You can have anything out of the fridge, and the townies leave us plenty of gift baskets and what not, which I urge you to help yourself to."

"Okay." Roxy sounds so deflated, so empty, I keep my body warm against hers.

Elle puts some bills on the bedside table. "It's not much, but I don't want you to be worrying. We'll figure it out. And I know you're not much for working the land, but maybe Mayhem can help me get ready for the market or something."

Roxy covers her face. She's never had a job that I know of.

Her job was keeping herself in the condition Lyle liked, baking cakes for the appropriate functions, laughing at his stupid jokes. But Roxy also has pride.

"Thank you," Roxy says into her hands.

"I've been living in this house this whole time. It's okay for you to take a little."

Roxy nods, face still covered, mumbles another "Thank you."

Elle comes to stand at the foot of the bed. "I do have one more thing to talk to you about."

Roxy looks up.

"I think we should go down to the station and file a report," Elle says.

Roxy blinks hard as though trying to bring Elle into focus. "Station?"

"Police station, Rox."

Roxy makes a sad sound. "Why in hell would I want to have anything to do with a cop?"

"It's not easy, and I know that, but we should document the abuse. What I mean is, if Lyle should come around—"

"He won't—" Roxy says.

"If he does—" Elle insists. "And I'm sorry because I know you just got here, but it would be better if the . . . uh . . . evidence were still evident."

"You're an expert?"

"Not an expert exactly." Elle looks embarrassed, sheepish. "I fell into it at some point, when the townies were still coming up here thinking I could work magic on their lives and relationships, asking about mugwort and eyes of newt. I started to see what was happening to them, started to try to make sense of it and to take some action . . . legal action. There aren't very many resources for victims of abuse, but we can do something. We can get it down on record, and maybe that'll help later on."

There's a silence so prolonged I start to lose focus. The words "victims of abuse" floating in the air around us, it's like none of this is real, like I must have dreamed it all. I must still be back in Taylor, in my bed, in the dark, with Lyle playing his music and dancing downstairs, holding Roxy by the hips long after she's ready for bed.

"It's nice you're a hero." Roxy closes her eyes again.

"Roxy, that's not fair."

"No, no, but it is. Always doing the right thing. Except when it's the wrong thing," she singsongs.

"I've apologized so many times."

Roxy puts up a hand. "I'll take your pictures and file your report, but I don't want to hear any more. That's the deal. Once it's done, we're done with this. Agreed?"

Elle's fingers coil around the camera; then she nods, but she doesn't move.

Roxy waits for Elle to leave, and when she doesn't Roxy says, "Now?"

Elle's face crumples. "I'm sorry, Rox, but it's already starting to fade. Every hour counts."

"Okay."

"But if you don't want to—"

Roxy uncurls herself and throws off the blanket.

"Nope," she says. "Whatever makes you happy, Elle."

"Rox—"

"No, no. Your house, your rules," Roxy says, and Elle follows quietly behind her and down the stairs.

SIX
YELLOW WALLPAPER

Roxy asks me to come with her while she has the pictures taken, and that's when I know things really are changing. Normally, she would make sure I saw nothing, or more likely, she wouldn't let Elle take the pictures at all.

She stands against the one blank wall in the dining room, which is painted a rich buttercup. There's a small crystal chandelier, a table made of redwood, its edges ragged with bark, the chairs crafted and thick, and opposite her, three large cases of china, stacked neatly. On one wall, a portrait of a woman in an old-style bathing suit, a cap on her head, hands on her hips. She stares outward defiantly, her bottom lip thrust forward.

Roxy takes off her jeans, gingerly, her skin sore and sensitive. She unties her blouse, undoing her buttons, and removes it. Her makeup has faded, she's still dirty from the car, and next to the yellow paint she's jaundiced. I wait out of the camera's frame, but close enough to save her if anything goes wrong. The top half of her stomach is flat and taut, with a constellation of moles near her right ribs. The bottom half is yellow and green, the bruises on her shoulder bluer and more purple. The worst kind of rainbow weaves all up and down her legs.

"He should go straight to hell." Elle hexes Lyle from behind her black Polaroid. "I could send him there for you. I will if he comes anywhere near here."

"I'm standing here in my underwear," Roxy says. "Can we just—"

Elle begins snapping the camera.

This is how we live in Taylor. We find excuses, ways to cover up so we don't have to admit the truth to each other. If I don't say anything and Roxy doesn't say anything, and we pretend that sleeping in the same bed is just mother-daughter bonding, we don't have to have conversations. We don't have to see anything and it's easy to lie, even to ourselves.

Now I see us through Elle's eyes and there is no hiding. I am looking at my mother. I am seeing her wounds. I want to tell her how beautiful she is, even now, while she herself avoids the camera, staring to the side and down so her features etch a sharp shadow against the wall.

Chikaw, the camera says, spitting out picture after picture. *Chikaw. Chikaw.*

Elle walks up close to Roxy and clicks right in her eye, so I almost put my hand between them. I stop myself, but glare at Elle as she takes another.

Chikaw.

"That seems like plenty," I say, startling myself with my own voice. "I mean, how many pictures . . . don't you have what you need?"

Roxy grips my arm and doesn't let go.

"Mayhem, you must think I'm a monster," Elle says.

"No." My lip trembles violently. "It's not that."

It's that she's pulling Lyle out of Taylor and bringing him into three dimensions, when I only want to leave him behind, in the past, gone forever.

Elle lets the camera fall to her side and considers her twin for a long while.

"I'm so sorry, Roxy," she says. "Shit goddamn, I'm sorry."

"My own fault, isn't it? I did it to myself." Roxy reaches for her shirt and her jeans, and disappears up the stairs.

SEVEN
THE ATTIC

Elle has retreated to her room and shut the door, so while Roxy takes her shower, I explore the house, munching on Nacho Cheese Doritos, sucking down a warm Coke. I run my fingers along the walls and take in the pictures of my family; paintings, black-and-whites where no one is smiling, then full color, fake Western shots, and finally my grandparents, my mother and Elle, grainy.

At the foot of the attic stairs, I smell incense and sweat. I tell myself I need to check out those kids and their private quarters for my own safety. They're strangers and I don't know anything about them, and we just came from being someone's playthings. I don't trust anyone, and I shouldn't. The world is full of crazy people. Anyway, no one told me I couldn't go up there. In fact, I was invited to move in. Sort of. I tell myself I am not like Lyle. I am not invading other people's privacy. I just want to see more, to see who they are in secret when they're alone. The stairs creak as I go up, and snaking guilt coils through me, but it doesn't stop me.

I see two beds, piles of black clothes everywhere, old band T-shirts, some smaller trinkets that must belong to Kidd; rings on a side table; an open duffel bag; backpacks strewn in the corner. I rifle through their things, again swearing to myself this is only a precaution.

I find some family pictures of Kidd and Jason with what

must be their parents, a nice-looking white woman and a pleasant-looking black man. Everyone is smiling. Jason is clean-cut, and Kidd's hair is in braids. They look new.

Kidd in a drum majorette costume.

Jason holding a football.

It's so all-American, so *healthy*.

I put the pictures back and move over to Neve's section of the attic, which I easily identify by the necklaces hanging from a nail in the wall. It's a mess, and I smell traces of tobacco and maybe weed on her dirty clothes. A couple of gallon-sized glass jars filled with water sit in the corner of the room, but there's nothing that gives me any hints about who she is, other than feather boas, glittery bustiers, huge crystal earrings, and some leather pants.

I wander toward the part of the room that's used for storage. Boxes and boxes. I glide my finger across their tops, come away dusty. Then I see the trunk in the back right-hand corner. It's shiny, its leather oiled and protected. A rusted lock hangs open from its center. I lift the lid. I smell lemon balm and rosemary and sandalwood, and my throat constricts. Memories of my mother's soft whiskey-laced whispers in the night.

Sandalwood is for protection.

Rosemary is of the sea.

Lemon balm? I can't remember anything but the smell itself. My nursery rhymes, incantations from another time and place. From before. I hear my father's chuckle, low. I see my parents' hands pass across my field of vision, see my own small one reaching.

Inside the trunk are four wedding dresses, each wrapped in clear plastic, some folders containing report cards. Underneath a neat pile of crocheted baby clothes sits a diary, a notebook covered in blue satin, finer than anything I've ever seen, definitely nicer than the composition notebooks whose pages

I have always filled with my secret thoughts. I open it, let my fingers dance along the edges of the pages.

Brayburn
Santa Maria, California

Letters are pasted in. Tickets. A couple of pictures. Some newspaper articles.

Diaries are sacred. They belong to their author. They are not to be touched by anyone else. I know what happens when you go poking around in other people's things. People get hurt. They get slammed into walls. People get bruised.

Sound ricochets across the attic, like something has fallen. I jump and look quickly out the window, but all I see is a black sky. I hear the noise again. It's a car door.

Elle's kids are back.

I flee down the stairs like I'm being chased, the diary clutched in my hand, all the way to Roxy's room. The shower is still going down the hall.

I open the diary.

I read until the water turns off and Roxy's feet creak along the carpeted floors, and then I stuff it under the mattress and pretend to be asleep as Roxy's body sinks down next to mine.

Everything comes with a price. Every victory has a trail of blood behind it. Maybe the sorrow I am dragging behind me means a victory is coming my way.

EIGHT

JULIANNA BRAYBURN

DAUGHTER OF THE WOODS

1940

Dearest Billie,

When I was young I swore to myself never to be the kind of person who carried secrets like an extra suitcase, as so many seemed to do; busy running from everything in their past. And now, ironically, I have a chest full of secrets I carry on my back that's so heavy it threatens to lay me flat. It's not what I want for you, my girl; a mother with worries she can't shake off. I know we've never picked wildflowers together as you have done with your father. We have never laughed together or baked a cake and iced it with colored sugar. There is something missing between us, something fundamental that should be between a mother and a daughter, and I wish for your forgiveness every day, for what I cannot muster that you need.

But we have stories, and our stories help us to understand each other. I write you today, knowing I am too cowardly to give you this story before my death, but I am comforted, knowing you will have it one day and then it will not be mine alone. It will be yours as well. It is already yours. I'm sorry I'm not brave enough to help you make sense of it.

I wonder what's inside you.

I think back to Alfonzo Luna, the great director with his wild hair and purple scarf, and I wonder, if I had refused to be in his play would I have saved myself? But I cannot undo one thread without undoing them all, and I'm afraid I'm far too selfish to live a life without having met your father, without having brought you into the world, consequences be what they may.

Everything in life comes with a price; every joy has a sorrow like a tail at its back. Every victory a trail of blood behind it. We keep getting up, child. As we must.

NINE
THE KIDS

I wake in the night, sure the motion sensor lights flashing on and off mean Lyle is here, scaling the outside wall, slipping through a window, wrapping his hands around my neck until I can't breathe anymore, even a little. I see the little hairs on his cheeks. I see the bowls of grapes.

He is coming. He's going to find us. He'll never leave us alone.

"It's just animals," Roxy says. "It's nothing."

I hold on to her. She holds on back.

I sleep through the rest of the night and wake to hot sun on my cheek, my stomach angry with hunger, Roxy gone from beside me, loud music climbing the stairs. I wait for the sounds to die down, but they don't, and my stomach grumbles fiercely, so finally I make myself go down to the kitchen.

Kidd's wearing a Mister Rogers T-shirt under a black leather vest, a fluffy tutu on the bottom, and she's eating a donut filled with raspberry jam. She catches sight of me right away and fixes me with a blank, open stare, red jelly at the corner of her mouth.

Jason and Neve are talking closely, but they stop as soon as I come in. Jason doesn't smile. He looks away. Maybe he knows I was in his stuff last night, that I saw his pictures. Maybe I left something crucial out of place.

"Elle doesn't allow sweets in the house except on Saturday

morning because of the market," Kidd says. "Mostly it's bulgur wheat and nutritional yeast."

"Ay," Jason says, quietly, "gratitude, Kidd."

"I know." She takes another huge bite of donut. "I'm just letting her know to have gratitude while she eats donuts, because they're only once a week."

"I keep my own private stash," I say. "If you're ever desperate."

"Her teeth are going to fall out of her head," Jason snaps. "She doesn't need any more sugar than she gets."

I redden and pour myself a cup of coffee. I grab for a donut, but I've lost my appetite. I'm about to leave, to take my food upstairs, but Neve stops me.

"Elle took your mom to get a few things. Some essentials you left behind. *But* . . ." Neve threads her arm through mine, drawing out the word. She has no idea how strange this is. I've watched girls coming together in the playground, deciding on each other so easily. It has never happened to me. ". . . she left us with strict instructions to take you to the beach. We need to be there—"

"In like an hour," Jason says. "Kidd was going to wake you up since it seemed like you were going to sleep all day."

"I was tired," I say. "It . . . it was a long drive."

"Well, let's go. Chop-chop!" Neve says.

"I don't even have a suit." My plan was to stay and organize my toothbrushes, maybe walk around a little with Roxy, perhaps reopen the diary.

Jason watches me for a second, then looks away.

"No worries about the suit," Neve says. "Santa Maria has about eighteen hundred places that sell swimsuits. Also," she goes on, "every kind of flip-flop imaginable, jellies, and every single thing you could ever think of with the words 'Santa Maria' printed on it. 'Best beach town in America,' don'tcha know." Neve corkscrews her fingers into the place where dimples should be and gives me a fake smile.

"I saw that on the sign, coming into town." There were mermaids welcoming us to Santa Maria, the caption between their welcoming naked torsos.

"Of course, no one mentions the other part," Jason says, darkly.

"What other part?" I sit at the table, interested.

"Leave her alone." Neve flops down beside me, grabs hold of a mug of coffee. "Ignore him. We call him the Awfulizer."

"Santa Maria has the most murders per capita in the whole country," Jason deadpans, popping a cinnamon donut into his mouth. "Most drug-related deaths. Most missing people."

I glance out the window at the bursting colors, the clean green, the fruit popping off the trees. "Seriously? Here?"

Neve nods. "It's an anomaly. Elle says it's because we're on a psychic vortex."

I would question what a psychic vortex is, but considering the books on the shelves and the crystals dangling from the ceiling, I let it go. Still, I half expect chairs to slide across the floor of their own accord.

"So why stay if it's such a scary place?" I ask, when all the furniture doesn't levitate.

Pain flickers across Jason's face, so quickly I might not have seen it happen, and then it all shuts down and he goes back to neutral and studies his plate.

"Because as far as earth goes, this is the best I've found," Neve says. "At least it's honest."

"Why would you come back?" Jason asks. "Maybe that's the better question."

"I always wanted to live here." I take a bite, lick powdered sugar from the corners of my mouth. "Even if it's a psychic vortex. Anyway, anything's better than Taylor."

"That's where you came from?" Neve asks, leaning over the table so I catch a glimpse of an elaborate silver vial between her breasts. It's beautifully engraved and looks ancient.

I nod.

"What's it like there?"

I think about it, aside from Lyle and Grandmother. There are good parts. "Cowboy boots and church and really perfect makeup and hair so big ferrets could live in it."

"Sounds kinda sexy," Neve says.

Jason makes a disgusted noise.

"What?" she says. "I like big hair. And I bet you didn't know I can two-step." She slides across the room with her thumbs hooked in her belt loop, then sways her hips and winks.

"The secret life of Neve," Jason says. "Where did you learn that?"

"Street Skills 101." She settles herself back at the table and holds her mug, blowing on the steaming coffee.

"Don't worry about Santa Maria. It's scary sometimes, but no one messes with us," Kidd says, and now I see she has the same vial as Neve, only hers looks like a bullet hanging from a chain. "And we never leave. We wouldn't."

We never much left Taylor, but there's something about the way she says it that's so . . . final.

"They do not mess with us," Neve murmurs, almost to herself. "For good reason."

Kidd laughs softly and plays with her necklace. "So stick with Neve," she says. "Right?"

Jason looks around the table, shakes his head, gets up, and stalks out. The screen door slams behind him.

"Awfulizer," Neve says, pointing at the place Jason has just gone. Then she turns back to me and wrinkles her nose, looking me up and down. "You're not going to the beach in that, are you?"

I look down at the worn *Peanuts* sleep shirt I pulled out of Roxy's closet and cross my arms over Snoopy's doghouse.

Neve takes another bite of donut, then unscrews her necklace to reveal a tiny atomizer. She sprays something into her mouth and replaces the cap. "Two things: one, we're supposed to be like sisters, remember? And sisters go to the beach together. And two, it's fun. What else is there to do? It's already almost three o'clock. Time's a' wastin'." She maneuvers me toward the stairs. "Totally not staying here. It's a beautiful day! It's summer! Santa Maria is *cool*! Your mom will find you. Trust me, the boardwalk is like two blocks. Plus she's a grown-up. You are not. Stop acting like one!"

I begin picking up the coffee mugs and dirty plates on the table, taking them to the sink.

"Shit," she says, "you need to learn how to have fun. Like, *really badly*. Like stat. Immediately."

"Okay, okay!" I turn off the sink water. "I'm changing."

I smile all the way to my new room.

TEN
REMEMBER ME

When Lyle knocked my head against the wall, I expected to shatter. I knew as soon as Roxy and I walked in that night, there was going to be trouble. The house was wrong. I could practically smell it, and so could Roxy. She grabbed hold of my wrist as soon as we crossed the threshold. The Patsy Cline version of "Crazy" echoed through the house. A bottle of Jack Daniels sat open on the kitchen counter, its top resting at its side. The bottle, which had been new that morning, was half empty. Roxy pointed at it as we searched the dining room, living room, bathroom, even the basement and came up empty. He had to be upstairs.

And I'm crazy for loving you . . .

There was a thick void as the record spun and crackled, and then the house went silent. Roxy and I stopped moving, breathing. And then she looked up, and that's when Lyle came.

Terrible things always happen when you aren't paying attention and you're just being. Roxy and I had gone to see *The Witches of Eastwick*. We laughed so hard when those witches got Jack Nicholson at the end. We were in a good mood. Almost happy. At first I thought that was why and that Lyle begrudged us our trip to the movies without him and wanted to punish us for it.

Well.

Lyle tore down the stairs, and this time instead of going for

Roxy like he always did, he came straight for me. He had never touched me before, though he'd been plenty aggressive over the years, so I didn't know what to do. I think he knew if he hurt me, it would really be the end for my mother and him, and that always kept him from doing it, until he couldn't hold himself back anymore.

He shook me so hard the house vibrated. The hairs on his cheeks blurred, and the perfectly hung painting of grapes in a silver bowl tripled above his head. That ugly thing. He took me by both shoulders and I collided with the wall and, dimly, as the world narrowed to a pinprick of Lyle and me and the wall and the wall and the wall and the wall, I thought how it should be different when someone holds your shoulders like that. It should be to keep you steady, not to knock you down.

I wish touch was love, not hate.

Slut. He kept saying it to me. *Slut. Slut. Slut.*

I kept thinking, *What does that even mean?*

Slam. Slam. Slam.

His breath hot on my face, him so close.

What did I ever do to you? All I ever did was take care of you and your mama and this is how you repay me? You're going to the cops? For what? What the hell you going to tell them?

And the pieces wouldn't connect. I thought, *Am I going to die now? Is it going to be over? All of it?*

And everything slowed down and I didn't feel pain anymore and it all got so clear it hurt in a different way. It ached. I gave up. That's what he had been waiting for. When I went limp, he started in on Roxy.

After Lyle had gone, closing the door gently behind him, when we were hauling ass to get out of there, we figured out what had happened. My room was torn apart, my journal open on the bed, every private thought, every wish, every confession right there, exposed.

He had hurt me and he had hurt Roxy, and I had done nothing to stop him. Again.

ELEVEN
THE BEACH

"Those are the punks." Neve points to the kids with all different-colored mohawks, bowler hats, piercings, and leather, hanging over the boardwalk railings by the beach. They're so uninterested in the ocean it's like they don't even see it.

It's a perfect day, warm but not too hot, and we are setting ourselves up.

One thing: sand gets everywhere. It's not like a pool, where you can keep yourself separate. The beach sucks you in so you're part of it. The shore in Texas has its charm, in fact it's stunning in its own Texas way, but it's different from this. This place has special meaning. My parents met here, and I picture them holding hands and running across the sand, stopping to make out passionately. This beach is my genesis.

"Valley girls over there." Neve points, oblivious to my epiphany. They're chewing gum, sunglasses on, eating frozen yogurt or sucking on sodas, lips so shiny I can see them from here.

Jason sets up an umbrella, and I take off my T-shirt and lay out my towel.

"Later, will you bury me?" Kidd asks Jason.

"Yeah," he says. "Here are your buckets." He hands her five containers of different shapes and sizes and a shovel.

She gives him a look, one hand hooked on her hip. "I'm *nine*," she says. "For God's sake."

"Come on," he says. "Don't act like you're too good for sandcastles. We'll help you."

"It's for babies."

"Not if I'm there, it's not. We're going tri-level, girl. We're going to make *the best* sandcastle. The whole entire town will be jealous."

"Okay," she says. "But you better not ditch me. You better actually do it instead of staring up at the sky and sleeping."

He pauses from where he's staking the umbrella. "I would never ditch you, Kidd," he says.

"Greetings and salutations," a voice croaks.

I look up to find two boys looming over me, dressed in full fatigues. One has a bandana, the other a beret, and they both look at me so severely I feel like I'm breaking a law being in my new black bikini.

"Hey," Neve says, as they slap hands and shake with Jason. "Mayhem, meet Eddie and Albert Gecko."

They're not twins, exactly. There's maybe a year between them, but they look nearly identical aside from their headwear, and the fact that the one in the beret, Eddie, has lighter hair than the other, Albert, and a slightly more upturned nose.

"Boardwalk security," Eddie says.

"Nice to meet you," I say. "Mayhem."

They both fold their arms across their chests.

"Welcome to Santa Maria," Albert says, unwelcomingly.

"Thank you."

They continue to stare down at me.

"It's our duty to inform the citizenry of certain pertinent facts about Santa Maria. By our count, five females have disappeared from Santa Maria in the last six months. The dipshit cops in town haven't put it together yet, but we believe it to be the work of one person. One *non-occult* person. As you know, the vampires in town prefer to prey on vagrants and small children," Eddie says.

"Vampires?" I say.

"Yes, vampires. Whether you realize it or not, ma'am, this town is a hotbed of paranormal activity," the other brother, Albert, says. "And there are certain factions we are no longer willing to tolerate. We're keeping you safe, doing the job the"—he makes air quotes—"*real police force* doesn't have the balls for."

I smile, but then quickly realize from their expressionless eyes, that's not the response they're looking for.

"You're new to the beach," Eddie says, flipping open a small blue spiral notebook, "so I'm going to have to ask you the purpose of your visit."

"Are you serious?" I say.

Neve grins from the side.

"Dead serious, ma'am." Albert makes a dead-serious face. "You do realize there are dangerous things happening. The beach is under attack."

Another glance at all the different groups hanging around and I realize people aren't as laid-back as they look. They're looking around. They're paying attention. They're nervous.

"Hey. This is Mayhem *Brayburn*," Neve says. "So check yourself. She's Santa Maria royalty, my friends. She is definitely not a threat you would object to."

They both nod and exchange a look.

Eddie scribbles something, then clucks, looking at his brother. "Another Brayburn. Interesting timing."

"Length of stay?" Albert asks.

"Forever," Neve says, "if we're lucky. Mayhem is home now."

"Mmmhmm, home," Eddie says. "In that case, we have rules, and we require you be informed."

"Knowledge is power," Albert says.

Now I do laugh, and they both look up at me, then back down at what must be some sort of list.

"One, no slaughtering innocent civilians," Eddie reads, making sure I'm listening. "You're more than welcome to have at the psychos. In fact, we would prefer not to have to investigate the man who's taking the girls. If you would handle that, we'd be grateful."

"Yeah, we'll get right on that," Neve says. I can't tell if she's being sarcastic.

"Two," Albert says, "no consorting with vampires. We don't need them feeling welcome, you know what I'm saying? Also, we ask that you leave them to us. We really enjoy a good staking, and we don't want to have to compete with you for our slice of the pie."

"And three," Eddie says, "no going weird. As a contributor to the town's, shall we say, unusual proclivities, we ask that you maintain your stance on the side of goodness and righteousness to serve our common goal. And if you don't . . ." He makes a slicing motion across his throat.

"Respect for your family business aside, since you're new, we'll be watching you." Albert takes two fingers, points them at his eyes, then back at me.

"Family business?" I venture.

"Seriously?" Neve pulls her sunglasses down. "You're going to start bossing Brayburns around?"

Eddie raises his arms defensively. "We're not trying to start trouble, we're just saying we do our thing and you do yours. No one steps on anyone else's toes and we have no beef."

"But if you do . . . ," Albert says.

"Nothing personal," Eddie says.

"Just letting her know how we do things around here."

"Fair enough. Message received. Now on your way, boys." Neve brings her hands to prayer at her chest and bows her head. "And we thank you for your service."

"Always looking out for the great citizens of Santa Maria," Eddie says. They nod curtly and in unison, and then continue down the beach.

Neve parks herself under the umbrella like nothing just happened and scowls at the rest of us, lying in a row in the sun. "In twenty years you're going to look like a bunch of raisins."

"Do you think we should be worried?" I ask. "About the girls who are missing?"

"Come over here, Kidd. Neve's right. You need some lotion," Jason says, giving me a nasty look.

"A serial killer?" I whisper to Neve.

"It's broad daylight. Those girls were alone on the beach when they were taken," Neve says, blowing into her bangs like she's bored by my line of questioning. "I'm not going to stress for no reason. It's summer." She's slathering sunblock all over herself, even though she's in the shade. Once done, she throws Jason the bottle.

"The . . . Gecko brothers or whatever," I say. "Vampires? That was a joke, right?"

Jason looks up from getting Kidd covered like he wants to say something, but he doesn't, just goes back to what he's doing. Which is when I realize he hasn't said anything directly to me this whole time.

"Their parents own the comic-book shop," Neve says, "and they're where you go if you want weed. Those guys are always high. Convinced there's some kind of conspiracy. Pay it no mind."

"But vampires?" I say. "And what did he mean about my family business?"

"There's vampires on that side of the beach, but they only come out at night," Kidd says. She points to the left. "They don't bother us because they're scared. They go over that way. And we go over here." She indicates the right.

"Kidd, stop telling stories." Jason looks at me.

"I'm not—"

"Kidd."

I don't miss the glance Jason and Neve share.

"It's nothing," Neve says. "But the dudes are cool, and if there's ever a fight or someone is bothering you, you want them on your side. We consider them allies. And okay, there *have* been some disappearances lately that have everyone in town on edge. But like, you need to relax. No one is going to hurt you," Neve says. "Change of subject. Time to look at all the pretty people in Santa Maria."

Kidd plops down next to me in her white bathing suit and plays with my fingers until I tickle her and she lies back laughing. My anxiety fades.

"For instance, the boys with the low-riders. They're over there. See all the chrome? Mmm," Neve says, appreciatively.

I thought she was dating Jason, but he doesn't react at all, just keeps looking out at the ocean. I have to squint, but I can see the light reflecting off a line of cars and trucks in the distance, and guys in white tank tops, mostly muscled, some in straw hats, staring out.

"And then there's surfers," Neve says. She lowers her shades to the tip of her nose. "If you like a more docile varietal."

The boys and a few girls are darkened and blondened and they're talking about water.

"When they're on land, some of them magically transform into skaters. You can identify them by their footwear."

Neve points down. “Converse or Vans only. There’s a few stragglers—some ballers and freaks—but that’s about it for Santa Maria.”

“In Taylor there was really only one kind of person.”

“Yeah?”

“Yeah, like not me.”

“Meaning?”

“It was all blond and blue eyes and clean clothes and white teeth. A few of us couldn’t make ourselves fit, but we didn’t hang out together. There weren’t enough of us.” It hurts to talk about, makes me remember walking alone through hallways, like everything was in slow motion and everyone was looking at me.

Why can’t you just try? Lyle said to me when he presented me with some Guess jeans and a lavender blouse and I wouldn’t put them on.

It wasn’t me.

I couldn’t.

“And so where do you guys fit in?” I ask.

“*We*,” Neve says, “roll with the Brayburns, and everybody knows it.”

“Meaning what?”

“Meaning we’re untouchable.”

“Because my family has been here a long time?”

Neve scoffs and shakes her head. “Wow, you really don’t know anything, do you?”

“Like what?”

“She doesn’t need to know anything,” Jason says. “She just got here.”

“Tell me,” I say.

“Maybe later,” Neve says dismissively.

“Elle seems so nice,” I say. “Why would anyone be afraid of her?”

Neve shrugs her shoulders.

"Why do people leave presents at the gate?"

Nothing. She looks bored.

"Neve?" I say.

Something has caught her attention. "You kids go play. I'm not in a swimming mood. I'm in a watching mood." She scans the beach with concentration.

"Come on!" Kidd says.

Jason eyes me for a moment, then puts Kidd on his shoulders and runs into the water. She shrieks as he flings her in.

I would press Neve for more, but years of living with Roxy have taught me when a door is closed. I walk into the water slowly, let the shallow waves nip at my ankles. I try to focus. In Taylor, the dimensions of the pool were clear, the lines in the lanes decided for me. Here, there are no borders. Anything could happen.

The water fills me up as I step in. I swim, avoiding the surfers, and after a while it's like everything else falls away and I am quiet, swimming in the direction my body wants to go. I swim. I swim. I swim.

I stop, far from the shore so the people on the beach look like sugar sprinkles on an ice-cream cone and the lights from the rides flash. Further along where the land juts out, cliffs kiss the sky. That's where my father died. I can see his body falling. There would be no surviving that. Behind the cliff tops, cars pass. He must have parked up there, or maybe he climbed up and then lost his footing. Maybe he was watching the sea and gravity pulled him downward. It's so quiet out here, it's like nothing else even exists. Which is why when Jason pops up beside me, I almost die.

"You all right?" he says.

"Yeah," I say. "Except for you terrifying me."

"Why'd you come this far out?" He looks annoyed, forehead creased. "I left Kidd."

"No one asked you to."

"I thought you were in distress."

"I was thinking."

"About what?"

"What?"

"What were you thinking about?"

"You want to know?"

"I mean, yeah."

"Hard to explain."

"Try."

"My dad . . ." I look to the cliffs again. A ball forms in my throat. "I don't want to," I say.

He looks to the shore uncertainly. "Well, don't come this far out. There's sharks and shit."

"I can take care of myself. I'm a good swimmer."

"I'm sure," he says.

My stomach whirrs. I expect him to go away now, but instead, we tread water and Jason keeps glancing at me like I'm going to talk.

"You can go, you know," I say.

He doesn't.

There are scars on his chest, and a small tattoo of the sun on his right shoulder. His necklace hangs heavy.

"You're not the only one with an ache," he says. "You're not the only one who's had bad things happen."

"I know. I didn't say I was."

He wipes some water off his cheeks. "Everyone here does."

"Does what?"

"Has a story. Otherwise they wouldn't be here. Just remember that. You're not special."

"Well, thank you for sharing."

No one asked him to come out here.

"And she's witty, too." He bends his mouth into a smirk, then shakes his head and kicks off toward the shore.

TWELVE
BONER

I'm still drying off, a little out of breath and a lot grumpy at Jason, thinking of all sorts of clever comebacks way too late, when Elle calls my name from the boardwalk. Neve looks out toward her and waves. Elle gives her a wave in return, then calls for me again. In the time it takes me to slip on a T-shirt and shorts, she greets several people, giving a gray-haired woman in braids a hug. The woman is still thanking her when I get there, but quickly disappears when Elle turns her attention to me.

"How was your first swim? You look refreshed." Elle smooths back my hair and looks into my eyes. "I wish I could have been there for it, but your mom and I had to get you two the basics."

I nod. "It was nice."

"Nice, hunh?" She looks past me to Neve, who has on huge sunglasses and an even bigger black hat. In the distance, Jason and Kidd have started on their sandcastle. "My babies treating you okay?"

"They've been great." Almost.

"Well, I'm sorry to mess up your day, hon, but your mom is refusing to do this without you."

I look at her blankly, still thinking about Jason and his odd behavior toward me. "Do what?"

"The report," she says. "I tried to talk her out of bugging you, but you know Roxy." A soft wind tickles her hair back from her temples. She closes her eyes and inhales deeply, then opens them again and takes my hand, watching me.

It all comes blowing back. The bruises. The pain. The road trip. My lack of clothes, of roots, of friends. That everything is new and we still can't get away from what happened.

And then a blanket of stress covers me, any remaining good smothered into silence.

The police station isn't dingy like I expect it to be. On the outside, it's gray slabs of concrete, set back a little ways from the boardwalk and surrounded by palm trees, plain and severe against the color all around it. But inside, there's a security gate and then the room opens up onto an archipelago of desks where people are typing and talking, holding cups of coffee, consulting files. There's a view of the ocean through one wall of windows, an abandoned, desolate corner of beach, but it's there nevertheless; a hint of seawater, the grit of the sand.

A little further in, I'm accosted by an entire wall of MISSING posters. These must be the disappeared girls the Gecko brothers were talking about. Girls with braids, with big hair, bangs, side ponytails. Girls with braces, with their names on necklaces hanging in the hollows of their throats, stapled into two black-and-white dimensions, hovering and frozen. I graze the paper.

They're dead.

The thought is fast and certain.

I examine the posters more closely.

LAST SEEN IN SANTA MARIA, CALIFORNIA

HAVE YOU SEEN ME?

MISSING FROM SANTA MARIA, CALIFORNIA

Over and over and over.

Roxy comes up from behind, so I'm startled and thrown off balance. I hold her hand, stumble, and my chest tightens. "The picket fences are a lie," she whispers in my ear, and I smell traces of wine.

In the main room a tall police officer with black hair is slapping another on the back, laughing. I went to the police station in Taylor so many times, such a different place than this. Small and quiet, disturbed for the most part only by the occasional drunk or some neighborly dispute. The stone steps, which also led to the courthouse and the one-room jail, had a statue of some war hero out front, the flag flapping proudly in the hot wind. How many times I sat outside, watching the two town cops come and go, blood pounding in my cheeks. I rehearsed what I would say, folded my mind around the words.

My stepfather is Lyle St. James and he . . .

And what might follow?

My stepfather is Lyle St. James and he pretends to be a nice guy, but . . .

The officers greeted me, got used to seeing me reading and writing in my notebook outside the building, probably thinking it was a good place to study under the shade of that tree. I drew the truth. I wrote it in haikus. I wrote it all out in long paragraphs. But I couldn't say it out loud.

Lyle St. James is a
Bully liar drunken punch
But oh he can dance

Everyone knew Lyle.

Best real estate agent in town, probably sold you your house, Officer. Probably your mom loves him because of that smile, and he sure does appreciate a cold glass of lemonade. If your mama is low, he'll make her feel like she's eighteen again, he'll two-step her right into the sunset. He might mow your grass if you're a helpless old lady. Plus he's a deacon in the First Baptist church and oh boy he can sing a hymn like all get out. He and the Lord are saving you together, one tune at a time.

My country 'tis of thee I once was lost but now I'm . . .

And if he loses his temper in a bar fight every now and then, well, a man's got to do what a man's got to do. He's got to be able to take a stand, to protect what's his.

And what's his? We are, that's what.

We *were.*

The front desk of the Santa Maria police station is piloted by a female officer in full uniform. She is not in shorts. Her body is tight and hard, and she is busily moving through a stack of manila folders, sorting them into piles. She nods at us with sharp features, her eyes glinting, unsurprised by our appearance.

"Elle." She straightens some papers and puts them in a manila folder, pats her afro reflexively. "Thought you'd be here earlier."

"Rebecca, honey." Elle leans across the desk and plants a kiss on her cheek. Rebecca's face contorts into what can only be a mix between stress and pleasure. "I'm sorry I'm late."

Rebecca picks up a pile of folders and drops them back down onto the desk. "I'm in paperwork hell." She purses her lips at me. "Oppression comes in many forms, young lady. I'm drowning in shit over here. All the interviews they're doing; the reports. Do they give this job to a man?" She slaps the folder on the table with an open palm. "Of course not. File your own damn reports." She smiles. "But you know what my mother used to say? *You don't need a man, girl, you need your books. Keep your head up and do your schoolwork, you'll be all right.*" She stops and exhales. "That's good advice."

"I hear you," Elle says.

Rebecca gives Roxy and me the up-and-down, taking time to pause at Roxy's attire for the day, consisting of polka dots, heart-shaped sunglasses, and red lipstick, plus heels to the sky.

"This your sister?" Rebecca's eyebrows are raised.

"Roxy. And my niece," Elle says. "Mayhem."

I shake Rebecca's hand. "How do you do?" I say.

"I'm so glad to finally meet you," she says, glancing at Roxy. "So." She eyes the office behind her. "You ready to make a report? We should get to it. You-know-who is here today and should be back any second."

"Oh no," Elle says, "I didn't even think of that. My damn stupid head." She turns to Roxy. "There's something I should tell you."

"He's harmless as a piece of felt," Rebecca says. "I don't know why you let him bother you."

"Boner works here," Elle says, as though she is delivering a death sentence.

Roxy claps her hands together. "*Boner* Boner? Boner is a cop? The last time I saw him he was smoking a joint on the beach!"

Elle waits for Roxy's mirth to burn off. "Things change when you're gone for a decade," she says. "Stoner Boner turned into a know-it-all cop." She throws her hands up, then rests them on her hips. "Well, speak of the pain in the ass," Elle says, "and he shall appear."

A man in plainclothes peers over Rebecca's shoulder. He's tall and in shape, hair shaved close to his head. I try to picture this guy on the beach with a joint hanging out of his mouth and come up empty. He is standing so straight he looks like he actually has a stick in his ass.

"Elle," he says jovially, settling his chin into his cupped hands and batting his eyelashes at her. "What brings you in on this fine day? Shouldn't you be out for an evening ride on your broomstick? Perhaps collecting goat fetuses somewhere?"

Elle folds her arms.

Rebecca snorts.

Roxy laughs.

"Oh, you're so hilarious," Elle says.

"I do try," he says. "Did you know I almost got onstage at the Comedy Store? Could have been the next Robin Williams. Alas. What about you, Ellie? If you weren't cackling the night away with your bats and spells, what would you have been?"

"Me?" Her fingers glide along her chest. "Why, Boner, I'm one of the lucky ones. I don't have a plan B, so throw a party, because you're stuck with me." Elle opens her arm wide to give the attention to Roxy. "Oh my goodness, I plum forgot. You remember my sister?" Elle is smirking so hard her cheeks might split.

Boner goes completely still and looks at us. Really looks at us. His smile drops from his face like someone slapped it off. "Roxy?" he says uncertainly. "Holy shit, Rox." He nearly sweeps Roxy into his arms, but holds back at the last second. His eyes are moist and shining. "Where the hell have you been? I can't even remember the last time . . . I mean of course I remember, but . . . you had a baby in your arms, a purple jacket on, and pigtails. You were so upset . . ."

"Hey, Bone," Roxy says. She moves in for a short hug.

"Is this your daughter? She looks just like—"

"I know, I know, she looks like my mother."

He's trying to absorb the magnitude of Roxy's beauty, and it's so awkward. "I just can't believe . . . I haven't seen you in . . ."

"Thirteen years. Boner's parents owned the closest house to us on the hill," Roxy explains to me. "We grew up together. More than that. We were like family. When we were little some of the other kids were scared of us because of the stories, but not Bone. Never him."

He beams. "Maybe the first time I snuck over there. But once your mom fed me those chocolate cookies of hers, I couldn't stay away."

"And he's in the next house over from ours," Elle says, "to this very day."

"Last time I checked you were exactly where you've always been, too," he says.

"Every damn time these two run into each other it's the same thing," Rebecca says to Roxy. "Bicker, bicker, bicker. Maybe you can make it stop."

"He knows why," Elle says.

"Oh for God's sake, Ellie, please let it go. I'm just doing my job."

"No, you are not doing your job. That is exactly what you are not doing."

"Well, how about this? I'll take care of things down here, and you pay attention to what's going on under your own roof is what I think."

Elle is suddenly serious. "What are you implying?"

"The kids. *Your* kids. People are talking, you know." He crosses his arms.

"What's new? People are always flapping their jaws. Nothing better to do."

"Some of my street guys are actually afraid of them. Can you explain that?"

It's like watching a game of Ping-Pong.

"Hmmm . . ." She taps her chin. "Easy scapegoating because you don't know how to do your job?"

"People are still going missing, Elle. And funny thing is, lately your kids are always around when it happens."

"Because they are out at night on the beach like every

other teenager in town? Great sleuthing, Officer." Elle points at Boner. "You watch who you tell that bullshit to. Those are good kids who haven't had it easy, and I will lose my temper if anything happens to them."

"You tell them to obey the law," Boner says, "and we'll be just fine."

"And you keep your speculations and lies to yourself."

"Hey," Roxy pulls her shades down, revealing what's left of her black eye, and Boner blanches. "Can you two cut it out?"

"My God, Roxy, what happened to you? Who did that to you?" Boner says, Elle forgotten.

"None of your business," Elle says. "Now shoo. We'd like to have Rebecca help us make a report."

Boner opens the gate into the desk area. "I'll handle this myself."

"We want Rebecca to do it."

"Officer Jackson has work to do," Boner says, tapping an index finger on Rebecca's pile of folders. He swings his arm in front of him to show we should go back.

"Fine." Elle sashays through the gate. "But I don't want to hear any of your usual hoo-ha."

Boner doesn't seem afraid of Elle, but he also doesn't seem like he's going to be doing any more arguing. He's in some kind of shock over Roxy's face, is suddenly hovering around her like he wants to be close enough to take a bullet for her should the need arise.

"Sorry about this, Roxy." Boner leads us into a small, windowless room. "It used to be quieter around here, but we're right on the cusp between town and city now, and we haven't had a chance to adjust. The hippies really fucked us over. And now we have some kind of potential serial killer loose in town? Ted Bundy's in prison, but there's always a new sicko there to take his place. We are *this* close to a curfew, and all the boardwalk shopkeepers are flipping out."

The Gecko brothers were wrong. The cops do think it's one person. Someone is out there right now, seeking out girls to take. Boner pulls a couple of folding chairs from the wall and sits down across from us at what amounts to a card table.

"Anyway, everyone's overworked and cranky and all our interview rooms are full. I'm sorry we have to be in here. It's the last space we have."

Elle refuses to sit, leans against the back wall instead.

"Can't say I'm surprised," Roxy says. "Santa Maria may always have been small, but it's never been sweet."

"So many drugs these days." He eyes me meaningfully, as though I am probably on them and he is onto me. "PCP, acid, heroin, ludes." He sighs. "Can't even keep up. If the free-love people hadn't drifted down here from San Francisco and set up camp, we might have been able to keep our little slice of American pie."

"Don't play stupid, Boner," Elle says. "It's just us here. The crime has nothing to do with hippies and you know it. Santa Maria is on a—"

"Vortex. I know, I know. Hang on a sec and I'll grab my magic carpet so we can go for a little cruise."

"Make fun if you want—"

"Fairy tales. Poppycock," Boner says.

"Is it, now?" Elle says. "Why don't you tell us more about this poppycock? Think back, Boner. Think real hard."

"Elle," Roxy says. "Please don't."

The room turns taut, pulled tight. The air conditioner overhead makes a noise like grinding teeth.

"Okay, then," Boner says, ignoring Elle, looking directly at Roxy instead, "what's going on here, and how can I help?"

"To be honest, I'm not really sure why I'm here," Roxy ventures. She's backing into herself.

"You're here because Lyle—" Elle starts.

"We're here because there was an incident with my soon-to-be ex-husband," she says.

"He beat the shit out of her," Elle finishes. "Not for the first time."

Boner nods, gets that simpering look that all men get around Roxy, like they're indulging her, going to protect her fragility. My hands ball up and I push my knuckles against my thighs.

"So your sister dragged you down here to file one of those reports she's so fond of." He leans back and the chair creaks. His biceps are too big. He must lift weights all the time. He must practically live at the gym, working on his physique and hanging out with those girls in striped tights with leotards that go up their butts. "Reports, by the way, Ellie, that don't do a bit of good in the end. A person practically has to die before intervention. Hell," he says, grinning, "I have guys who won't even go near a domestic situation. People go crazy when they're in love."

"Boner, you fucking insensitive prick," Elle murmurs. "You really call that love?"

He straightens, glancing up at her, then at Roxy. "Of course not. You know what I mean."

"Yes, I know what you mean, and I also know it's bullshit."

"Of course I know it's important for us to take these things seriously. I'm just saying there are holes in the law when it comes to the goings-on between a man and his wife. There's not much we can do. And Elle, you and your obsession with this paper trail? It's not the answer. It just puts you in the system, on the books, you know what I mean? It can even work to your disadvantage. Questions come up. How long has it been going on? Why would you allow it—"

Roxy pinks up.

"Are you kidding?" Elle says. "You don't have the first clue what it's like to be a woman in this world. How dare you?"

"Elle, let me finish," Boner says. "I'm not saying why would she allow it. Obviously most women can't defend themselves against an abuser or control their behavior. I'm saying why would *she* allow it."

"You know, I'm about sick of people talking about me like I'm not in the room, like I'm some dumb little girl," Roxy says.

"No one's saying that—"

"Yes you are, Elle, even by making me come down here when I don't want to, making me feel like I have to appease you." She turns to Boner. "I made some decisions and maybe they weren't the best ones, but I did what I did. I didn't defend myself because I didn't know what would happen next and I didn't want to come back here. Maybe that was the best I could do. But I'm here now."

"You don't have to do this if you don't want to," Elle says. "I'm just trying to protect you. What if he comes here, tries to take you back?"

"He won't do that," Roxy says. "He's got too much pride."

He will come *because* he has pride, not in spite of it. I don't know how she could really believe what she said, if she's lying to herself or if I really know him better than she does.

Lyle St. James smiles sun
Teeth white and straight and shiny
Clenched against blood lust

"Roxy." Boner makes a steeple of his fingers. "I'm going to give you my best advice here, okay?"

"Go ahead," Roxy says.

"You do not deserve to be hit. Any man who hits a woman

or a child is subhuman and should be crushed like a cockroach, which is what he is. And especially to hit someone like you, like your kid." His face is becoming more flushed with every word. "But I just want to make sure you get what's happening here. This means you're starting something, a trail. You need to be sure you're willing to take that risk."

"He's never going to let her go." The sound of my voice surprises me. "He's going to come looking for her." I'm shaking so bad. When I get mad I cry. I'm so mad right now the tears are pushing at the edges of my lids. "You don't know him."

Boner looks at me, at the pictures of Roxy and all her bruises on the table between us.

Roxy finds a smoke and lights it. Boner slides the ashtray on the table over to her.

"Just make the goddamn report," Elle says.

Boner stares at the Polaroids for a moment.

Roxy takes a drag and puts her sunglasses back on. "Last time I saw you, things were bad, and now they're bad again. You must think I'm crazy, that I'm just a mess of a person."

"It's not like that, Rox."

"Sure it's not."

"I think you're a sight for my sore eyes, that's what I think."

"Oh please," Elle says from the corner.

"Your mother was the belle of the ball," Boner says, I guess to me, but not looking at either of us, just staring at Roxy. "And then poof . . . she left all of us, just like that. Just like that, she was gone."

Elle steps up to the table. I haven't known her long, but I know enough about her to understand that she barely has hold of her temper. "Get the report," she says, teeth visibly clenched, "and fill it out. Right now. Right now, Boner. Paper. Pen. Go."

He looks to Roxy, who nods. "It's for the best."

Boner pulls a notebook and a pen from a corner file cabinet. “Okay, Rox,” he says, “why don’t you tell me what happened?”

I decide again that I like my aunt Elle very very much.

THIRTEEN
RAPE

When we get home, I need to be alone. Roxy too, I guess, because she takes a couple blue pills and disappears, and Elle goes into the garden. I find a quiet spot in my grandmother's study, amongst all her books, and I pull the diary from where I've hidden it, behind *Chaos Magic* and *The Electric Kool-Aid Acid Test.* I open its pages, find my place in my great-great-grandmother Julianna's story, and read.

I was raised in a small house in a big forest, with my father and mother. They knew the plants and the land and wanted nothing from other human beings, they thought people were a scourge. When they died of an influenza virus I somehow survived, I came down from the forest hill, and I found myself in a small boarding house. That's where the director Alfonzo discovered me, when he was out looking for a fresh face for his play.

Your father was Romeo, and we were to perform at the Trident, the sea stage, the creation of the madman who had come from

Spain to be the art darling of the entire coast.

A stage, he had said, that gives the impression of being in the sea.

It wasn't in the sea of course, not exactly, but it was close enough to pretend. He bought the finest stage curtains, the most elaborate lights and chandeliers, and he built his stage on an inlet. Romeo & Juliet was the flagship play.

Your father came from a homesteading family, but he was an actor at heart. Still is. I catch him reciting his lines to the furniture. He was so happy with all the strutting and fencing and the sounds of the language.

By the second performance, I knew he loved me. Truth be told, I knew it the moment I met his gaze and found it burning. He held me at my waist and with Alfonzo sitting in the front row reciting every line along with us, hands gesturing wildly, and how soft his touch. I knew I would be his wife. I would bear him children and we would have a cat and work the land at the top of the hill that he inherited from his father.

He told me I was beautiful.

It never made much mind to me whether I was beautiful or not. In the woods it was of no concern. I didn't grow up with mirrors or fancy dresses, but for him, I would be beautiful.

Your raven hair, he said, a little unoriginally, but with so much passion I couldn't help but smile.

We would meet in the cave behind the stage where no one would look for us. We would let the water trickle from the wall. The sin was assuredly temporary. I knew he loved me with all he had to offer and would leave me with my reputation and dignity intact. It was for that reason I could forget that dignity entirely with him, forget everything as though there was no world and there were no brutalities, as though it was not a terrifying and daring thing to come down from the mountain without my rifle in hand, an orphan surrounded by the savagery of human beings. I want you to know how much love there was between us, how vast and innocent, and that some touch is kind even when it is passionate and of the flesh. I hope that for you: one love.

Julianna, you are a spitfire, my father used to tell me. What are you going to do with that spark?

I don't know, I used to tease. Burn everything down?

That night, I was preparing for another visit from your father in the cave behind the stage. I brought a blanket though the ground was warm in the cave, for it was winter and the warmth of the summer theater days were behind us. I made some little cakes with delicate flower icing. I poured petals from fat peonies on the ground. I was so lost in my romantic vision, I didn't hear the stranger's footfalls. It was dark, and perhaps it was stupid, but I felt safe, as you do before you are violated and never again afterward.

I thought it was your father, but only for a moment. When the man hit the back of my head and I in turn fell to the ground, I knew I was going to die. He lifted my skirt from behind. He told me I was beautiful as your father had, and then he took everything from me. I never saw his face, though I felt him, his reeking breath.

It hurt. God be, it hurt. And that may be how you were conceived, though I have never wanted you to feel any less than Lawrence's daughter, for that is who and what you are.

I was decimated by my lack of ability to simply leave. We are so trapped in these human bodies for the duration of our lives, even when our spirits are screaming to be let out. I did pray to die, and then I prayed to live. I could not make up my mind then, and I cannot now.

Juliet, he said.

This is the part I have always wanted to tell you, because I fear it will affect you, that you will have to pay for my communion with strange forces.

I performed witchcraft. I did. And in doing so, I think I cursed us both.

My blood dripped into the dirt below me. I staggered to the stream that had poured over us. It was cool going down my throat. I splashed it on my face, but I couldn't hide my shredded skin and I let myself bleed into the dirt. Then, when I was strong enough, I went to the shore and found your father there, tied up, with a bump on the back of his head.

I went back the next day to search for clues about the man's identity. Finding none, I prayed for the gods to destroy the place, to destroy the man who had hurt me. I raged. I did. I put my head into the water and I screamed.

And would you believe the very next day the gods sent an earthquake to rattle the Trident right off the earth, to sink it into the ocean. The whole stage. Gone. Just like that. I swear to you, I willed the earth to come apart as I had. And it did. On April 18, 1906, the earth did as I had asked and it took the theater and the stage down.

In San Francisco, three thousand souls lost their lives. Here, the only damage sustained was the Trident breaking off and falling into the sea. The land clean sunk, like an old pirate ship. For the longest while, I would go and look at the place it should have been, trying to understand how and why my prayers were answered.

And then I went back to the cave.

I knew right then that there was something about that water, my blood, my cries. After that, when I found the water and the cave intact and my belly growing with child, I could feel that man. I knew just where he was and I found him. I went into his living room where he was taking his dinner, and I murdered him with no more than these two arms and these lips and left him with his cheek resting in his roast and potatoes. Imagine his surprise when he realized it was me. "Juliet," he said again, and it was his last word.

The next morning, the crows came, and they have been with us since. I do not know why, but it cannot be coincidence. I fell into the cave's arms accidentally, but now it is mine.

What I have gifted you is something I must apologize for even as I have placed it in your palm. Imagine my surprise when you went to it so naturally, when you drank and saw and took to it like it had always been yours. You tried to keep your discovery from me, but the sight makes it impossible. You shine differently from the rest, and there are no honeycombs for us. And so I knew. And I also knew I could never say anything to you about any of it.

We plant. We sow. If we mind what grows from our sorrows, we can only call this life mysterious and we can only hope to worship that mystery properly.

Don't deny evil, Billie. Crush it. That is your duty.

Your eyes are strange, your voice filled with determination and spirit. Carry on.

Your mother,
Julianna

PART TWO

Take your man and curse you, too

FOURTEEN
SAND SNATCHER

I've barely seen Jason or Neve or Kidd in days. I had been having fantasies that we would be best friends, that we would be inseparable and I would never be alone again, but as quickly as I thought that, I found myself loafing around the house alone. Everyone sleeps all the time, Roxy in her old room with the door closed, the kids up in the attic. I get hard thoughts when I'm alone too long, remember too many things, let myself linger on Taylor, Texas, and Lyle and whether or not he's going to drive up any second, so I stick close to Elle, who always has lots going on, taking phone calls and leaving at random to do her work with the women in the community, but who also picks lettuce and flowers and peruses the property.

She puts an arm around my shoulder as we walk to the gate and collect the gifts and the thank-you cards that have been left there. The birds caw and coo and hop along next to us. There's one with a brown patch on his beak who seems to be watching me and who is always there when I look.

"Oh, aren't you lovely?" Elle says, sniffing a bouquet of stargazer lilies.

I make a stack of the thank-you notes and slip them into their designated folders in what was once my grandmother's desk. "Why do they leave presents?"

Elle regards me searchingly, then goes back to sorting papers.

"I know Roxy doesn't want you to tell me anything, but I want to know," I insist.

She looks at me surprised, then sighs. "They leave presents because myths make people feel safe. Get that crate of oranges, would you? We can make fresh juice."

We place the creamy scented soaps in the bathrooms and store the chocolate-covered almonds and colorful rock candies in the pantry. We stack the vegetables in the fridge and the succulent fruits in bowls. I take these quiet moments with Elle and I store them away. She is steady and strong and certain. As she walks through rooms, curtains wave in the breeze as though reaching for her. This is how I want to be a woman, not like my mother, who is constantly reacting, whose very self seems to be a hostile presence, toxic to her own body so she has to medicate to keep herself blurred.

Oh, Roxy.

My mama.

Waking up at dark, rifling around in all the rooms, crying when she thinks I can't hear. Since the police station, Roxy has been hitting the Valium hard and is mostly parked on the couch, reading or napping.

Does this mean she thinks Lyle will come, too, that she wakes up shaking in the night?

Does she wind her mind around all the ways he might be able to find us? Old phone bills; some acquaintance of Roxy's who knew where she was from; process of elimination?

Worse, does it mean she misses him? Would she ever take us back to Taylor?

So far it seems like Neve and Jason and Kidd come in almost at sunrise, then sleep and leave again in the afternoon, which would explain why they were eating breakfast at two p.m. my first day here. They spend most of their time in the attic, and I don't want to go up there uninvited.

They don't invite me.

I wonder if I did something wrong. I wonder if that day at the beach, that moment out in the water with Jason—if they decided I was a mismatch. Not cool enough. Not dark enough. Just a girl in a pair of shorts and a T-shirt from Texas.

Today, alone, I amuse myself by digging deeper into my parents' closet, looking through old boxes of paperwork. I find a pipe in my grandmother's desk and stalk about the house with it in my mouth, pretending to say important things. I pet Millie and let her knead me for so long I expect to rise and then bake. Finally, I flop on the bed and stare upward. Not having a TV is hell.

With nothing to do, I imagine lives for the kids upstairs from before Elle found them.

In my mind, Neve made a shank out of a toothbrush, melting one end to a deadly point. She stabbed a girl at school with it. The girl died. No one ever found out, but the guilt ate away at her until she started setting things on fire, which is how she wound up living under an overpass, which is how she wound up here. In my mind, Neve glows. She bares her teeth. She is covered in blood.

I start awake. The house is completely silent. No lights are on.

I can't be here another second, in the shadows of the sunset.

Somewhere, life is happening.

"Come on." I throw a rose-colored cardigan I found in my grandmother's closet over Roxy, who is sacked out on the seafoam-green sofa in the living room. "Let's go into town." I still haven't recovered from scraping together the last of our change to fill the gas tank, but Elle gave me a fifty-dollar bill I haven't broken yet.

"Mmm, baby?" I hear a slight slur in her words that means

she isn't a hundred percent sober. Probably not even seventy-five percent.

"Hey, Roxy? Mom? Did you hear me? I want to go to the boardwalk. Please."

Her eyelids flip open and flutter. "Where's Elle?"

"I don't know. Not here."

She sits up, hair askew, and pulls her tank top over her stomach. "The car . . . we're still out of gas. I don't think we could make it to the station. Have to get a can or something."

"We can walk."

"You want to go to the boardwalk?" She nods out again, relaxes back against the cushion.

"Yes! Please!" I tug on her so hard she falls to the floor in a heap and bursts out laughing. She's awake now.

"I bet we still have bikes in the storage shed," she says, pulling the cardigan around her shoulders. Seeing her on the floor like that, legs flopped in front of her, hair tousled, smiling, I could almost believe there's hope.

"Bikes! That's perfect! Come on!" I jump up and down to wrangle enough energy for both of us.

"Okay, maniac. Hold your horses." She's brightening, looking excited even. "Let me get my face on and we'll go."

While Roxy gets ready, I follow her instructions to the bikes, which are covered in cobwebs. I wipe them down, and when Roxy comes out she's in some cutoff shorts and flip-flops and her hair is in short pigtails. She's not so done up and has less makeup than usual. She howls as we fly down the hill. She's going too fast, and her yipping cries hurt. It's like she's calling herself back from somewhere far away.

Once we reach the bottom, she slows so we can ride next to each other. Crickets chirp, and cars pass us by. The night is warm and inviting. Roxy seems spent and content, hardly pedaling at all, letting her legs fly out to the side so the wheels click beneath her.

"Thanks for making me leave the house, baby."

I don't say anything.

"I know it's been tough lately . . . again. I'm just so tired. I need a minute to recover. But it's not fair. I should be with you. I should be helping you." She looks at me, and between the streetlamps and the waning sunset I see her right down to her guilt. "I know you're worried about me, worried about Lyle coming for us, making us go back. But you know how I know Lyle isn't going to come here, May?"

I stay silent and listen.

"Because he'll never leave Taylor. He's homegrown. I landed in his lap and vanished just as quick," she says. "Plus all I ever did for twelve years was tell him I never wanted to come back here no matter what. He probably thinks we went back to that shelter and they evacuated us or something. He probably thinks we're in Timbuktu."

"There are a million ways he could find us. He's totally crazy—"

"He's selfish and lazy. Trust in that."

"He's obsessed with you. He's bad. And he's an asshole."

"Yes," she agrees. "He's an asshole."

We ride a minute in silence, and then she pedals ahead, and it's like years are peeling off of her with every turn of her wheels, until I can see my mother shiny, as she must have been when everything was ahead of her and her heart was whole.

At night, the boardwalk is different from in the daytime. There are still all the people the kids showed me, but there's more underneath it, like it's all being powered by an electric current. A group of boys ride over its wooden planks on motorcycles, hooting as a cop on foot runs after them, yelling. It sounds and smells like you would think. Roasted nuts, cotton candy, trash, seawater, hot dogs, popcorn. There are people standing outside little stores with cute names, offering up T-shirts and bathing suits. In front of one of them, two older people in afghans, the man with long hair and a beard, are totally passed out on each other's shoulders. Along the sides of the boardwalk, people play guitars and fiddles. They sing familiar songs and rattle jars filled with loose change. One guy has a sign painted on cardboard that reads NEED MONEY FOR BEER. The Gecko brothers pass by, nodding militarily as they say, "Evening, Brayburns." Everyone looks tan and a little sweaty. Above us, the Ferris wheel spins its slow tour. Any tourists that might be milling around in the daytime are gone.

"Come on, baby." Roxy tugs on my arm.

A man in a yellow G-string and a top hat whizzes by on roller skates and opens up a deck of cards, showing me a spread made entirely of hearts.

Roxy fluffs her hair, but I am transfixed as we pass wall after wall of more MISSING posters. They're everywhere concert and event flyers should be. It's impossible for me to ignore, and I'm not the only one. There's a buzz as people stop to crowd around, commenting to each other.

I look into the girls' eyes again, try to see their souls. Their families must be falling apart. They must be going crazy. I flash on what Roxy would do if it were me, taken from the beach. She'd pluck out her eyelashes. She'd cry and starve herself to death. She would never recover. She's told me before, told me outright she couldn't survive losing me and my dad both. It would be the very worst thing.

What I would do if something happened to you, Cookie.

It's like I can actually hear the mothers of these lost girls crying, like I can hear them screaming for their babies.

"May, stop," Roxy says. "It's morbid."

I shrug her off even as the pit inside me grows and whispers that they are dead, they are dead, they are dead.

"May."

If this were happening to Roxy, and I were gone, she would expect the world to stop its self-indulgent spinning to find me, to help her.

"Roxy, don't."

"They probably just took off."

"They didn't."

"*We* did."

"One of them is thirteen. You think she just took off?" I cross my arms. My breathing is rough.

"Fine," she says, "suit yourself." She pulls a Red Vine from her purse and munches.

HAVE YOU SEEN THIS GIRL?

I say their names.

KAREN DELANO, 16

JESSIE CASTRO, 14

KIMBERLY RAEL, 13

BENITA JACKSON, 14

TINA CHAPUT, 16

LAST SEEN IN SANTA MARIA

LAST SEEN IN SANTA MARIA

LAST SEEN IN SANTA MARIA

Five of them. All last seen here on the beach after dark. I sear their faces into my memory.

"You have to tell Boner to do something about this," I say. "We all should be doing something about this. Where are the cops?"

Roxy looks at me sternly, knitting her brow. "They're interviewing people? Detecting! How should I know? Having cops crawling all over the boardwalk is not the Santa Maria way. I heard they have extra lifeguards or something, that the beach is being watched twenty-four hours a day now."

I look at the pictures again. It's like there's a Lyle to worry about everywhere I go. Maybe worse than him. I can't imagine him killing anyone other than us, and then only if he was real mad. But someone coldly planning? That's something else altogether. That's bad to the power of ten. Evil, like Julianna said.

Don't deny evil. Crush it.

Roxy clucks. "Quit obsessing over this stuff. You're going to give yourself nightmares. And me, too."

"I'm not. All I'm saying is there must be something we can do."

A group of girls in bikinis walks by chattering and laughing. The beach itself is not lit up at night. It's nothing but darkness out there, except for the swing of the occasional flashlight.

"You don't think it's the tiniest bit pathological that all these people are acting like this isn't even happening?" I press.

Roxy looks at me. "Mayhem, you're exhausting me. This is not our concern. Why should everyone stop living? Life should go on. Anyway, Santa Maria can take care of herself. She's got her defenses in place."

KAREN DELANO, 16

JESSIE CASTRO, 14

KIMBERLY RAEL, 13

BENITA JACKSON, 14

TINA CHAPUT, 16

"But—"

"No buts. Lord, Cookie. I know it's upsetting, I really do, but you can't spend all your time focused on negative things. You have to keep living or you let the bad guys win." Roxy drags me forward a few paces. I'm about to point out that she hasn't been living all that much, and has actually mostly been facedown on the couch, when she stops and stares ahead like someone just slapped her into shock.

"This used to be a thrift store," she says. "I got pants here once, all leather with fringe down the sides. Matching bra. They were amazing. Damn Elle," she mutters to herself. "You'd think she'd give me a warning at least."

Inside the store, a woman with huge, teased red hair is making scooting motions to a couple of kids, obviously trying to get them to leave. One has a mohawk and a jean jacket covered in safety pins, and the other has on big baggy parachute pants and a net shirt that barely covers his abdomen. His pink baseball cap is slanted to the side. He grins at her, flips her off, and runs past Roxy and me with a videotape in hand.

"Marcy," Roxy says.

"You know her?"

"Ex–best friend."

Roxy with a friend? Roxy with a *best* friend?

"Why ex?" I say, as Marcy, who is shaped precisely like a potato, rushes out after the thieves.

Roxy ignores me in favor of watching Marcy chase the kids. By the time Marcy's on the boardwalk, she's out of breath and they're long gone, having disappeared into the crowd.

"Little shits," she wheezes. "If it weren't for the goddamn asthma . . . Now I have to get security gates?" She squints at Roxy, elbows resting on her knees. She watches us a minute or two, trying to connect the dots that are obviously flailing around in her brain.

Roxy crosses her arms and waits. "It's Roxy, dummy," she says, softly, then when Marcy still doesn't speak, "Yeah . . . it's me, sugar. How goes it?"

Marcy pauses like the bottom just fell out of her reality. Her friendly, bright features settle into wariness. "My God," she says finally, "I honestly thought I'd seen the last of you."

"Well, here I am."

Something is passing between them, something old and mired, like a current of water, one filled up with trash and seaweed.

"Your hair's platinum?" Marcy sticks a hand out to touch Roxy's head. "I always thought of you as such a brunette. Didn't even recognize you."

Roxy grins, and I can tell she's relieved. "I needed a change when I left. Anyway, your hair's red!" Her hands search around in her purse. She comes up with a couple of butterscotch candies and hands me one.

That's when Marcy's attention shifts my way and she gasps. She pushes her hair back from her face as though to see me better, as though to see me at all. She steps forward, eyes getting larger. Now that she's up close I think she has the biggest eyes I've ever seen, a watery green, swimming between her lids. She purses her lips and clasps her hands. "Lucas Machado's baby girl."

I'm aware of myself in the overalls from the big bag of stuff Elle gave me, of the black T-shirt underneath, of my emergent tan, the way the ocean weather has loosened my curls so they spiral down my back and the saltwater has lightened the blue tips.

She pulls at my hands and rests them in her own. They're pudgy and soft, and I am immediately comforted, reminded of the three fairy godmothers in *Sleeping Beauty* who always screw everything up with their magic. She's like a more punky version of that, as though one of those sweet ladies fell into a bag of makeup and a leather skirt.

"You're a vision," she says. "An absolute vision."

When she skims my cheek, I don't flinch, which tells me something.

"We all loved your dad, you know. He was a very special man with a big, warm heart and a laugh that made anything seem possible." She purses her lips again, which I'm already taking to mean she's thinking. "You have that heart, too. Deep." She pushes an index finger into my chest and I half expect it to go through my skin. "I can see it."

"Stop harassing my kid with all your woo-woo crap," Roxy says, but she's smiling. "Marcy isn't any good at small talk, May. Ask her the weather and she'll predict your future."

"Be that as it may, you know what I'm saying is true," Marcy says. "It's impossible that you look at her without thinking the exact same thing. She has his heart, and that's a blessing."

Until it's not. Deep hearts dive off cliffs with no water to catch them.

She's welling up again. "She's beautiful, Roxy. Just gorgeous."

"I know," Roxy says, and it seems like she's about to lose it, too. She sniffles. "Shit." Roxy finds a cigarette, sticks it in her mouth, and glances inside the store. "So you own a video store?"

Marcy nods.

"That's great, Marcy. I love movies."

"Me, too."

"Really?!" Roxy threads her arm through Marcy's. "Tell me everything."

And then they're chatting and it's like I'm not even there and every three seconds or so, one of them says, "*What?*" and the other one says, "*No way!*"

I head into the store, start scanning the shelves. Roxy is into kung fu movies with bad dubbing, so the mouths aren't even close to moving at the same time. I like comedies where people fall in love and everything is bad and then in the end everything is good. Movies are something we have always done together, Roxy and me, something that has kept me from feeling so lonely as I sometimes do.

This store has a pretty good collection.

". . . you just left us and . . . you could have . . . ," Marcy is saying.

I stop and listen without turning my head. Roxy has a way of knowing when I'm being nosy.

"After what happened to Lucas . . . I . . . ," Roxy says, and I strain even harder. They're talking about my father.

"Good movie."

I almost jump at the sound of a deep, throaty voice right next to my head.

I glance down at the box in my hands. *Aliens.* I didn't even know I picked it up. Neve, Jason, and Kidd are right in front of me. Neve looks highly entertained by my sudden fluster. She takes the box from my hand and considers it while I consider her: her breasts cinched into a black lace corset, the necklace resting between them, a row of black rubber bracelets climbing up her left arm, the dagger tattoo running down the right so she looks like a pirate.

"I like this one better than the first." She hands the box for *Aliens* back to me.

"The first one is quieter, but better tension," I say.

"Both stupid. That's not even a real Latina playing Vasquez in the second," Jason says.

"Still a good movie."

"No, it's not. The whole thing is bullshit."

Kidd reaches into the bubble-gum machine and shakes it, trying to get a ball to come out. After a few seconds, a yellow one drops into her palm. "Works every time." She fixes Neve with a severe glare. "You said if I went and did the one thing you guys would—"

"Kidd—" Jason's voice is filled with warning.

"I heard what Elle said. I'm not going to spill any beans to Mayhem." She fiddles with the machine again. "All I'm saying is you said if I went to watch that creepy guy's house you would take me on the roller coaster, so let's go to the creepy guy's house so I can go on the roller coaster."

"I don't want her going," Jason says.

"I need you there," Neve says. "What if something goes wrong? There's got to be at least two of us."

"Not Kidd."

"We have a job to do," she says. "I'll just take him to the tunnel, no big deal. I'm not going to let him—"

"Neve." Jason looks in my direction.

Neve stops talking and pouts. "I was really looking forward to this. You're ruining all my fun with your rules."

I glance outside. Roxy is telling some kind of animated story. "How long are you guys going to be gone?" I ask.

"Forty-five minutes, tops," Neve says.

"I'll take her," I say. "It'll be fine."

"Really? You're the best!" Neve tries to pull Jason to the door, but he doesn't budge.

"I'm not even a baby," Kidd says. "You guys are rude."

Jason shakes his head and stands firm. "Yeah, right. I'm not leaving Kidd with her. She's a—"

"Brayburn? Hardly," Neve says, rolling her eyes.

"I was going to say stranger."

"Come on. Look at her. You can see plain and simple that there's nothing going on. Let's go, get it done, boom, bang, bing, we'll be back in a jiffy and Kidd will be right here, safe and sound."

"On the rides," Kidd corrects.

"On the rides," Neve confirms. "Having a total blast."

"I'll make sure she's taken care of," I say. "We don't have a car, so you guys will be back?"

"*Totally!*" Neve says. "This is great. Perfect!"

Jason looks unconvinced.

"Ugh, oh my God!" Neve says, with a heavy emphasis on the *d*. "Let's get this over with. What's your favorite color?" She looks at me expectantly.

"Um, red maybe?" I say, trying to think.

"How do you like your eggs?"

"No eggs. They make me gag."

"Excellent answer. Seconded, and thirded by Jason himself. And are you going to harm Kidd in any way, shape, or form?"

"No!" I say. "Of course not."

"Well, then." Neve curls herself around Jason, leaning into him. "What's the problem? Jason, she lives in the same house as us. If we can't find her, we only have to walk down a very short flight of stairs. Anyway, she's supposed to be our sister now, or cousin or something."

Jason keeps his body stiff. "Kidd, it's up to you, I guess."

Kidd pops a second bubble-gum ball into her mouth, this time a pink one. She scans me up and down and then says, "I'll go with Mayhem." She smiles. "And if she messes with me, I'll just kill her."

FIFTEEN
THIS IS YOUR BRAIN ON DRUGS

The roller coaster is a rickety thing, made of white wood, and I regret it the second I'm on board. I tell myself I'm ridiculous. I don't know why anyone would ever want to do this. I don't know why I am trying so hard to impress a little kid who, judging from the way she's giving me the side-eye, thinks I'm a total moron.

As we climb upward, I catch wave after wave of paralyzing fear. I can't get back to the ground. Kidd fixes me with open curiosity and some smugness as we climb into the damp air, as though she wants to observe my cowardly ways. Either that, or she's watching me like my entire being is a car wreck. The lights around us are a pink and indigo rainbow, and they blur into the cries coming from below as we climb. That's how high we're going. If I weren't gutted by my own anxiety, I would be mesmerized.

"I've never been on a roller coaster before," I squeak as we approach the summit.

Kidd pries my hand from the bar and rests it in her own. "You don't have to be scared," she says. "And if you are, you can scream. It will make you feel better."

Then I do scream. We round the hump and fly downward and then up again and through the night and I yell and I laugh until I choke.

This is the opposite of swimming, which is all me, every

muscle moving toward an end, my spirit controlling every move. I don't have any control at all here. The fear is gone as we round corner after corner, hands gripped. When we pull into the loading zone, my whole body is vibrating.

"You did a good job," Kidd tells me as the safety bars lift up automatically, and the guy signals us to move along and out so the next group can get in.

"You did, too." I am fully exhilarated as Kidd bounces next to me.

"How did you never go on a roller coaster before? How is that even possible?"

"Taylor," I say. "It doesn't have roller coasters. There aren't even any anywhere nearby."

She wrinkles her nose. "I would never live anywhere with no roller coaster."

"Agreed," I say, deciding that's an excellent way to assess a town's appeal.

"So what did you do there? In Taylor? If there was no roller coaster, I mean?"

I think about this for so long she finally says, "Are you hungry?"

I nod and tousle her hair. "Where are the tacos everyone has been talking about?"

Kidd points to the end of the boardwalk, to a beat-up old ice-cream truck. There are still pictures of rockets and Fudgsicles glued onto its sides, but now a boom box sits in the window blaring some music with words I can't understand, and the guys with the shirts buttoned at the top and the hot cars we saw at the beach crowd around, laughing and talking. Another trail of people passes, jostling by, heading somewhere beyond, off the boardwalk. It looks like they're following the Pied Piper or something, jumping over each other, skateboarding, elated.

"What are they in such a hurry for?"

"Sax Man," she says. "He plays every Friday, and then there's always a party on the beach. Fires and stuff like that. Sometimes people surf or get naked and swim." She shrugs.

"And you go every time?"

She nods.

"And what do you do at a party? Do you have friends?"

"I like the fires. I like watching them. And I don't need friends. I have Jason and Neve."

"Nine's pretty little for going to parties."

"Jason doesn't like me to be away from him. He says I'm safest when we're together, even though that's not true anymore. I take care of myself." She looks away.

"Don't you want to be at home, drinking cocoa in your pj's?"

"I was in my house when the men came." She stares straight ahead. "Being home doesn't make you safe."

I think of Lyle, of how I felt in that house.

"Yeah, I know that's true," I say. "Being home doesn't make you safe."

Kidd eyes me shyly, then licks at her lips. "I can see it. You don't have to tell me about it."

"See what?"

She pretends not to hear me.

"See what, Kidd?"

She sighs like I'm boring. "You getting pushed into the wall. That guy standing in your room at night. The mean lady leaving you in the basement."

That's an unexpected jolt. Grandmother. I must have been four years old when she found me putting on her jewelry and left me in the dark for hours. I haven't thought about it in years.

"How do you know about that?" I ask her, trying to catch my breath.

"I just do."

"What do you see?"

She stops and folds her arms in front of her. "You going to tell someone on me? Because I wouldn't do that if I were you. You would ruin everything and then Neve would get mad. And you don't want to see what happens when Neve gets mad."

I don't have to think about that for long. "You are correct. I do not want to see Neve mad. I just want to understand how you could know about that. Did my mom say something to you?"

She softens somewhat but refuses to answer, then says, "We know the truth, that's all. Everyone's truth."

I stop walking because my thoughts are swimming. I'm awash in Sunday school, in rules and Lyle and Grandmother, and Roxy swinging her hips to Frank Sinatra in the living room and my father falling from a cliff's edge and Lyle with murder in him. Things keep coming together so they almost make sense, but then they split apart again before I can get to them.

"You okay?" she says.

I nod, wanting her to say more. "So you were telling me about the men in your house?"

I wait.

"I was telling you about the parties, not the men," she says finally. "Can I get a soda?"

"Sure."

She's so upright, so alert, watching everything, our handholding on the roller coaster as far behind us as the adrenaline rush from the ride.

"Do you want one, too?"

"Yes."

"And how hungry are you?"

"You don't want to tell me what happened," I say. "That's okay. Sometimes it's hard to talk."

She stops walking and throws both hands on her hips. "You want to know what happened?"

"I do."

"Okay, but I'm used to it so it's not hard for me, but it might be hard for you."

"Okay."

She makes a gun from her fingers and pulls the imaginary trigger. "Banging on the door. Men coming in. No more Mommy. No more Daddy. Got it?"

We've reached the truck, the Latin music coming out, and the best smell ever.

"It's okay," Kidd says. "No one is ever going to do anything like that to me ever again. No one could."

"What do you mean?"

"Neve says it's not time for telling you that yet," Kidd says. "But don't worry, you'll find out."

I float the rest of the way to the truck's window, everything around us, from the music to the smells to the soft swells of the waves and the people screaming as the roller coaster tears downward, steeped in surreal hues.

"*Buenas noches*," the guy at the window says to us. He's sweaty, bandana tied around his head, AC/DC T-shirt on.

Roxy used to make meat with cumin and oregano and all kinds of other spices that would fill up the house on good days. It smells even better than that now, which almost distracts me from the crazy conversation with Kidd. It has definitely distracted her. She's reading over the menu board tacked next to the window.

"*Buenas noches, señor*," Kidd says. "*Dos Coca-Colas, por favor, y cuatro*"—she looks me up and down—"*seis barbacoa tacos*."

"*Bien*," the guy says, beaming at her Spanish.

A few minutes later he hands us a couple of cardboard boats filled with tacos. I grab our drinks and my change.

"You girls be careful of the Sand Snatcher, now," he says.

"Sand Snatcher," I repeat.

The guy folds his arms. "You never know when he's going to strike, but all those girls were on the beach, so just look out."

"We're not scared," Kidd says.

"You mean the girls from the posters?" I say.

The guy nods. "Everyone knows it's one dude. They keep saying the girls ran away because there's no bodies, but then how come they were all last seen on the beach? That would be a hell of a coincidence, don't you think? First girl gone a year ago, then no one for six months, then bam, bam, bam, bam." He motions to a red baseball bat in the corner behind him. "I'm looking out."

"I told you, we're not scared," Kidd says, with a mouthful of taco.

I thank him and shuffle her along before she starts a fight with the taco guy, and soon we're too busy eating to think about much else.

"Tacos are the perfect food." I rub my belly. "First crunchy, then the meat, and then there's cheese and whatever that salsa was."

"Chimichurri, duh."

I spot Neve, coming down the boardwalk, using Jason's arm as leverage as she bounces and bounces. She is glowing and wide-eyed. Not him. He has gone dark again.

"Come on!" she says. "Let's go let's go let's go, slackers!"

She dances me to the video store, where Roxy and Marcy are still talking, an ashtray filled with cigarette butts on the table beside them.

"Miss Roxy," Neve says, "can Mayhem have permission to come out with us tonight?"

Roxy looks happier than I've seen her in a while. Even with the Sand Snatcher and all the weird shit going on in this town, joy seems to be leaking all over everyone. Including me. Neve is like some kind of sprite, and here she is, holding my hand, batting her eyelashes at my mother because she wants to spend time with me.

I expect Roxy to say no. She likes to have me close by. Usually I don't mind that, but right now I want to be close by Neve.

"Well, where are you going to be?" Roxy asks.

"We thought we'd listen to some music. We'll be safe, I promise."

"You won't be drinking?"

"No, ma'am."

"And you won't be doing drugs?"

"We don't do drugs. Swear." Neve puts up two fingers. "I've seen those commercials with the egg and the guy with the frying pan." She shudders. "Terrible stuff."

"What about the beach? I don't want Mayhem walking out there tonight." Roxy looks outward to the sea.

"You said not to dwell on that stuff," I say.

"That doesn't mean I want you to walk into the lion's mouth. It's so dark. There isn't even any moon at all."

"We'll stay strictly on the boardwalk," Neve says, "and we have our bus if anything comes up and she wants to go home."

Roxy hesitates.

"We'll make sure she's safe," Neve presses. "We're not going to disappear. Mayhem isn't going to be alone. She's with us."

Roxy runs a hand across my cheek. "You want to go, baby?"

"Yeah," I say. "I had some tacos, rode the roller coaster. It's actually pretty fun here." It's heaven, but I'm not going to tell her that. Showing too much excitement would be detrimental to my goal of staying here forever.

"Let her go, Rox. You're only young once," Marcy says. She lets her lids fall shut and puts her index finger into the center of her forehead. "I predict this night is going to turn out fine." She opens her eyes and winks at me.

Roxy looks at Neve so sharply for a moment, I feel a trill of fear. She puts a hand on my shoulder. "Okay," Roxy says. "Go have some fun. Just be careful. And can you grab the bike and bring it back to the house?"

"We can totally do that. We have a bike rack on the back of the bus and everything." Neve smiles obligingly.

I don't know her very well, but I know this version of her right here is total bullshit, and I'm pretty sure Roxy knows it, too.

Marcy has gone inside and comes back with a couple bottles of beer. She twists them open and hands one to Roxy. "See you, girls."

Roxy takes a long sip and looks at me one more time. "You sure?"

I nod and kiss her gaunt cheek. It's cool and smooth.

Neve and I walk a few paces and then Neve grabs my hand and we run down the boardwalk, weaving through the crowd. I probably look so dumb laughing and running, but everything is alive and possible and rushing through me, as good as a movie.

A few paces back toward Jason and Kidd, Neve drags me onto the beach, away from the boardwalk. She gave my mother her word and it only took her two minutes to break it, because here we are standing on sand in the dark.

"What's going on?" I say.

"I once was lost but now I'm found, was blind but now I see."

Neve sings to the world, tugging me further down the sand toward the water.

"You said no beach. I mean, you promised. What about the Sand Snatcher guy?"

"Oh my God, don't worry about it. I would kick his ass." She stops. "Also, rule number one, adults need to be placated. You tell them what you need to tell them to get them to behave. They think it's the other way around, and you let them think that. Common sense." She twirls herself under my arm. "Come on, Mayhem, don't you want to be found, like us? Don't you want to see?" Neve opens her hand. In the center is something shriveled up and terrible-smelling. "Mushrooms."

"I'm not eating those!" I cover my mouth and try not to gag. "I think they're rotten."

"No, dumbass. *Mushrooms.* Like, see reality and other dimensions and your true spiritual self . . . *mushrooms.*"

"You just told my mom we weren't going to do drugs!"

"Mushrooms aren't drugs." She spins in a circle and stops just in front of me. "Mushrooms are a revelation. They're medicine. They give you access to what's really going on. Don't you want to know what's really going on, Mayhem?"

I have heard about mushrooms, but I expected them to look red with white spots or something, like the ones in the movies, not brown. Plenty of people get drunk in Taylor. They get in fights, shoot each other's houses up on occasion, even murder someone every once in a while, and I know there are some who love their weed, too. More than once Roxy has muttered curses under her breath while someone swerves around on the farm roads at nine a.m. But mushrooms aren't really in the mix.

Also, I'm pretty sure they are drugs.

Neve shakes some from her palm into mine. She measures out an amount equal to what she gave me. "It'll just be a little boost, you know? It's not that many. It's not like it's acid or something."

"Who's going to take care of Kidd?"

"Jason. He's abstaining so he can be there for us if we need him, which we're not going to."

"And they're going to come with us? We're going to do drugs in front of Kidd?"

"Stop saying that word, Jesus!" She looks irritated all of a sudden. "You think we're going to sprout wings or turn into demons as soon as we take them? We're still us, just with sparkles."

When I stare at my palm, she says, "Give them back. I'm not twisting your arm. You either do it or you don't. I'm sure you can still find your mom and she can take you home to bed."

"No."

"Well, then."

I shove them in my mouth, which fills with the taste of cow and dirt. I gag but then force them down, freezing to make sure they don't come back up.

"That's my girl," she says.

I've heard people jump off buildings, thinking they can fly.

Maybe I'll drown.

Or swim.

As though she can hear my thoughts, Neve says, "Mushies make you see things for what they are."

"They taste like literal shit."

Neve doubles over, giggling. "I like you." She pats me on the back. "Try not to puke." She hands me my can of soda. "Wash them down with the Coke."

Beside us, a couple throws down a blanket, settles into the sand, and turns on a black and silver boom box. Hardcore blares out as the couple starts kissing.

"People really rut everywhere in Santa Maria, hunh?" The last of the mushroom flavor disappears and all I taste is sugary sweetness.

"Summer love." Neve shakes her head. "Crazy kids."

"Ladies." A flashlight shines on us. "You doing okay over here?"

"Yes, sir," Neve says.

The guy puts the flashlight down. When my eyes adjust I see he's not that much older than us. He's in a red sweatshirt and shorts with the word LIFEGUARD across his chest in white. He has the full-on surfer accent, drawing out all the vowels. "We're walking the beach to make sure if there's some guy bothering the ladies he knows someone is watching."

"Well, thank you," Neve says. "We're grateful." She bows and he smiles, then walks past the couple and on down the beach.

"The beach used to shut down and there were no guards on duty at night," Neve explains. "Not like people didn't party anyway. It was just more low-key, I guess. But all that changed a few years ago when they decided to keep the boardwalk open until two in the morning and like one million people started skinny-dipping and stuff. This one guy, Brent Lutsker, drowned. The lifeguards don't really do much except make sure no one dies. They never tell us to put the alcohol away or anything." We start back to the boardwalk. "It's a new moon tonight. There's a meteor shower, so this is going to be perfect. You can see the stars when there's no moon, you know? But first, I have something to show you, something really, epically Santa Maria."

"What's that?" I say

"Sax Man," Neve says, then makes devil-horn fingers at me. "Kidd told me about him."

As it turns out, I've never seen anything like anything.

As soon as we find Kidd and Jason again, Kidd reaches for my hand, and though I am surprised, I take it and give her an extra squeeze.

"I promise you've never seen anything like it."

Jason has an arm around Neve again, and I'm grateful for Kidd skipping beside me. It isn't hard to find where we're going. We follow the throngs of people, and Jason throws Kidd on his shoulders when we get close so she doesn't get tripped over. Everyone seems agitated. We finally stop at the top of a makeshift arena. Crates are stacked on top of each other in tiers, and in the bottom center is a band playing metal. The lead singer is sweaty and in spandex pants, his hair waving in the wind. The guy drops his guitar and picks up a sax. He is literally oiled from head to toe.

It's not so much that people are immersed in the music, although some definitely are. Instead it acts as a soundtrack while they do other things. They drink, make out, lean over to whisper in each other's ears, smoke weed. I see no sign of police, or of anyone over the age of eighteen. To my right, a skinny kid attacks a kid with a shaved head and they topple to the ground at my feet, so I grab Kidd and we scoot out of the way.

At center stage, the guy thrusts his muscular pelvis against the sax, greasy curls bouncing along his shoulders, and wails out a solo as the part of the crowd that's there for him claps along.

I check Neve's face to make sure she has an appropriately judgmental look, but she's busy scanning the crowd as though looking for someone. I'm starting to get a little nauseated, a little tingly in my fingertips.

"This is Sax Man?" I say. "Really?"

"I know he seems crazy, but he's an innocent," she says.

"Sax Man is his actual name. Changed it legally last year. And you know what?" She hands off a soda to Kidd. "If you're going to be here on the beach at night for your first time, you are going to have to understand that cheesy cock rock and beach treats are part of the deal. Tacos, low-riders, surfboards, the carnival. I don't want to misrepresent Santa Maria. This is it."

"Hey, sweetie." A guy with a leather jacket and a spike coming out of his nose weaves toward us, and Neve kicks out her leg so he trips over it. He flexes his arms. I think maybe he's going to brutally murder all of us, but instead he looks from Jason to Neve and back again and straightens. "I didn't see you there. I'm sorry." He leaves immediately, hands in his pocket. No. He scurries.

Kidd wedges in between us and looks from one to the other. "So are we taking her?" she says to Neve.

"No," Jason says.

"Why not?" Kidd scowls.

"Didn't you hear anything Elle said?" Jason flickers his eyes to mine, then looks away.

"Well-behaved women seldom make history," Neve says to Kidd. "Some smart chick said that. We shouldn't always listen to what people tell us to do."

"Neve—"

"I think it's time. She's supposed to be with us. Elle will understand."

"You're playing with the roof over our head," Jason says.

"What matters is what's right here." Neve points from her heart to Jason's to Kidd's. "What we have right here is sacred, and no one is going to mess with it. We could be under any roof so long as we're together."

"What about Mayhem?" Kidd says. "Doesn't she get to be sacred?"

"We'll see," Neve says.

The guy in the band is gyrating over his guitar now. "Christ on a cross." Neve watches as Sax Man humps his way across the stage. "He's our pride and joy, but sometimes I wish he would calm down a little."

"But are we taking her to the hideout?" Kidd presses.

"Hideout?" I ask.

"It's in the ocean," Kidd says.

"*In* the ocean?" I say.

Kidd nods. "You don't walk there. You can't even run."

"That's enough, Kiddo." Neve puts a finger across Kidd's lips. "Let's take a vote. All in favor of showing Mayhem our hideout, raise your hands."

Neve lifts hers, and so does Kidd. Jason doesn't move. I put mine up high.

"Three to one," Neve says. "It's decided."

Behind me, the ocean whispers. Maybe I can step into the water and find my dad. Maybe find my mom, too. A memory yanks me under. Sun, a bright day, the sky perfect blue. A surfboard. My mother, her hair brown in pigtails hanging off her shoulders. Her smiling. My father, the color of a redwood tree. Roxy laughs. *Perfeito, amor.* His arms are around me as I balance on the surfboard, hands out like I'm flying. His hands steady everything as I bob on a small wave.

My dad.

I take a full breath, lungs open, and sigh as I exhale, which is when I realize my eyes are closed.

I snap them open and Neve is grinning at me.

"Girl," she says. "That hit you quick." When she turns her head, another head follows, licking its lips.

This is your brain on drugs. Any questions?

I nod, but the music has gone from bad to way too loud, though when I dare to look at the band again, Sax Man's golden spandex pants do sort of make him look like a superhero.

I mean, for just a second, he is glorious. A rainbow halo dances around him.

"You're hallucinating," Neve says. "It's nothing. Just tracers. Your pupils are dilated, so light does strange things. What I do is try to let it happen. If you fight, you're screwed."

I need to get away from here, all these people. I need to get to the water. I'm covered in dirt.

"I want to go to the hideout," I say. "The hideout in the ocean."

Neve throws an arm around my shoulder. I feel it in my legs.

The ocean pulls at my belly again like there's a cord attached. I have always wanted to live in the water. Die there, too, swimming laps back and forth. No more back and forth. I want to go somewhere, to *go*.

"I'm ready," I say, unfamiliar certainty surging. "I'm ready."

Jason pulls his necklace out, removes the cap, squirts his mouth, then pulls Kidd's chin downward and does the same to her. Then he replaces the silver under his shirt.

"Okay, then, it's decided. Come on," Neve says. "Let's head out."

SIXTEEN
HIDEOUT

I can't see it at first, even though Jason tells me he's shining a light right on it, something directly below the cliffs where my father died. The water is almost still. There's hardly a wave. It looks like all the other cliffs jutting from the water at a hard angle, unreachable and treacherous.

In the distance, the sounds of the carousel, of Sax Man thumping the night away.

My feet sink into the sand, and when I look up, the stars swirl. It's not real. I know that. I strip to my underwear and a bra, and Jason takes my clothes and stuffs them into a dry bag they carry with them.

"Right *there*!" Kidd's curls bounce, and I want to pull on them and watch them boing back up.

Neve gets behind me, takes my arm and uses it to point. "See through my eyes."

I try to let her eyes be mine, and within seconds, the split in the cliff is obvious, how the rocks are covered in moss and there is an opening underneath, like a howling mouth.

"Oh," I say.

"Good." Neve lets go of me and starts gathering things that are hidden under a nearby rock. "It wouldn't be a hideout if everyone could see it. There'd be all sorts of people trying to live there. Jay, will you take this?" She throws him a bag he straps around his waist. "I'm going to make sure Mayhem gets there okay."

"Alleeoop!" Kidd climbs up onto Jason's shoulders, and they speak to each other in Spanish for a minute.

Neve nudges me forward, firmly.

As I step deeper and deeper, the water is not all around me, it is all the way through. I push off the ocean floor. I follow Jason, his head dipping in and out of the water as he takes long, measured breaths. Kidd throws one fist in the air.

My feet hit the craggy rocks at the entrance of the hideout, and Neve pulls me up into the cave. It's narrow, and then it's not. A few feet through a tunnel and it's wide open.

Neve lights candles that border all the walls.

There are tapestries, and a coffee table sits balanced on two flat rocks. Blankets are everywhere—purple, pink, brown. Little cups and saucers. The floor is flat and warm and I sit, following Neve and Jason. There's space, the room is open, ceiling high. Water trickles from somewhere out of sight, and other than that, there's nothing but the swish as the ocean brushes against the rocks outside and the sound of towels rubbing against skin.

"How'd you get all this stuff here?"

"Dry bags. Some of it was already here. People probably brought it by boat at some point."

"It's so warm," I say, palming the floor, which is at least eighty degrees and keeps me from feeling the chill of the swim.

"We're on a hot spot, baby." Neve looks bright and less menacing with her hair wet and no makeup on. "Come on, I want to show you our treasure. Jay, bring the flashlight."

He guides us down the tunnel.

"They say the caves run under all of Santa Maria. If we kept going, who knows where we'd end up," Neve says.

We follow the thread of yellow across the flat rocky ground.

"If the tunnels are the arteries, we found the heart." Neve points back into the darkness. "And it bleeds."

"Wouldn't it be cool if you could climb out of here into someone's closet?" Kidd says. "You could be the bogeyman and you wouldn't ever have to be scared again because you would be the scary one."

"Duck," Jason says, and Kidd lowers her head as we cross into another part of the cave. It does look like arteries leading into ventricles, as a large room separates into quadrants that are nearly walled off from each other. The room they lead me to is no bigger than a toilet stall, and it's all mud and rock. Water flows from the wall. I've been here before. I'm sure I have. The earth rolls under my feet.

Jason lets Kidd crawl off his back to stand. We are all crammed in together, and Jason breathes from behind me.

"Are you okay?" Kidd says. "You look weird."

Neve laps. Her body leans into the wall so she can get closer. Water drips down her chin and chest. Her head hangs back at the neck so her throat is exposed, mouth slightly open. Then she snaps up and takes the flashlight from Jason.

"It's magic," Kidd whispers, but her voice echoes through the cave.

Jason takes a drop from the wall and lays it on his tongue, then does the same to Kidd. She shudders.

"Go ahead," Neve says to me. "I'll hold the light for you."

"Aren't you even going to tell her?" Jason says. "Before she does it?"

"Tell her what?" Neve says.

"Elle didn't want us to bring you here," Jason says. "You were supposed to find it by yourself or not find it at all."

"I saw her, Jay," Neve says. "She made straight for it as soon as she got in the ocean. She's a Brayburn."

"Once you drink, you'll have to keep drinking," he says, ignoring Neve. "You can't stop. I wish we never had."

I laugh a laugh that loops through the air around us so I hear myself, brash and ugly.

"It's not a joke," Jason says.

"You just don't want me to be one of you," I say. "You don't like me."

"He likes you," Kidd says. "I do, too."

"Look at her," Jason says, pointing to Neve, her dazed euphoria. "Look at all of us." He grabs at his necklace. "We're slaves to this place. That what you want?"

Neve's eyelids are fluttering like it's an effort to keep them open. "There's nothing better," Neve says. "Nothing in the world."

"It changes you," Jason says. "You can't ever go back."

"I'm thirsty." I take a step forward, and Jason pulls Kidd by the hand.

"Remember this. Remember I warned you."

"Bye-bye, Jay." Neve waves him off, peeling herself from the wall. She takes a finger and dips it into the water, then comes over to me and runs it along my lips.

"Lick," she says.

I do.

"Good girl."

For a moment the only sound is of the water falling across the rocks. Then Neve says, "Who needs boys?" There's a smile in her voice, but there is also something animal coming from underneath it. It forms from her shadow on the wall. She's a crow, with a winged expanse that is frightening and absolute and stretches over me.

"I see now," I say, bliss moving through every cell. "You're a bird like the ones at the farm. A beautiful, scary bird."

This stops her. Now that I've seen it, it is impossible to unsee. Her feathers. Her beak. Her beady black eyes.

She runs a hand along my arm. She points the flashlight to the wall over the water. BRAYBURN is etched, carved there.

"This place belongs to the Brayburns. Or it did. Now maybe it belongs to us, too. We can be a whole new generation. We can make it ours."

I don't understand everything, but some pieces are coming clear. Somehow, I am in Julianna's cave. The letter from Julianna to her daughter, Billie, the gifts at the gate, people being afraid and worshipful—it has something to do with this. I am proud for no reason, proud of my name.

Brayburn lady coming for you
Take your man and curse you, too.
Brayburn lady knows your sins
Reads your mind and kills your friends . . .

Neve smiles. "You never heard that before?"

"No."

"You don't know yourself yet," she says, "but you will. People want to keep secrets from you, but it's not right. You need to know everything."

"I don't know anything."

"I get it," she says. "It's a way for people to control you. They're afraid that if you know everything, you'll turn into someone they don't want you to be. But I believe in you. I believe you're strong enough to handle it. The question is, do *you*? Here's the truth, Mayhem. This water is the first step. I know it sounds fucking crazy, and it is. But it's also something so powerful, you can't even believe it. This water is everything, and it is made just for you. You can turn away from it. You only had a little tiny bit. Like Jason said, Elle didn't want you here, because your mom will have a monumental-ass freakout. But ask yourself why. What are they trying to keep from you? What are they trying to hide?"

"Is that why you guys have been ignoring me until tonight?"

"Here's another truth. After the day at the beach when you swam all that way out? You almost made it here. Elle lost her shit and sent Jason to get you. She told us just to stay away from you. Said your mother would be angry and she didn't want to do anything to upset her. She's scared your mom might take you."

Back. To Taylor. That will never happen.

"Everybody's keeping secrets," I say. I see all the webs spreading out, everyone trying to block each other, trying to exert control, but it's useless because life is chaos and there is no protecting anyone, especially from themselves. I see Taylor now, all the barbecues and cinched-in waists, the constant efforts to keep everything tamed.

We are all beasts and there is no taming anything.

"What's going to happen?" I ask. "If I drink more."

"Everything." Neve smiles sagely. "Everything that has been closed is going to open. And the best part is, no one will ever be able to hurt you again." She hugs me, body pressing against mine. "I'll make sure of that. You'll be one of us."

She guides me to the drip, so the water falls into my mouth, courses down my throat. It's cold and clean. I want more. I can't get enough. I drink until I'm filled up. I want to lick the wall. I stay there until I'm completely sated.

"I love Santa Maria," I say, wiping my mouth, "and I love you."

I mean it more than I've ever meant anything.

"I love you, too, Mayhem," she says.

We fold our fingers over each other's hands, press our foreheads together, our wet bodies.

"The world will try to lie, will try to hurt, but we will always be there for each other. We're family now."

"Family." Like a wedding vow. "I do," I say.

"I do, too," Neve says. "You don't have to be scared. Use your voice. Use your strength. Be everything you are."

"I will, Neve. I promise I will. Thank you," I whisper. "Thank you."

SEVENTEEN
ONE OF US

In the distance, the town is dark. There's nothing, no roller coaster, no thumping music. It must be more morning than not. Neve and I are at the mouth of the cave, facing outward, legs kicked out over the rocks. The occasional breeze is warm, and my insides are the quietest they have ever been, as though exhausted into a thick and delicious rest.

Behind us, inside the cave, Kidd and Jason are two piles of green and mustard-colored blankets. They've been sleeping for hours while Neve and I talked and watched the lights on the boardwalk go out, one by one, while we climbed around on the rocks and meteors blasted across the sky. The more she talks, the more she tells me, the more I see how beautiful she really is—honest, fearless. She's in a black sports bra and matching shorts, dry now. Her hair hangs down past her shoulders. She hugs her knees in and turns to me. She looks almost placid.

"I have to go," she says quietly, just as I'm thinking maybe it's time for me to find some blankets and lie down on the warm rocks for a little sleep. "Jason will take you back to the farm, but I have something I have to do before that. It's really important. You'll be okay."

There's an edge of sadness to her voice, of weariness.

"Are *you* okay?" I say.

She smiles. "Yeah, just a busy lady."

"Isn't it like four in the morning?" I don't want her to go. I am afraid for her and I don't know why. I imagine the whole world as a predator and that I am the only one who can protect her.

She blinks, lashes kissing the tops of her lids. "I can't tell you all my secrets in one night. I have to save something for later." She takes the chain from her neck and places it around mine. It dangles against my chest. "You'll need this. You'll know when. Don't panic, okay? It's going to seem like you're dying at first. You're not. You're going to be fine."

"I don't want you to go," I say.

"Jason and Kidd are here."

"Jason hates me."

She smirks. "Is that what you think?"

I nod.

"He doesn't want you corrupted. He's mad at me, not you. Don't worry. He'll mellow out eventually, once he sees how much you're meant to be one of us."

I look up at the stars dancing above us, the meteors flying across the sky, and I let her words glide over me without sinking in.

Neve runs a hand up my arm. I shiver. "I'll see you tomorrow. Get rest. Drink water. I'll be at the house when you get there."

And then she drops, and a few splashes later, everything is silent again.

It's a moan that startles me from the sky, from trying to make sure Neve gets to shore in the dark. Kidd is shifting back and forth against the wall, still asleep. Her breathing is shallow. I pull myself up and go over to her. She seems especially small, her white hair wild and big. Beadlets of sweat have popped out across her forehead. She shifts around and moans again. I don't know whether to wake her or not. I take a pillow, prop it against the stone wall, then wedge myself under her head so she's on my lap. I stroke her cheek. She wraps one arm over my legs and settles.

Jason sits up groggily, sees me with Kidd snuggled against me, and leans himself against the wall. "Thank you," he says after a moment. "That's nice of you."

"You're surprised I'm nice?"

"I'm surprised when anyone is." He rubs his eyes, still trying to get oriented. "Kidd's been having nightmares." He hesitates. "We had some bad things happen. It's been a minute since it all happened, but she still tries to stay up at night. Night is when she can't keep herself from getting scared, you know?"

"Seems like she's in the right household, then. I don't think anyone gets up before noon over there." I stroke Kidd's hair back.

"Where's Neve?"

"She just jumped into the ocean and left. You think she'll be okay?"

"Oh yeah," he says. "As long as she wants to be, she's going to be fine."

There's a moment of silence.

"Kidd told me a little about what happened to you guys, to your parents, when we were hanging out earlier. I'm sorry."

"Yeah, how much did she tell you?"

"I don't know, because she said it in Kidd-speak. But something like someone broke into your house?"

He gets a flask and takes a drink of water and wipes at his mouth. "You drank the water, right?"

"Yeah," I say.

"Well, no going back now." He offers it to me. "Might as well chugalug."

I take a sip.

"I thought the water would solve everything," he says. "Just made new problems. It's an addiction."

"Addiction to what? We're already addicted to water just being human."

"No," he says, shaking his head. "An addiction like a drug. Like heroin or crack or something, except it's an addiction to being powerful."

"From water?"

"Yeah, from water."

I think for a minute. The letter I read in the Brayburn book comes back to me. About Julianna being raped in the cave, and the water, and how she cursed other people but also herself. She said she murdered people. Lots of people. Elle didn't want me to come here. I did anyway. I am a Brayburn.

"What's going on over there?" Jason says. "Many many pennies for your thoughts."

"Too many pennies for you."

He grins.

"How about you? What's happening in that head?"

He readjusts Kidd's blanket. "I wasn't home. When the guys came in to rob the house. Kidd was under the bed. It's how she survived. She bit herself until she bled to keep herself quiet. My dad got in an accident." Jason wraps a blanket around his shoulders. "A few months earlier. He had some money from the settlement. Had some of it in cash. I guess people found out. My dad tried to fight and it went awry. I should have been there. I could always calm my dad down when he started to lose it. I could have convinced him to hand over the money and deal with it later. But I was out with my girl, Pamela." He looks at me. "I was having the best night. Feeling all the curves in the dark. So selfish. Whenever I think about that, it makes me sick."

Jason in a room with a girl, feeling curves, giving himself, taking. And all the while his family was being attacked, killed.

"I should have been home," he says. "I broke curfew. If I had come back on time, none of that would have happened."

That's crazy talk, of course. He might have made it worse. He could be dead, too. What if he'd tried to run out of the house with Kidd?

"I'm sorry," I say. "That's a terrible thing to think. But it's not true." He starts to protest, so I add, "It's *probably* not true."

He accepts this enough to nod almost imperceptibly.

"I let my mom get beat up for years." It's the first time I've ever said it out loud.

Jason's expression doesn't change.

I go on.

"Seemed like the whole town was conspiring for me to keep my mouth shut about it. Like, at first I was too little to know what was going on. And it didn't happen very often, either. But as I got older and it stopped making sense to me, it was like everybody from church to school to my mom and especially to Lyle, my stepdad, were all keeping themselves blind and deaf; like they were so determined not to see anything that they convinced me there was no way we would ever get out of it. But it kept getting worse and worse. A few months ago we went to a shelter a few towns over. We never talked about it even then. Roxy just went about getting us in somewhere so we wouldn't have to sleep in the car. Then Lyle found us because he followed me from school, and he and Roxy had some long talk, and then we went home. That's all I ever knew about it. It was awful in that place, even though people were really nice. Babies crying. Everything smelled weird."

"Why didn't she just come back here?"

"She was scared, I think. I'm not sure of what, but I think she ran away from something here. Maybe this. She was afraid of what would happen to her if she came back. Plus my dad died here. I think she wanted to forget Santa Maria even exists."

"You hear about people running away from the sticks to

L.A. or New York. You never hear about people running away to a small town in Texas."

"Yeah, well, that's where the needle fell on empty and the money ran out, and where she stopped to think about what she was doing. She got a motel for the night and ended up staying. Taylor is cute, I guess. There's a square and a Main Street and a Church Street and everyone tries to be kind to one another. All the same families have been there for so long. There was just this one place at the edge of town where people came through or stayed and paid by the week." I glance at Jason, who is watching intently. "I guess there were some hookers there, maybe some drug stuff going on. I know my mom was scared of it, but I was too little to remember. We had to stay there at first. Lyle, my stepdad, that's where he got us. He took us out of that motel and he never let us forget that's where he found us, like that motel and our bad luck was who we were, like he was any better just because he had some money when we didn't."

Jason nods. "That's how the worlds runs—money and status and what kind of car you drive."

"And fitting in. Everything about my mom bothered the people in town. And it was like everyone thought Lyle saved us and we should be so happy about everything because we were lucky enough to have that kind of guy to take care of us. Roxy would come sleep in my room sometimes. But she wouldn't leave him no matter what he did."

I don't know how to explain in words the feeling I have now, about how a person's history affects their standing with themselves. About how in Taylor my mother and I were peculiar and nonsensical, but here we have the strength of all the Brayburns behind us and it runs like a current under our feet. Makes us stand taller.

"So what changed? What made her decide to come here?"

"Lyle hit me," I say. "Rammed me into a wall."

slut slut slut slut

"He . . . found something and he came after me. I'm pretty sure every time he ever hit Roxy, he really wanted to hit me. I think I drove him crazy, and he'd get mad. It was like he was relieved when he finally got to, like he was finally doing the thing he'd always wanted to do." Lyle's grunt as he laid hands on me is something I've not talked about since it happened, and now it seems to me that grunt was the bliss of a thing clamped down for years finally being allowed to snap open its eyes and come to life, finally being allowed to breathe.

It seems like the mushrooms have worn off, but I'm still able to find words without fear. My usual awkwardness is gone for now, and instead there is a vibrating trill, like something is trying to make itself heard.

"Shit," Jason says, after a minute. "That's heavy."

"I just can't ever figure out why it was okay for him to do it to her all those years but not me. I mean, why did she let him?"

"You never asked her?"

"You don't know Roxy." I think for a second. "I don't know Roxy either."

"She's got the dullness," Jason says.

"What's the dullness?"

"Something people put on themselves when they don't want to look at the truth about anything. You'll see soon enough. But also, I get where she's coming from. I could see taking some punishment myself, but if anyone ever did anything to Kidd it would be game over, you know? Maybe your mom thought she was keeping a roof over your head, clothes on your back. Maybe she thought that was the price."

"I didn't even get to know my real grandparents. I didn't

get to make any decisions for myself. All because . . . what? What's so bad about Santa Maria?"

Jason looks down for a minute. "I guess I can't blame her. I sometimes wonder about the choices I've made for me and for Kidd. Choices I can't take back."

"I guess we all do things."

"Yeah."

"You know what was the strangest thing? It's the thing I've been trying so hard to understand. When he hurt me he called me a slut." It seems funny now. "I never even kissed anyone."

Do I imagine Jason catches his breath, that the air changes in the cave, brings everything closer, into focus?

"Never?" he says. "Not even at a birthday party or something? No truth or dare? Nothing?"

"What birthday party? I went to one at the roller rink when I was ten. They all held hands in a line. I was the last one. They went as fast as they could and then they let go so I fell. I was going so fast. I bruised my ass so bad. I never went to another one after that."

"Damn," he says.

"So why slut?"

"That's just something guys say."

"That's stupid."

"*Real* stupid."

It seems so ridiculous I even laugh, and then Jason is laughing, too, and it's a cool sound that bounces around the cave and lands in my ears, then rushes to my toes. I let out a little gasp.

"What?" Jason says.

"Your laugh," I say. "It's real. It's . . ." I sink further against the wall. "I thought the mushrooms were done, but I guess not."

"You're past the visual part. Now you're onto the doors-of-perception part, like Aldous Huxley wrote about."

"Says the expert."

He shakes his head. "I've only done them once. Once was enough for me. I got enough doors open already. But since you're there, you might as well get the benefits, right?"

The sound of the ocean rushes into the cave, but otherwise it's silent. I almost want to leave it quiet like that, but Jason has barely talked to me and now he is, and I am happy and interested, and other words I can't think of right now but can feel all over.

"Jason," I venture, "what if everything is exactly the way it's supposed to be and you can only know things at the right time?"

"I'm listening, tripping girl."

"No, for real though. I don't want you to get mad, but think about it. What if you weren't at your house the night your parents died for a reason? What if your life was supposed to lead you here? All the pain and tragedy and the terrible things that happened with your family?"

Jason's face closes. "Are you trying to say there's a silver lining to my parents getting shot in their own house? Because I hate that."

"No! I'm just saying you wouldn't be here without that having happened, and maybe you're supposed to be. Just think about it for a second. What if?"

He relaxes his neck backward so he's staring upward at the curves on the ceiling. I take it as a sign he wants to hear what I have to say.

"What if the same is true for me? All those years of misery and that big fight with Lyle had to happen so my mother would have to bring us back here. What if everything in both our lives has brought us to this minute, in this cave, for a reason?"

This concept makes so much sense, I have to close my eyes

to take it all in. If that were true, no time would have been wasted, no bruise would be for nothing. There would be purpose and then the question would be about what's to come, not what's already passed.

"You're starting to sound like Neve, you know that?" he says.

"We're practically the same human."

I say it as a joke.

"I hope not," Jason says. "She's so fucked up, Mayhem. Don't let her pull you in."

I can't hide my shock. "I thought you were friends, *family*. I thought you . . ."

"I'm loyal," he says. "That doesn't mean I can't see what's really going on here, and you should make sure you're watching, too. Don't let the *idea* of people overshadow truth."

Neve's arms had encircled me as she put the necklace over me. I saw her heart-shaped face and the way she was looking all the way into me and didn't avert her gaze the way other people do.

"And I got another what if," Jason says. "What if I'm selfish and you're a coward and that's how we wound up here? What if we're stuck on some crazy-ass planet where people are savage and want to pretend they're something else? What if it's pure chance that has us here and nobody's looking out for us and it's every man for himself, so I'm going to care about Kidd and look out for me, and you're going to keep trying to get your drugged-up mama off the couch and keep her from going back to your sadistic stepdad, and that's it? What if there's no meaning to anything?"

In real life I might be mad he said that about Roxy, but right now I'm only thinking he looks so sad, it's like I can see every bad thing that's ever happened to him hovering around him, holding on to him, not letting him go. I reach my hand out for his, and he takes it, rubbing his thumb against my knuckles.

Sensation travels all the way up my arm, down into my belly. He keeps *doing* that.

"I like you," I say. "A lot."

He lets go of my hand. "Sorry."

"What just happened?"

"Let's just say you answered a question I was asking you in my head."

The same thing happened when Neve took my hand when I first met her. I take his hand again. "Anything else you want to know?"

"No," he says, grinning, "not at this time, but I reserve the right to change my mind."

"I have a question. Does it work both ways?"

"You'll have to take your chances, I guess."

"So what happened to Pamela, the invisible girlfriend?" I say.

He tilts his head, wistfully, like he's listening to a favorite song.

"Pamela, my girl. I don't blame her. The whole thing got to be too much with the cops and everything and me not having a home and trying to deal with Kidd."

"She broke up with you?"

"That would have been nice," he says. "She didn't say anything at all. She was there and then she wasn't, like she was going invisible a little at a time. I didn't really have the space to go looking for her. I figured if she didn't want to be there, she shouldn't have to be. But it was like getting my heart broken a slice at a time, and I was already broken, you know?"

"Yeah."

"I missed her though, for a while, like missed her so much I thought the hurt would never stop."

"Did it?"

"Yeah, but I miss being able to find a girl in the dark, to

recognize her by smell, to know her skin and body so well, being able to know everything about what she's thinking just by looking at her, without any tricks . . . belonging with someone. The last time I saw Pamela, Kidd and I were on the boardwalk, and she was there with some of her friends. Had on this little halter top and cutoffs, her hair blowing around her. She was so beautiful. But she looked at me and it was like a layer was missing, like she had turned into some kind of paper doll. I knew she wasn't, and I know that's not true, but it's like whatever had been between us was shut down. Gone, just like that. And then I didn't miss her anymore."

No one has ever looked at me any special way or tried to know my body. Roxy, I guess. She's been the person I've kept track of in the dark, whose thoughts I've known. But not for romantic love. I'd like to love someone, to have someone love me, if it were possible for that to exist without it turning into a nightmare. Without Roxy how she is, would it have happened for me? There might have been someone in Taylor who would have wanted to wrap himself around me. There could have been dark rooms and lips and hands touching. My breath is coming short just from the thought of Jason, running his hands up thighs and over bellies in shadows. It's so private and he gave it to me and now I can't make it go away.

Jason takes his hand back, yawns, and throws me a pillow and blanket.

"Listen, it won't be long now," he says. "You should get some rest while you can. When you wake up, if I'm not right here, go back to the water and you'll be okay. Just remember that."

I don't know what's going to happen to me. Part of me thinks nothing will at all, that I'll wake up in the morning and this will all have been some silliness, Julianna's letter the fantasies of a bored wife and mother, Neve and her warnings some drugged-out joke. The rock beneath me heats me from the inside out, and as I fall asleep with Kidd snoring beside me, I decide no matter what happens next, I will never regret being here, taking mushrooms, drinking the water, holding Jason's hand. I'm glad we came to Santa Maria. Things are finally real, they're finally happening. I can finally sleep.

EIGHTEEN
WAKE UP

"Mama!"

I feel two things as I come to consciousness: heat and pain.

I unglue my eyes and then immediately shut them tight to block out the light. I barely register Kidd, who has nestled herself into me even further since I fell asleep.

I crawl away from her. I don't want to hurt her. I don't know where to go. I scuttle across the floor, knees bruising where the rocks separate and come together unevenly. At the mouth of the cave, I want to throw myself back into the water, but the light is too much, needles digging under my skin.

I retreat, blinded as reds and blues drum against the backs of my lids.

Then the thirst comes, choking me, like all the air and life is getting squeezed out. My throat is dry, parched, painful.

A swarm of bees fills my head. I scream from somewhere, scream to let the bees out. They don't get out.

They buzz harder.

Jason is up, he is next to me.

I can't see, but I can smell him, salty.

He is shushing me.

The rushing water in the cave. It's all I can hear, and I pull myself from Jason's grasp and crawl to the sound. I find the stream. The first drops hit the top of my head. I open my mouth. Water trickles onto my tongue. I flatten myself against the rock wall to get more. It pours over my tissue skin, a relief. I open wider, let it slide down my throat.

It's like balm on a burn, ice on fire. I drink and drink. I drink until I'm full, and then collapse and crumple. I lean forward, push my wet hair back from my forehead.

When I open my eyes, Jason is squatted across from me, face pinched with concern. The colors around him are bright. I see his sadness. I see his goodness.

I am panting.

His longish hair cuts into his face. It's so black it's blue. His skin is smooth, the color of a penny. Pillow burns run across one cheek. He blinks hard. He waits.

"What is it?" I whisper.

"The water," he says.

I nod.

"Once it's in you, it keeps wanting more of you. Right now, it's introducing itself to you. It wants to be your friend."

The world tilts, then tilts again.

I lean my head back, let the water slide over my chin. Every heavy drip makes its individual mark. Sounds come violently.

"You'll be okay, Mayhem," Jason says. "Especially you."

After a minute or two, things calm. I breathe normally.

"I have to go home now." I pull myself to my feet, lurch toward the front of the cave.

"You're not ready." He follows me. "There's so much. You need us to watch you."

"My mother," I say.

The sun burrows into the back of my skull.

Jason grabs my elbow and tries to pull me back. It hurts.

"You're going to do something you'll regret," he says. "It's like being a baby. You have to learn everything all over again. You can't be around civilians right now."

I wrench myself free.

"Hey," he says, "do you have any idea what Elle will do to us if anything happens to you? Do you even know what this could cost us? Do you care? Sit down and chill out. You'll be better in a few hours, and then you can go home without hurting anyone, mostly yourself."

I lunge forward. "Don't tell me what to do. And don't touch me ever *ever*."

He takes two steps back as though I've hit him. Behind him, Kidd sits up.

"No," she says, "you can't go." She throws off the covers.

A wheel of emotions whirls over Jason: sadness, regret, anger, fear.

I turn, lift my arms over my head, and launch myself into the sea.

NINETEEN
AUNTIE ELLE

Swimming has always been work. Now it's nothing. It's less than nothing. I have to think hard and focus to stop myself from smashing onto the rocks. I reach the shore and I'm creeping, keeping to the side of the pier. My dripping torso leaves a trail of seawater. The boy who works the Ferris wheel yawns, raises his hands above his head. He is pungent. He catches sight of me, takes me in head to toe, eyes lingering at my midriff.

I am having trouble breathing.

I am pulled to him. I want to give him a hug, but not in a nice way, to hug him until he stops smelling so much like want.

"Um, hey," he says, as I approach. His skin is thin, with a voice to match. "You okay? You need some help?"

My movements are jerky, like my body wants to go faster than it can. Ice starts to form around the boy. Honey fills my throat. I am choking. The ice can make the choking stop. I get close to him, look at the ice that's getting thicker. Inside it, pictures of the boy. If I put my mouth over the boy's and I inhale, if I put my arms around him and take the ice, it will be better.

His lips are red. I put one arm around his neck to get closer, *inside.*

He's paralyzed. I am the one paralyzing him. Sweat leaps to his skin. I smell his breath, sour with fear.

I inhale. He moans. "I'm hot," he says, letting his forehead fall against mine. "I'm burning up."

His knees give.

"There you are!" It's Jason, with Kidd right next to him. She is looking up at me, eyebrows knit together. Jason yanks me back away from the boy just as the desire to rip him apart has started to overwhelm me.

I might have gnashed my teeth.

The boy collapses to the ground.

"Sorry. I had to," Jason says. "You can't . . . It's daylight. There are people. And he didn't do anything. Let me take you home."

He pastes on a smile as Kidd grabs hold of my hand and urges me back.

Jason helps the boy to his feet. He looks around, bewildered, like he's shaking off a nightmare.

"Jake," Jason says, "this is Mayhem."

"Mayhem?" Jake says, looking stupidly from side to side. "As in, Mayhem *Brayburn*? As in *Brayburn lady coming for you—*"

"This is not the time, dude," Jason says.

"I don't mean anything by it. We're psyched you're here. Town's been crazy lately." He hesitates. "We need you." He rubs at his lips. "If legend is true, I mean."

I take a long look at Jason, at Kidd, at the boy.

"She all right?" The boy takes a step closer. "If what they say is true about the tunnel, you can." He leans forward like he's waiting for me to hug him again, and I recoil.

"You don't want to do that, Jake," Jason says.

"If it's more of what she did before, maybe I do." Jake searches around. "Where's Neve at?"

"Dammit," Jason says, as I run. "Mayhem, get back here!"

Climbing the hill is nothing. Fruit trees are orange and yellow blots of paint, spattered green and brown. The front door is wide open when I get back to the farm. I force my legs to slow down. They want to go fast, but I tell them to take normal steps, to have patience.

Elle is walking toward the door when I stumble in. She's all in white like she was the first day we got here, skirt falling over her legs, hair slipping over her bare shoulders, eyes flashing. I haven't seen it until right now, but she doesn't look human at all.

She comes over to me, puts her hands on my arms. She looks me up and down. "Welp, your mother is going to kill me. Teenagers can't fucking follow directions for shit."

Millie meows from the chair, indignant that her all-day nap has been interrupted.

"Mama." I try to pull myself away so I can go to my mother.

"No you don't." Elle doesn't let me go. "You're going to scare the shit out of your mom if you go up there like this. And then, frankly, if you can even wake her up, all hell will break loose in a way I just can't have right now. There's too much at stake. So you come with me."

"I want my mom."

"I'm sure you do. And she wants her mom. That's the way it goes."

"But—"

She raises one finger to silence me. It works. "Aside from your current mental state," she says, "you look like an absolute disaster. Don't make me put you in front of a mirror. I promise you won't like it."

I look down. I'm dry now, but still in my underwear and bra. My hair snakes down my back in damp clumps. "We slept in the van. We were safe." I focus on keeping my appearance normal, my voice steady. "There was a meteor shower. We just . . . watched it."

"Stop it." Elle fingers the necklace Neve gave me, runs her hand over the heavy metal. "There are some things you can't hide, especially from me."

"We fell asleep," I protest weakly.

"Neve's been back here for hours," she says. "She tried to sneak past me, but honestly . . . for God's sake, it's *me*." She shakes her head. "I'll tell you what. Let's make a deal. Let's have that be the last time you ever lie to me, and I will try to help you sort through this mess without traumatizing you or your mother any further."

My eyes well. I steel my jaw against the tears. Elle goes to the closet and returns with a towel, which she drapes over my shoulders.

Elle sighs. "Come with me."

I look up the stairs.

"Now," she says.

I follow Elle out the door. I search for signs of the ice coming back, but I find no traces of it and begin to relax a bit. I do see more light, *extra* light, especially around Elle.

"Frankly, when Neve got home and told us you were sleeping in the van somewhere, your mom took enough Valium to knock out a gorilla, so you're not going to be able to talk to her right now anyway." She sniffs. "Neve wouldn't admit to the rest until Roxy was out, but I knew as soon as she showed up here without you. She wasn't going to bring you back here for your first morning with the water in you, especially if she was trying to keep me from knowing, as if that could ever happen." Elle peers at me as we step on wet grass and weave through the orchard fruit trees. "Did it hurt much?"

I shake my head.

"Good. You seeing things?"

"Light," I mumble.

She nods. "That's normal. It's a little different for all of us depending how our systems adapt, but the basics are the same. Light, feelings, the honeycombs."

"Honeycombs?" I say.

"We can talk about that later," she says. Then, "You should know it's not a good idea to pollute your system, though. A person with our lineage should not put foreign substances in our bloodstreams. No pot or beer for you. And definitely none of that business you did last night. You think it damages a regular person, you have no idea what it will do to you."

Roxy's always drinking or pilling. We have the same lineage. There's an unpleasant pressure in my skull.

Elle gives me a side-eye and tries to take my hand. I pull away.

"No," I say. I'll tell her what I want to tell her when I'm ready, not because of some weird spell.

"Fine. Do you really think Roxy's behavior is an accident?" She sighs. "Because it's not. She's been trying to un-Brayburn herself since the day your father died, and just look at this unholy goddamn mess. My twin sister, keeper of the Brayburn lineage, is a junkie."

The words sting, but she moves past them, not noticing. Light trickles off behind her and melts into the ground as I put some of the puzzle pieces into place. They are beginning to form an image, of my mother and Elle and what was given to them in the cave that started with Julianna. Elle wanted it. My mother ran away from it. I don't know about my father, but I think his death had something to do with it, too. And now I have it, or I'm getting it.

Here, trees and plants are separated into neat rows. There's nothing wild, only sweet smells and warmth and soft dirt under my feet. I breathe easier. The sun waterfalls over me, and sand dries off my skin and shakes to the ground as I walk. Elle leads me to a stone bench that overlooks the whole valley. Birds sit on either side and pepper the trees, chittering softly. We can still see the driveway, but with our backs to the house, there's nothing but us, watching.

"I'm sure Roxy can fix herself," she mutters, lost in her own thoughts. "The question is whether she even wants to."

"You're leaking light," I say.

She smiles. "Damn right I am. There are some positive side effects. It sure can be pretty."

"Beautiful."

"This is where I always come when I need to think. I used to bring you here all the time when you were little. Do you remember?" she asks hopefully.

I shake my head.

"Well, Brayburns have been sitting in this exact spot trying to suss the world for more than a century now. You can see everything from here, and there's something about it that lets you think in peace. Just listen for a minute. Let the quiet fill you up."

We sit there, overlooking the valley, and I hear the whispers of the world, the swaying trees, the welcoming earth, and my own breath coming long and even.

"Being young can be confusing. It can be exciting and wild and frightening, but it will never be as much for most as for you. And now, for better or worse, you've taken a step toward your own life story that you can't take back."

"I don't—"

She puts up her hand. "There's so much to sift through, and you're not ready to hear it now. I just wanted to give you a place to think, somewhere all the Brayburn women have done it before you. You can come here, sit in the sun, and let it heal you." She looks out into the distance, body tense and lean. She stares out over the expanse, tucks one arm over the back of the bench. "Did you know that royalty used to keep their castles at the top of hills like this so they could protect their citizenry, defend themselves better, have a bird's-eye view if someone was preparing for an attack?"

I try to see the valley through her eyes.

"It's so important to pass things on." She turns quietly toward me. "Roxy never got that."

A new heat travels up my neck.

"I'm thirsty," I croak.

"Of course you are," she says. She reaches for the necklace Neve gave me last night, looks at it fondly, the engraved flowers and birds. "Do you know what this is?"

"Not really."

"I had a drawer full of them upstairs before the kids came. My grandmother had them specially made many years ago. She loved being what she was. Anyway, this one was mine when I was younger. And then I passed it to Neve when she got here."

I wrap my hand around the silver.

"Unscrew the top. Spray it on your tongue and hold it there."

I do.

"Good," she says.

Relaxation slips downward until my whole body is warm. "You only need a little bit. We keep extra jars of water in the attic. Only put it in glass or metal," she says. "It eats right through plastic."

I lay a flat hand on my belly.

"Why don't you have a necklace?" I ask.

She has the bird, like my mom's, no secret compartments I can see.

"Oh, I don't need it," she says. "And soon you won't either. There's nothing like getting it from the source, but it's best to keep some of the water around while you're transitioning because it's really a drag going all the way to the cave every time you need it, and you'll need plenty for the first few days. It'll be best if you stay here until the first phase has passed, and then we'll work on getting you acclimated." She is about to say something else, but the orange van comes rolling into the driveway. We both turn.

Jason gets out. Just the sight of his skin and his bright yellow T-shirt are enough to start a riot in my insides. The car door closes, and I fight to keep my attention on Elle. She is bright laid against the greenery, the flowers. Around her, shiny tendrils climb from her skin.

"I can help you, Mayhem," she says. "I didn't mean for it to happen this way, but now it's done. You're a part of the Brayburn legacy, and you don't have to do it alone."

I can't respond. My mouth won't make words.

"One more thing. Don't be an asshole about this. I know you're going to have mixed feelings about it, but Roxy left once before thinking she was protecting you, and I think she'll do it again, so we have to be strategic. We won't have to keep it a secret forever, just for now. Fortunately, she's so doped up I don't think she can see at all anymore. She's done it to herself, and at this moment that works to our advantage."

It's like Roxy and I are standing across from each other and our whole story is cracking the earth between us and she's too asleep even to know it.

"Sorry," Elle says. "That was insensitive." She clutches her head and smiles. "I've just almost had it with people not listening to me, careening off the rails and taking me and my entire town with them. We have a job to do." She takes a long, deep breath. "So go upstairs, use my bathroom, get yourself cleaned up, and then go take a nap. When you wake up, you won't be so out of sorts."

She looks over my shoulder, to where Jason and Kidd are

approaching. I can see the concern on Jason, and I feel how afraid he is that Elle will kick him out and he and Kidd will have to sleep on the beach or in the cave from now on.

"Be a love and go get Nevie for me. I need to have a word," she says. "Do you mind? We'll talk more later."

I hardly look up as I pass Jason and Kidd.

"Are you okay, Mayhem?" Kidd asks.

"Fine," I say, staring at the ground.

"Hey," Jason says. "It's okay. It really is. We'll be okay," he says, and runs two fingers down my arm, quickly.

I am so tired I hardly make it upstairs. Millie follows me and meows as I open the door to the attic, contemplate the stairs, and decide I can't even make it that far. I call for Neve to go downstairs. I wander through Elle's bedroom, run a bath in her claw-footed tub, dip under hot water and back out again, then fall onto her bed and into the deepest sleep ever.

TWENTY
CHOICE

When I wake, it's dark. The smell of incense wafts through the air, and the scents of rose and lavender creep through the open window. Crickets chirp. Elle's room is large and clean. Black-and-white photographs cover the walls, all of them old and worn, but lovingly framed. Trees and their shadows. Moss on a rock. A woman's figure. Two small girls holding hands. A cat that looks just like Millie. Sprays of white flowers burst from vases on the dresser and bedside table, where a bottle sits with a note taped to it that says *Drink me*. I chug it all at once. When I am strong enough, I get nosy. Oils and candles and silk scarves in a silver tray cover the vanity. I open the top drawer to find small boxes lined up, most empty, but two with beautiful necklaces like the one I'm wearing, one with an owl and the other a tree.

Music comes from the attic. Maybe that's what woke me.

If Jason and Kidd hadn't showed up when they did, I don't know what I would have done to the guy from the Ferris wheel. The scene with him plays briefly in my mind, but I shake it off. I am still wrapped in the towel I was in when I fell asleep. I find a black T-shirt and leggings on the bed next to me. I slip them on and pad toward the room I share with Roxy. I have to tell her what's happening to me, about the cave, about everything Elle said.

I nearly trip on the phone cord running across the floor into the bathroom.

I smell smoke and hear the slosh of bathwater.

I put my ear to the door. Roxy's slippery voice is saying, "Mmmhmmm."

I stiffen.

"No, I'm not," she says, voice mushy. "Lyle, I told you, I wasn't calling you because I'm coming back. Stop saying that." A pause. "Well, because, I want you to know I'm fine but that my decision is firm."

Lyle. I swivel the doorknob and knock. "Let me in, Roxy."

"Oh," she says, then, furtively, "I gotta go." She hangs up, and I hear the phone drop to the floor with a clang. "Oh shit," she says.

My face pounds as I keep my hand on the knob. I want to rip it off the door. I want to rip her apart. I try to gain control of my breathing, to make the air come in and out evenly.

"Why did you do that, Roxy? Why would you call him like that?"

I bang my forehead lightly against the door.

"Why would you go out at night and tell me you'd be back and then stay out all night when there might be a psycho on the loose?" she returns. "Do you have any idea how scared I was?"

"Why would you call Lyle?" I say again. "Don't try to turn this back on me."

"I shouldn't have to justify myself to you. You're a kid and there are some things you can't understand." There's the sound of water as she sits up in the tub. "I have screwed everything up, I know that. But I wanted to tell him I had decided once and for all. And you didn't even bother to come home. You left me here alone." It's like she can't decide if she's blaming or apologizing.

I'm afraid to ask my next question, but I do it anyway. "Roxy, did you tell him where we are?"

"No," she says. Then "No!" again.

I sink to the hardwood floor, look up at the fairy lights strung along the hallway, and bring my knees to my chest. I rest my head against the wall.

"You hear me, Mayhem?" she calls out. "I didn't tell him anything."

Lyle used to tell me the story of the woman who called him up needing help to find a place even though she had no money and no family, so she could have an address and get a job. As soon as he saw Roxy, he knew she wouldn't be living in the apartment or the motel at the edge of town. She was too beautiful for such a sad fate.

"I know you don't understand why I was ever with him. I don't expect you to." Her voice evaporates into memory. "He took me out dancing that first night. You stayed with Grandmother. You know her house. It was clean and tasteful, and she was nice at first. We laughed, Lyle and me. I had been so sick, crying all the time, too. I missed your dad so much I could hardly breathe. It was the first time in so long I'd felt even a little bit better. He was strong, knew which way to turn me so I could two-step even though I'd never done it before."

Again I almost vomit. "I don't really want to hear about any of that right now."

"He gave us a car and bought you clothes and didn't ask any questions," she says. "He took care of you like you were his own, mostly. At first he allowed me to try to go on living without your dad."

She goes quiet, and we sit there for a while. This day. This is a day I'll remember forever. How it started. How it's ending. How I'm not the same person I was last night. How I cannot *stand* my mother right now.

"Why did my father kill himself? Because that's what happened, isn't it? He didn't fall or slip or anything else. He jumped, right?"

No answer. I'm breaking our tacit agreement, the one where I tread carefully around Roxy so she doesn't break down.

"Why did you leave here and take me away from my family?"

No answer.

"Why did you let Lyle hit you and go back with him when you could have come here?"

Again, quiet.

"Why did you steal me from my own life? You only thought about yourself is why. You only *ever* think about yourself."

Nothing. A sniffle.

"You know," she says finally, "you don't get over things like losing your one and only. You just learn to live around the loss."

"I'm sick of living around your losses." I hit the wall. "They're my losses, too. And you didn't even give me any choices. You won't tell me anything at all."

"This is why I didn't want to come back here," she says.

"Well, I don't get that," I say. "Because coming back here is the only thing you've ever done right."

"May," she says, voice cracking.

"You only care about yourself. Don't lie to me anymore. I'm only important to you because I make you feel less lonely and because I always do whatever you want."

I don't know when the last time was that she sat with me, completely sober, and listened to me talk about my life. Maybe it's that she's afraid of what I would say if she asked. Maybe she's a coward.

The door to the attic creaks open. "Oh, good," Neve says. "You're up! I've been waiting all afternoon." She bounces over to me. "Come on. Elle said she would literally murder me if I woke you."

Neve doesn't hesitate or wonder what I'm doing here or why I might be sitting in the dark. These things are not important to her, and I love her for it.

I put my finger to my lips.

"Okay," she stage-whispers. "But we talked to Elle, and she isn't even mad anymore. You're one of us now!" She jumps up and down so the fairy lights tinkle. "We have so much to talk about." She waves the Brayburn book at me. "So much to teach you."

She motions for me to come, tracers swooping from her hands.

"Where'd you get that?"

"Where you hid it. I'm good at finding things."

"May?" Roxy calls. "You still there? You still listening?"

Neve lets out a little giggle and tugs on me.

The water sloshes again, and the door to the bathroom unlocks. Roxy's blond head peers out across the hall. She is dripping wet and swathed in a towel.

"May?" she says, blinking hard. Her makeup is smeared. And now I see. She is a little blurry. The dullness, Jason called it. It's like she's shrouded in a see-through blanket. The sight saddens me with a sudden, unexpected weight.

"Go to bed," I say softly.

Neve leans into me.

"You're not going to tell me where you're going? I thought we were talking." Roxy scans me as though looking for something.

"Do you want to talk? Because I'm here if you do. But only if you're actually ready to say things that matter, not give me excuses about Lyle, because I'm done talking about that."

She hugs the doorway and drips onto the floor.

"Didn't think so," I say.

Normally, I would run to her. I would comfort her and

make sure she was warm and safe, but I don't want to do that now. I'm not sure I ever want to do it again.

Roxy's pain.

Roxy's battles.

Roxy's needs.

I stand there, one hand in Neve's, and I see my mother. "I'm going up, Roxy."

"May?" she says.

"Good night, Roxy!" Neve trills.

"Night," Roxy half-whispers.

I close the attic door behind me.

TWENTY-ONE
BILLIE BRAYBURN
DAUGHTER OF JULIANNA

1928

Mother told me yesterday that Father has been run over by an automobile. I can't picture it. Did his face come to pieces? What does a body look like after that? I don't know and I can't get my head around it properly, so I've given up. It's because of the way I work, the way that I figure through things slow as syrup. But I get there. I get to an understanding. I just have to be patient with myself.

And meanwhile, Father is the person I would have asked for help in this sort of situation, for advice. He would have been the one to tell me how to go step by step until I understood how he could be here one day and gone the next as though he had never been at all. He would have tried to explain to me about the body being a temporary home for the soul, and I would have been able to understand it. But without him, I can only imagine him putting his things away in his drawers, turning off the lights, going out the front door, and disintegrating into nothing, ceasing to be.

When I close my eyes, I hear him saying to chin up, to put my best foot forward. Still, I don't quite know what to make of death. One time I saw Tommy Havershaw shoot a deer, saw the hole from the gunshot, all the blood coming out and leaking everywhere. Why, I feel like I've got one of those holes in me right now, that bits of me are leaking out all over the place.

But Mother.

Oh, Mother.

She recited lines from Romeo & Juliet for hours last night. That's the play Mother and Father were in when they met. She lay down with her scarred cheek against the sofa in the drawing room, and she sobbed. And I ask you, where do I belong in this? I do not.

I first saw the hideaway last week. Maybe finding it meant something. Maybe it was a foreshadowing of Father's explosion, of his corporeal departure from this fair world and of something new for me.

And I don't know.

I don't know what made me get my swimming costume on and put my hair up in my cap and go all the way there, to the place where the cliffs come apart.

Well, I do know why, and I shall endeavor to be honest here, in this place, writing just for me. Perhaps that way, life won't be such a puzzle.

The hideaway opened to me, showed me its existence, and I remembered Mother talking about a dangerous place filled with magic, built into the cliffs. The curtains made of mountain drew back, drew apart. Can you imagine? I think most would run, but I did not. Or I did, but I ran toward.

I saw something that shouldn't even exist, and I believe in magic, and I believe when magic comes a-knockin' at your door, you have no business doing anything but answering the call.

Of course, Father always told me not to swim out past where I could put my foot down to touch the rocks and the sand. But he's not here now, is he?

We're not supposed to do anything, ever, and it's just ghastly, unfair, ridiculous, if you ask me, which nobody does.

And by we, I mean girls.

Well, I don't like it one bit.

I am the best at holding my breath in the water. Tommy Havershaw says he is, but he is not, and I know that because the last time we had a contest he was gone, sitting on the shore having himself a ham sandwich by the time I came up to the surface.

Yellow-bellied.

Father once told Mother she was a stunner, with black hair to her waist like she has now, though she never wears it down, and skin that browned in the sun and eyes that sparkled and twinkled like she was made of stars and flame.

Mother always cleared her throat when he said that.

Oh, Mother would be so angry if she knew about the hideaway.

Well, she doesn't, and she didn't want to look at me because of Father dying and so there.

It's true the hideaway is full of ghosts. But I am better than fear. Mother says, when she's having her good days, that being brave is being afraid and doing a thing anyway.

It's how I found the spring in that cave, going deeper toward the fear, to my very own private well.

And would you like to know something? The word "Brayburn" is scratched right into the wall. That's my last name. My heart nearly gave out when I saw that. It truly, truly did. And now I have made a decision. If I ever have a child, she will be named Brayburn. A woman is just as good as a man, and she can want to pass on her line, too. The more I drink the water, the more I understand that things as they are make no sense.

I will tell you a secret about that cave.

It's not seawater. It's clear and sweet like you wouldn't believe. I tested it. And then I felt strange the next day, like I was going to die if I didn't get more. But then, then I felt just fine, better than fine, because then I could see.

There is the part of me that doesn't want to see so much. Sometimes I'd rather not know that the good are quite so outnumbered. Fortunately, I have figured out how to turn it off, just like a tap. I am thinking how I love this water and this place, and how I want to stay here forever, because here I can pretend there's nothing but me and the earth and this water, and that is better than people. Things look different now, and no one can keep a secret from me anymore.

Of course, it is a little mysterious. I don't understand it when I put my logic brain on, like Father tells me to when he says I'm being irrational and sighs to the sky.

Sighed to the sky.

I sit on the shore and I can see the big wheel they're building across the bay. I can see everything from here, and I like it that they can't see me back. I pretend that this place exists for me alone, that no one else can get here, even if they try. It is mine.

It seems like my body is awake, my mind sharp and deadly. It seems like maybe this is the start of a whole new Billie Brayburn.

TWENTY-TWO
MAYHEM BRAYBURN
DAUGHTER OF ROXY BRAYBURN
MINE

1987

"I mean, it's a fucking *gold mine*," Neve says. "A veritable *treasure trove* of information. I can't believe it was just sitting up here this whole time and I didn't ever even see it."

I remember back to that first day up here, not so long ago and yet forever ago, the way I was pulled to the trunk right away, how I *had* to see what was inside. Like the women who lived in this house were all steering me there, like that journal was calling to me.

"I mean, isn't it fabulous that Elle is so monumentally rad that she took the time to think ahead, to gather information and put this together so it would just be sitting here, to pass on, so everything's in one place?" She flips through again, scanning the pages. "Your mom even wrote stuff in here." She holds it up so I can see Roxy's scrawl across the page. "Everyone relevant. This is a historical document!"

My face reddens. I reach for it and Neve tucks it under her arm.

"Can I have it?" I say.

"Why?" she says. "Why can't we read it together?"

Because it's mine.

"Because I haven't even gotten the chance to read it by myself yet and I . . ."

I want to discover it. I want to be with the women in my family without anyone watching me. I want to take my time. More stupidly, I want to be alone in the dark with it, to hold it close if I want, to understand the mysterious pieces of myself. "Can I just see it by myself first?" I try to keep my voice calm.

"I mean," she says, slinging her legs over mine, "not really." She opens it and begins to read out loud again.

"Holy shit, give it to her, Neve," Jason says. "It's her family. It's hers."

Kidd looks back and forth between them, nervously.

"I don't know what the big deal is. We found the cave on our own," Neve says, closing the book. "That's why Elle took us in. It was a sign. And we're being adopted in. We're family, too. The book is just as much ours as hers."

"It was a sign we were hers," Kidd tells me. "We found the cave and then she found us. We're special."

"Of course you are," I say.

Jason sits on his mattress in the corner of the room, flipping through a magazine. "It's because you weren't here yet, Mayhem. If you had been, we never would have found it."

"What?" Neve looks incredulous. "That's so stupid. What does Mayhem have to do with what happened to us?"

"She's a Brayburn," he says simply. "She wasn't here. Now she is. You know whatever's in that cave likes them best."

"Like it's a person," Neve scoffs.

"What*ever* it is." Jason pauses. "It's something alive."

I picture the water rolling down the wall into the spring, feeding itself.

What if it's waiting?

"What, it likes our blood or something?" I mean for it to sound like a joke, but it comes out panicky.

Jason shrugs. "We know we all carry our past around with us. If we can see that, what can *it* see?"

"I don't even know what you're talking about," Neve says. "Anyway, the point is, if the cave wants you to find it, you'll find it. We found it, it found us, and here we all are. And they all lived happily forever after in love and glory." She tosses the book, more at me than to me, so I have to catch it before it slams into my nose. "But take it. What the fuck do I care?"

As soon as it's in my hands, I calm. Just having its edges against my palm is soothing. I smooth it down, make sure it's safe.

Neve lies on her bed and rests her legs against the wall so she's watching me, upside down. "So anyway," she says, "more importantly, this Sand Snatcher piece of fuck is wrecking this town, and Elle has decided we have to handle it."

I nearly laugh, but Neve's thoughts are shifting, ungrounded, and now she's onto this. She's not smiling, she's concentrating. I flicker to Kidd, as does Jason, and our eyes meet on the way back. He shakes his head almost imperceptibly, that helpless drowning look I'm beginning to recognize. Kidd seems oblivious for the moment, sifting through a box in the corner. She pulls out a top hat and puts it on so her frizz sticks out the bottom, then continues to search the box, neatly placing each item beside her. An old corduroy jacket. A silver flask. She runs her hand over each thing after she puts it on the ground, like she's petting it, taking care of it.

"We?" I say, bringing my attention back to the conversation. "What can we do about a kidnapper?"

"You haven't put it together yet, even after reading that journal?"

"I haven't read it all the way through."

"Well, you should. Because we have to handle this. Just imagine what it must be like to be them."

Them. The poster girls. *We are sitting on the beach. We*

see someone approaching. And then we're taken. We're in the trunk of a car. We're tied up. We're strangled or stabbed. We're helpless. When I look up again, Neve is giving me that look, like she knows so much more than me and I am a little slow.

"What do you think we do around here?" she says. "Sit on our asses and watch the beach go by? We earn our keep, chickadee."

Jason flips a page in his magazine noisily.

"So first we have to find this asshole, and then we have to see if we can find the girls he's been stealing, and then we have to take him out."

The world wobbles as I contemplate what that means.

Neve perks up with interest. "Looking a little swoony there, my fine friend." Her eyes glimmer as she smiles. "Going to pass out or barf or something?"

"When you say 'take him out—'"

She swipes across her neck with her index finger and lets her tongue loll from her mouth. "End his ass."

Jason slaps his magazine shut and sits up. "Just be straight with her, Neve. Quit playing games. This could not be more serious." He turns to me. "We're supposed to train you so you know what you're doing, but Elle wants us to find this dude and end the threat." He hesitates, then motions to the book in my lap. "That's what you guys . . . what we do. As long as all of you . . . us . . . are here, fucked-up people are going to come and do fucked-up things. This whole place is a trap, and we're the monsters."

"But why doesn't Elle just do it herself, then?"

"Because she can't." Neve bounces up and down. "Because *apparently* when the cave gets new people, the older generation starts to lose it. It's a matter of resources."

"I'm not going to hurt anyone," I say.

"You should. You should want to kick some major ass after what your stepdad did to you. And if he comes back, you should be ready to make sure he isn't allowed to be a bully anymore." Neve hops up. "Anyway, you're thinking about it wrong. If the Sand Snatcher is allowed to run around doing whatever he wants, Santa Maria is going to be his hunting ground forever. Just plucking those beach wildflowers."

Kidd looks up, and I think I see her shaking a little.

Neve doesn't notice. She's pacing. "The cops have their detectives or whatever, and that might work, *might*. But we have something else." A tunnel is forming around her. It's opening and swirling, gawping. "We can see people's secrets. Which means we have a responsibility. We'll be able to find him so much faster than them and take care of it."

"You haven't seen him yet?"

Neve shakes her head. "Sometimes when people believe their own stories, it's harder to see. But he's here. He's close, I know it."

I think about Julianna's story, about how she said she had had to kill so many. She was talking about murder.

Oh hey, nice to see you. I just found out I come from a long line of supernatural homicidal maniacs. How's your day going?

Jason comes over to where I'm sitting on the floor. "You're not looking so good."

Neve motions to Kidd, who goes over to the glass jars in the corner, fills a cup, and brings it to me. After taking a few sips, I look up.

"Why didn't Elle just tell me all this herself?"

"You know how doctors make their nurses give the shots so the kids won't associate the pain with them?" Jason says.

I smile.

"Yeah, I think it's something like that." He puts an arm around me. "You don't have to do anything you don't want to."

"No, no, of course not," Neve says. "Let's just let this predator have his way. Wouldn't want to upset anyone's conscience."

Neve squats down in front of me and lifts my chin. "The truth of the matter is that there really isn't a choice here. You drank the water, you owe the cave. You owe the women in your family, and you owe the people of Santa Maria. They're our flock, and we are their protectors. They deserve to go to the beach and be young and beautiful and careless without having to think about some psycho violating them. Maybe you didn't ask for this, but you have it now."

"You're okay with this?" I ask Jason.

"Yes . . . and no."

"We get to be *strong*," Neve says. "Nobody anywhere can fuck with us. Ever."

"You can still say no," Jason says.

"Say no? No, she cannot say no. The clock is ticking. I was up all night looking for the guy. Nothing. But I know he's near," Neve spits. "He has to be."

"Mayhem can't go anywhere for two more days," Jason says. "That's what Elle told us. You going against her? Again?"

Neve flops to the floor. "No. I guess not. But that doesn't mean we can't do something while we wait."

Even with the water, my lids want to close. What I need is for time to stop so I can adjust. Time doesn't stop. I don't adjust.

None of this should be real, yet it is.

Again I think of the boy, Jake, at the Ferris wheel, the ice forming around him. I close my eyes, struggle to remember what was in the little compartments. Honeycombs, Elle said. I slow it down, breathe in deeply, ask the water to show me. And then I see. Girls, naked, running away from him while he chases. They are fantasies, but he could be dangerous if those thoughts were set loose on the world. The images fade and my eyelids snap open.

Neve is still standing over me, while Kidd and Jason are on either side.

"Be one of us," Neve says. "Save your town. Live your destiny."

"A little dramatic," Jason says.

Kidd settles her head in my lap. She looks up at me. "Do you have any candy?"

"I don't," I say.

"Here you go, Kidd." Neve tosses her a lollipop she pulls from her pocket, then puts her hands on her hips and looks at me expectantly. "At least let us show you how it works. Let me show you what you're made of." She throws out her arms. "Because it is *incredible*!"

I think of the poster girls. Karen, Jessie, Kimberly, Benita, Tina. The probably dead girls. Girls like me with shiny hair and hopes and pain. "Okay. Teach me."

They make a bed for me in the corner of the room, next to Jason's, out of sleeping bags and a green plastic camping mat. They offer me pillows they pull from boxes in the corner. They burn incense and play soft music, and fans whir. I fall asleep almost immediately and dream of swarming birds. I hear the flapping of wings and nattering caws. Black shapes push at me. When I wake up, Neve and Jason are gone and my whole body is filled with anxiety. The feathers and the busy beaks are still pecking at me. I can't calm down until they come back in, until I hear material rubbing together and zippers coming apart and stitching back together again, and Jason has gone to his bed while Neve has gone to hers. I lie there, my body charged, mind unloading thoughts like a rushing river.

"You okay?" Jason whispers. He is only a foot away. He is so close.

"I think so," I say. "You?"

It's absolutely silent for a moment, the kind that rings in your ears where all the usual sounds should be. Then his hand snakes from his blanket and lingers in the space between us.

I don't know if the hand is meant for me, but I take it anyway, and I hear a little exhale from him. Surprise, maybe, or maybe it's relief like it is for me, like I'm exhaling after holding my breath for always. At first our palms are only close to each other, but slowly he pries my fingers apart and wedges in his own, so our palms kiss. When I wake, many hours later, we are still holding hands.

TWENTY-THREE
SLUAGH

The sun is already more than halfway across the sky when I sit up, and the day is scorching. When I try to stand, my legs wobble. Jason brings me water and then gives some to Neve and Kidd.

"Bottoms up," Neve says, makeup smudged around her eyes. "Always first thing. Night takes it out of you, so you have to put it back."

When I get downstairs, I check the bed for Roxy, a little on edge about what she might have to say to me, and there's only a note:

Gone to Marcy's.
-R

Yup, she's still pissed. Well, so am I. Every time I think about Lyle's caramel voice saying things to her, I want to hurl.

The table downstairs is laid with green juices and fruit. Usually, the sight of that much produce would send me into a panic, but I gulp it down and eat a warm, fuzzy peach. Slowly, my depleted cells fill up. Every time I meet Jason's eyes across the table, or we accidentally touch, I heat up, but he always either looks away or holds my gaze for too long. Finally, I can't take it anymore, so I go outside to find Elle.

"Hi, love," she says, and holds her arms open to me. I fall in, then out, suddenly shy.

She is in the tomatoes in jean shorts and a top, wearing brown canvas gloves, and though I can still see little strands of light around her, when I focus I can also make them go away so she looks pretty normal. Normal for a super-beautiful person, anyway.

"The tomatoes are still green," Elle says, wiping at her forehead, "but this heat is going to make them so sweet you'll be eating them whole off the vine before too long. You have to water them, then you have to starve them. It's their fight for survival that gives them the special flavor." She looks up, maybe noticing I'm not saying anything. "You all right?"

"Fine," I say.

"Why don't you go get some gloves and we'll work on this together?"

We get baskets and a wheelbarrow and go to the fruit trees. The peaches are perfect, so we start collecting. I take a ladder and follow behind Elle while she talks about the farm and what amounts to a small family business. She survives on the farmer's market and the things the town leaves at the gate as payment for the favors she does them. She doesn't need much sleep anymore, now that the water isn't calling her to action.

She climbs the ladder, swiping away a crow that's snacking on a peach, then pauses to wipe the sweat from her brow as the crow flies up, then back down and lands on her shoulder.

"Of course I got curious at some point," she says, as though we were in the middle of talking about something completely different, "tried to find some sort of source for what was happening to me, what had happened to our entire lineage. I went looking for the details of every kind of mythical creature, every old wives' tale, every fairy tale, searching for something, anything, that would explain the Brayburns and the water to me in a way I could understand. It was like we'd been given this mission to keep Santa Maria safe, because it's the kind of place that needs it. I could accept that, but I needed more. Roxy was never like that. She loved every bit of it. Even before we got the water she picked every fight she could and lived to take down anyone who ever even thought about being a bully. Everyone loved her." She sighs. "I was different, more introspective, I suppose. I wanted information so we would know what we were dealing with. Bits of our history were scattered everywhere, in drawers and the backs of books and in musty boxes. All the Brayburn women have been diligent record-keepers, fans of the epistolary relationship, and I was able to pull from each ancestor's journals and compile them into a history that has taken on some sort of shape. I needed to make some sense of it."

I redden. That book is under my mattress now.

"Oh, don't worry," she says. "Much as I wanted to respect Roxy's wishes, I'm so glad you found it. You should have it, get to know it since you'll never know them directly. I wish I had had a book like that when I was younger. Of course I've read through it so much it's practically falling to pieces, and I still haven't found all the answers. One of the mistakes I think we've made over time is not telling each other about what's to come the way we should. Each woman passed along a bit of something to her child, but not enough, nothing comprehensive. Maybe if we had all talked about what was happening instead of hiding it, it wouldn't have been such a disaster."

She climbs down and pulls a jar of mint iced tea from the garden bag on her wheelbarrow.

"Anyway, the water can't speak, though it does have its ways of communicating. I think of it as a sort of guardian of Santa Maria." I wait while she strokes the bird, who is still sitting on her shoulder watching everything carefully. "Handsome, isn't he?"

I nod.

"He's our resident king."

The one with the brown on his beak.

"Have you ever heard of the sluagh?" she asks.

"Sounds like something you get stuck in your throat."

"It does, but it's not. I hadn't heard of them either, of course. Some obscure Celtic creature. They were thought to have been rejected by both heaven and hell. Some myth has them as fairies, another as ghosts. I don't think I'm either, do you?"

I shake my head.

"But there are similarities. For instance, lore has it that they would take the form of birds and swarm on the nearly dead, that they would suck their souls from their bodies." She indicates the bird on her shoulder. "I don't turn into a bird, but these guys are sure around in large number, and they stick close by us."

The necklaces she and Roxy wear.

"All I know is the crows are ours," Elle says. "Or we're theirs."

Neve was a bird in the cave, or very nearly. All around the house, crows. Crows hold grudges; they sense fear. My dream. The pecking. The birds always hanging around on the fence and in the trees.

"There's something to it. Every myth has a kernel of truth. So that made me sit up and take notice, and then there's the fact that the sluagh fed on the souls of the nearly dead. Although I don't think it's what they meant in the myth, people who exist on this earth preying on people who are just trying to cope with being on this planet are empty inside. They are nearly dead. And we do . . . relieve them of their souls, I suppose."

"You think there are more people who are like this?" I manage. "On earth, I mean?"

"I don't know," she says matter-of-factly. "At first I thought so, of course. Where there's one or five there have to be many. But we're not ourselves away from Santa Maria. We hurt. We lose the sight. I've done some traveling, tried to see some things, but I've found being away from Santa Maria difficult. And often not worth it." She smiles. "I spent some time in a commune in Massachussetts in the sixties. It was painful and eventually boring, too. After a while I gave up and watched the occasional travel video instead."

"So you never came to Taylor."

"Yeah," she says. "I guess that's part of it, although I would have parted the seas to get to your mom at one point. But she was so adamant about all of it. She didn't want me around. Anyway, your mother and I didn't exactly end on a good note, though we came to a place where we could talk sometimes after our parents passed away."

"And that's why Roxy left?"

"It's not quite that simple."

I wait.

"When you leave Santa Maria and you have had the water, you get sick. Sometimes very sick. It depends on the person."

"That's why Jason says he can't leave."

Elle brushes the crow off her shoulder, and he comes and settles on mine. I'm afraid at first because he's close enough to peck an eye and I'm not totally over my dream, but once he's comfortable it's no big deal.

"Roxy must have been terribly ill by the time you got to Texas," Elle says. "It doesn't take long."

"Roxy has been sick my whole life. Not bad, but she's had a bellyache since I was little."

"And not since she's been back, right?"

"That's true, I guess. But seems like she's sick in other ways."

Because of the drugs.

We're quiet a second. "The family is buried over there." We walk to a small hill. "Everyone is here. Julianna and Lawrence, Billie and Thomas, Stitcher and my father, Tobias."

Their tombstones are all in pairs. I feel dizzy, like I'm caught in a giant, spinning machine.

"Do you have a true love?" I ask, remembering what Roxy said about each Brayburn only having one.

"I do," she says. "*Did*. Her name is Melissa." She checks me for a reaction. "Her family was opposed, though we did have two beautiful years up here after my parents were gone. Then she left. The Brayburn line is neat and clean as a whistle. I'm a deviation from the plan, you see? Each woman has one girl child and one love. But my mother had twins and messed everything up, and then Roxy up and left with the heir."

She wipes the dead leaves off her mother's grave.

"It's all right. Don't feel sorry for me. I know who I am. When I was your age I did as much research as I could. I found out that a lot of people out there believe there are six or seven points on the planet where the energy is higher and more intense than other places, and this is one of them." She sighs and looks around. "Assholes and broken souls are drawn to this place like hummingbirds to sweet water. The kids finding the cave is proof to me that if it's not us taking it on, it'll be someone else, and who knows what kind of person that would be. I don't think that's a risk I want to take. I'd rather be in charge, wouldn't you? And here we are, me and you. And you're back. You're so different than Nevie. She was running all over trying to test it, asking me so many questions I could hardly manage. She is more like your mom was. I had to stop her from wreaking vengeance on everyone at once."

I flush.

"It's good to be an innocent," Elle says. "Gives you restraint."

How do I tell her I don't want to be an innocent anymore? Innocents get hit. I want to hit back.

TWENTY-FOUR
TRAINING

Jason, Kidd, Neve, and I are lined up at the edge of the property. It's midnight. Kidd is jumping up and down and looking ahead. Elle stands beside us, arms crossed in front of her, wearing a serious look.

"Welcome to Stalking Your Prey 101," Neve says.

"Murder humor," Jason drawls. "Love it."

"Please take this seriously. We have to speed up the plan. Here's what we know about our Sand Snatcher, or at least what the profiler thinks, according to what Rebecca shared with me. He's likely a psychopath, not legally insane, knows the difference between right and wrong but is driven to hurt. He will have no lack of intelligence, no brain damage, no frank psychosis." Elle seems to be thinking. "He is probably attractive, charming, and between twenty-five and thirty-five."

"That's everyone here, practically," Neve says.

"Exactly," she says. "So chop-chop."

Neve makes stabbing motions behind Elle.

"Okay, my experienced ones, you know how this works. The point of this exercise is what?" Elle says.

"To win," Neve says, coming back to attention.

"Not exactly." Elle walks down the line.

"Kidd?"

"It's to learn to see where you want to go and just go there."

"Yes!" Elle says. "Mayhem, think about the tree on the far

side of the property by the bench and go. I don't want you to think about your legs or moving. You just think about that tree as a destination." She comes up behind me.

"But I can't see." I hate the sound of my voice, timid and sweet. *I want to hit back. I want to hit back.*

"You aren't seeing with your eyes, May. You're knowing with your body. Your eyes are only a small part of your vision. If you let the rest of your body see as well, it will," Elle says. "Think about the tree's leaves. Ask it to let you come to it. Listen."

My mind is full of questions and other noise; Jason and what may or may not be. My mother. She has been gone to Marcy's since this morning and hasn't come back, and she's taken all the pill bottles with her and even the mini white-wine bottles she keeps around in her underwear drawer. Then come thoughts of my father and what it must be like to fall that way. And then that silence blankets me again, thick and full.

"Good," Elle croons. "That's it."

The trees whisper to me and I search out just the right one, with the plums just beginning to make their way to its branches. I hear it. And then, the birds. *We're here*, they seem to say. *Come find us.*

"This is taking forever," Neve complains loudly. "Hopefully you won't be this slow when it's real."

It almost breaks my concentration, but the line between myself and the birds in the tree is strong and it holds.

"Go," Elle says quietly.

I let myself be taken. Trees and grass and tomatoes and wildflowers whiz past me. I am sharply aware of Jason on one side and Neve on the other. I see their legs moving in a blur, and then Kidd blazes past me, hair flying in the wind she's making as she rips through the tall grass, then past the house. I see the tree coming and I think to stop, and I am face to face with its bark, arms out, a millimeter away from smashing into it.

I freeze where I am.

"You almost pancaked yourself," Neve says.

My arms are out to the side and I am suspended in midair. With each intake of breath my chest meets the tree. That was close. I look up to find Neve and Jason and Kidd perched on branches that should be too weak to hold their weight. The crows sit between them, watching. They tut and squawk.

"You okay?" Jason says.

"I'm fine." I take a step back, fully land on the ground. And I am okay. I'm not winded or anything, just have a thumping heart. Still, if I had hit the tree going as fast as I must have been, my insides would be on the outside right now.

"Isn't it so cool?" Kidd says.

"*So* cool."

Elle materializes with sparkling eyes. "That's how you speed in the dark. I knew you'd be a natural. Now"—she claps her hands—"again."

We practice like a hundred times, running all over the property to different destinations until I can think about a specific purple flower and get to it in half a second. If I let the scared human part take over, it doesn't work. But I learn if I believe I'm invincible, that's what will happen. Elle points out that Kidd is better at everything than all of us, because she is youngest and her pathways are less formed and more open to suggestion. She doesn't necessarily believe the world is a single way, so for her anything is possible. For us, we have to fight the part that tells us this can't be true, that this can't be happening.

Elle is making everyone do it. Jason is good, but he's tolerating, not enjoying, and Neve seems bored. She's perfect at everything, smooth and skilled as she lands her targets. She doesn't sweat. Her breathing doesn't change.

"Wait till you get the real thing," she says. "That's where it all happens."

I am sopping wet with sweat and finally exhausted when Elle gives us our last set of instructions. Neve and Jason and Kidd will camouflage themselves somewhere on the property and I will find them.

My stomach is grumbling and it's nearly morning and weakness is setting in, but Elle insists. This is the most important part, being able to find someone who doesn't want to be found in the dark. That is where people prey on others. It's where they hide and wait for the unsuspecting to ignite their interest and desire. And when you are the one chasing after that desire, hunting the hunter, you have to be extra on your game because their senses are on high alert. Those people are basically dead, Elle reiterates, except when they are about to hurt someone. That's what brings them to life, fulfills them.

Once they're all hiding, Elle tells me, "I know you're tired and don't want to do any more. This is exactly when you should. You're getting weaker. The sun is about to rise."

I want to eat and drink and sleep.

"Buck up. Go find them. Don't think. Take yourself there." Elle pats my cheek. "I'll go make you some food for when you're done."

It's still dark, but the sky is lightening some.

The farm is fifty acres, and they could be anywhere. I flop down onto the porch. The only reason they aren't in bed themselves is because of me, or I would curl up and pass out right here. I think of Kidd, of her moaning as she sleeps, of her penchant for sugar and the way she ran ahead of me, lithe and serious, of her contours against the sky, a shadow set loose. And then I feel her. I perk up. She's lying somewhere. Not far. She's a pinprick, but she's there. I stand, let my body go, and in a minute I'm with her, hands on her back. She's fallen asleep, white curls against the dirt, and so I pick her up and take her back to the house, into her bed. Elle is putting finishing touches on a salad, and a pot of rice steams on the stove.

"Very nice," she says, as she lays out avocadoes over lettuce and pumpkin seeds and cucumbers. She makes a motion toward the door.

"Now?" I say.

"Bring them home, May."

I focus on Neve. She's darkness, but a bouncing kind, never still. She is corsets and lace and leather and hair and red lips and bangs. She's hurt and loyalty and selfishness and manipulation. In a second, I have her. I know where she is and I will my body to her. I go outside. Exhausted. Stomach rumbling. And so, so thirsty. When I appear in front of her, she's in a tree, swinging her legs below her. She claps and bounds to the ground, then takes a knee.

"I bow before thee, Mayhem Brayburn of the Brayburn Clan, Feeler of Feelings, Holder of the Elusive Brayburn Blood."

I pull her to her feet.

"No, seriously," she says, "it took me weeks to do all this, and it's taken you one night. It's impressive."

"Thanks," I say.

"Anyway, you found me." She yawns. "Shall we to bed?"

I hesitate, eyes flickering further into the orchard.

"Ah," she says, grinning knowingly, "saved the best for last."

"I didn't mean to."

"But you like him, right? He gives you goosebumps in all the right places. He makes you feel funny." She is behind me now, weaving. "He pushes all your buttons. And the way he ignores you sometimes just makes you all steamy inside. All you want is to go for walks in the park and share ice-cream cones." She claps her hands so I jump. "You want him to win you a big ol' teddy bear from the county fair," she twangs.

Her words land and ripple. "I don't know what I want."

She brushes herself off. "Listen, here's a piece of free advice from me to you. I know I'm a bitch sometimes, but at least I'm honest. Stop telling yourself lies, because this little-miss-demure tortured thing is a bunch of bullshit. You know what you want. I think you *always* know what you want. So go get it and don't apologize for it. No one is going to come beat the shit out of you for having desires and ambition. He can't any-more, get it? That means it's all you. Your mistakes and your victories." She releases me. Looks upward. "Now get out of my face. Jason's waiting for you."

The night goes still. There is no nattering. There are no cicadas. There is only Neve and me. I want to ask her if she loves Jason or at least what's between them. I've been wanting to ask this since the first day, her head leaned on his shoulder. The un-believable jealousy I felt for the ease between them, even then.

Neve hugs me so our bodies are tight to each other. Her breath is shallow as she takes my cheeks in her hands and drops her forehead in close to mine. "Oh, Mayhem, I have feelings for everyone." She pecks me on the lips. And then she's gone. I touch my mouth.

When I search for the house I can see lights off to the east, and they're far away. Neve has unnerved me. I try to focus on Jason, but the scattered thoughts are back. My mother. She's at Marcy's? What are they doing? What is she planning? Is she go-ing to show up in the morning and try to take me away? Does she want to go back to Lyle? Where is Jason I am hungry I am lost I don't know who I am I am never going to find him and I won't be any good andthesandsnatchersandsnatchersandsnatcher.

A man. Brown hair. In his twenties. Arm around a girl. He's not far from here now. She smells like cheap perfume, sharp, sour at the edges. He leans in and sniffs. The smell makes him hun-gry. He saw a girl before on the beach. They're all so stupid they don't even notice him there, watching. When he breathes in, it is with all his unsatisfied desire. He'll have to fake it tonight. He has studied normal, has learned how to bend his mouth up to smile, how to get just the right amount of moisture in his eyes to approximate empathy, and how to soften his features in order to imply he's capable of love. And while he does what he has to so he can survive, he lives on his memories, so many lovely memories that carry him through. He is up high. He is up high. Up. A girl in his hands, her neck.

Hiding in plain sight.

My eyes open. I can hardly breathe and I bend over as my mouth fills with water. Nothing comes out. My stomach is empty. I'm alone and there's no one to help me. Birds land nearby and watch.

Jason.

Jason will help.

I need to get to him. He has ancient eyes. He has long muscles. He chooses his words carefully. He seems calm, but he's not. Everything in him is happening all the time. He is split. He doesn't know what's the right thing to do. He doesn't want to kill. He wants to kill everyone. His hand. His fingers between mine.

And I'm there. In a flutter of feathers I find him.

He's almost to the house, his jeans loose around him, torso long, and I am just next to him. He stops. "I heard you coming," he says. He sprays the necklace into his mouth and nothing comes out. Empty.

"Here you go." I give him some of mine, realizing I haven't wanted any all night.

"Thanks." He winces. "I wish I didn't have to."

"I know," I say.

The sun is coming up around us, the urge to sleep powerful, and I want to explain what happened before I found him, but my legs are giving out and the world is going crooked.

With Neve's words echoing in my ear, I stand on my toes and let my lips touch his. He doesn't respond—not a muscle moves. His eyes don't close.

"Sorry." I pull back and start to turn.

"Don't say sorry," he says. "I've been trying not to do that for days. I wanted to make sure I was invited."

"You are." I let my fingers wrap through the hair at the nape of his neck and press my body against his. We kiss, and bark scratches at my back. He runs his hands over my hips and I light up. When we come apart, he's searching my face. He brushes my hair back with one hand.

I'm pretty sure my entire chest is about to burst open and have little happiness babies all over the place, but his brows suddenly knit together, a look I'm beginning to recognize as guilt and I am afraid. He is such a good thing. I don't know if good things can stay for me. I am too nervous to ask him outright.

I look up at the marmalade light coming from the house. I can smell food even from here. Family.

The sound of crickets and the trees buckling under the breeze seems to rise around us as the sky lightens even more.

Jason tugs on my hand and we walk to the house. He pauses just before the front porch steps. "For a while it was just me and Kidd and Neve. When I met her she was dumpster diving and these guys . . . she couldn't defend herself. All we had was each other. I was just trying to stay with Kidd, keep my house. Until we found the cave and everything changed."

"It's still changing."

"Yeah, it is. And that's why we have to take care of each other. It's nothing to do with you. I just don't want Neve to—"

"—think you're going to stop," I finish.

We hear the front door creak open, the sounds of footsteps on the porch, and we glance at each other. Jason steps away from me.

I understand.

Elle is spooning rice and beans into bowls and Neve is finishing her food when we walk in, keeping a civilized distance between us when all I want to do is glue myself to Jason.

"I was almost worried," she says, not looking up. "Almost."

Neve pops a piece of a roll in her mouth. "*Finally.* You guys are back."

Elle puts the bowls in front of us and sprinkles them with lime juice.

I sit down to eat, but once I'm in front of the food, what I saw by the trees comes back to me with so much force my breath catches.

"What is it?" Jason says.

"You're not going to eat?" Elle puts her hands on her hips. "Because I know you and your mom aren't used to it, but processed food is poison. Your body needs actual nutrients—"

"I saw the Sand Snatcher."

Jason and Neve look at each other and Jason's face twists into a question.

"Right before I found you," I say to Elle, "I saw the Sand Snatcher when I was looking for Jason. I know who he is." I shake my head. "I mean, I know *what* he is."

"You *saw him*?" Elle is standing completely still. "Visually?"

It's like time and everything else in the world have stopped, waiting for my answer, and it scares me. My stomach starts pulsing with something thick and dangerous.

"I saw him, or I *was* him or something," I try to explain.

Neve shoves her chair back from the table and puts her elbows on her knees. Her hair falls over one eye and the one that's left is a dark slit. "But that's not how it works. You have to see them in person, so you probably didn't even—"

"Neve, let her finish." Elle leans over her and takes Neve's bowl, in motion again. "It's not likely, or usual, but it's possible. Julianna had that level of sight. Maybe Mayhem has it, too."

Neve grabs a lettuce leaf out of the salad bowl and munches on it. “Because she's a Brayburn?” I don't miss the tinge of bitterness.

“This has nothing to do with blood, Neve. It's a little different in all of us. Maybe it's more developed in her in this one way. All I'm saying is it's possible.” Elle places her hands on my shoulders. “Go on, Mayhem. Find him for us if you can.”

Elle's fingertips seem to send energy through my skin. I try to find the image again, the way it came before. It's like I'm searching a dry-cleaning rack for the right image. And then it's before me. I let myself dive into it, and even though it's disorienting and sickening, I invite it back in. “He was up high or something,” I murmur. “He was with a woman and then—” I pause as the images come crashing in like waves, down my throat, push into my lungs, and squeeze.

Up high. Up high.

It's so cold in him. It's lonely and plastic, fake and empty.

“Well?” Neve throws one foot up on the chair next to me. “Spit it out!”

I press past the discomfort, make myself come back here, to the kitchen in the house on the hill, to the warmth and the smell of beans and flowers, and I choke out the words.

“It means he's up high,” I say.

A lifeguard.

“What do you mean up high?” Neve says. “What does that even mean?”

“He's a lifeguard.”

“Watching everyone,” Neve says.

“Hiding in plain sight,” Elle says. She takes a breath. “Well I'll be damned.” She spoons some food into a bowl. “Eat, then get some rest. You're going to need it.”

TWENTY-FIVE
LYLE

The phone rings through the house. Everyone is asleep around me, and Kidd has found her way to my side and is holding on to my waist. The phone rings again and no one stirs, only me, and I can't even move my body. I glance at the clock on the card table. It reads 7:02. I pry myself out of bed, wobbling. I stumble back down. I grab for the nearby jug of water and drink. By the time I can breathe properly and there's sensation in all my toes, the phone has stopped ringing.

I stretch my arms over my head and look around the room. Hopefully there's some kind of laundry day coming, because it's starting to smell musty.

The phone rings again, clanging around the house so loudly the birds start up from outside. When no one answers after the third ring I make it down the stairs to the phone in the hallway and pick up. "Hello," I say.

"Good morning," Lyle says. He says it like it hasn't been a month since the last time we spoke, like I didn't run from him to save my own life, and Roxy's. His voice is the same old smarmy ooze as it ever was. "May, that you?" He waits, then chuckles. "Good thing. I was afraid it would be that aunt of yours, and I don't think she likes me much."

I almost drop the phone. My hands want to let go.

"Third time's the charm," he says. "Sometimes you just got to let the phone ring-a-ling, you know?"

I hold the phone so tight my knuckles are turning colors.

"May," he says. "You're not being very considerate. You're not even going to say hello?" Consideration. Respect. Submission. Lyle's rule of three.

"No," I say, letting the word dangle between us.

"Your mama there?"

"No!" I snap, not knowing whether it's true. I'm not going to tell him I haven't seen my mother in days.

"I'm just checking on you all," he says, acting like I asked him a question. "To be honest, May, I've been wanting to see if you're ready to come home." There's a pause. "Your room is all set for you, your mama's new car just sitting here waiting for her." I stay quiet. "May, can I talk to her?"

"I told you she's not here." I look to the bedroom door, which is closed, weave my finger through the coiled black cord.

"At seven a.m.?" He pauses. "Well, I guess there's a silver lining, because it gives me the chance to talk to you." His voice softens, goes from that aw-shucks, well-meaning tone to something more intimate. "Can I talk to you? Really talk, me to you?"

I don't answer, but I don't hang up.

"I know it all went wrong," he says. "I lost my temper. I would never argue with that. I shouldn't have done that. I know, I know I shouldn't have put my hands on you, but you have to understand, that journal was a shock for me. The things you said? They were nasty. But now we can put all that behind us. Everyone has had some time now, to think."

"Behind us," I repeat, looking out the window to the treetops and the sky, anywhere that takes me away from this conversation.

"Thing is, if you forgive me, Roxy will." This is an admission he doesn't want to make and I can hear in his voice how it costs him. "She told me she doesn't like it there, that it's a strange place and her sister's in charge and God only knows what you're up to."

This brings me back to the moment with a sour-tasting jolt.

"You're lying." He has to be. Roxy can't want to go back to him again.

"Well, that's just plain rude." The arrogance is back. I can hear the victory in his voice. He got to me. Consideration. Respect. Submission. "You know it's what's best for your mother. She's not going to make it there. Between you and me, May, she was drunk as a two-dollar hooker when she called me, just begging to come on home. I told her I'd come get her. You think anyone else would put up with that? No. That's the answer. But I do because I love her and she is my wife in spite of her flaws. And you know what she said to me?" He laughs, savage as a hyena. "She said she couldn't come unless you told her it was okay. You believe that? My wife said she needs her daughter's permission to come home to her *husband*." His voice is a snarl now. We've only been on the phone for a few minutes and he's already run through all the versions of himself.

"If she said it, she didn't mean it. You think she would say that if she were sober?"

There's a small snorting noise.

"No way, Lyle. She's done with you. I heard her tell you to leave us alone."

Lyle takes a deep breath. I hear him trying to steady himself, can picture him leaned into the kitchen counter back in Taylor.

"Sweetheart," he says, "you don't understand what's between me and Roxy and you never did. It's complicated and it isn't always easy, but she's my girl."

This is his final injury, the last knife he has to throw: that he somehow knows my mother better than I do, that he's secretly more important, and that Roxy would choose him over me.

I swell with all the things I want to say. I don't know how he can believe his own words, be so dead set against his part in all of it. And then the voice saying maybe he's right. Maybe Roxy really does love him more than me. Maybe she misses him so bad, she would go behind my back, sober or not. And the worst is, if he would just leave us the hell alone, I wouldn't have to think any of these thoughts at all.

I want to hurt him. I want to hurt him bad. For every time I have been wounded by him, for every time he has hurt my mother. I also want to hang up, but I can't because I have more to say and I hope this will be my only chance to say it, that I will never have to speak to Lyle St. James again. I hope I can say this in a way that sticks to his ribs even if it's something he doesn't want to hear.

"She's not your girl." I grit my teeth against the words. "You gave her a house and a car and a place to run when she was mourning over the man she *actually* loves. My father. She *used* you and you fell for it and she let you beat the shit out of her because she felt guilty you were such a sucker."

He lets the words settle over him. If I was smart, I would hang up right now, but we have each thrown the other on a meat hook, and neither of us can climb off, so we hang there in the empty space of the miles between us and every wrong thing that has ever happened in the time we've known each other.

"No respect," he says, but his voice is weak.

"*Respect?*" I pick at the wall in front of me. "No, Lyle. There's no respect here. Not from me. Not ever. I do not respect you. I do not consider your feelings. And I will never, ever submit."

That's when the hold we have on each other breaks. There's a series of loud smacks as Lyle bangs the phone against the counter or the wall or maybe even the stove. I hold the receiver away from my ear and smile. It feels good to make him lose it. I know just where he's standing, how the white tiles on the counter will be clean and stink of bleach, how the dish towels will be perfectly symmetrical and he will still fix them as he walks by to calm his mind. His jeans are tight and his hair is tight and he's probably clenching everything.

"I ought to come over there and wash out that filthy mouth," he says, low. "You need to be taken in hand, Mayhem *Brayburn*."

"You mad, Lyle?" I ask. "You losing your temper?"

"I'm going to see you soon," he says. "Real soon. And I'm bringing a bar of soap just for you and your dirty, ugly mouth."

My stomach rolls. "I'm looking forward to it," I say, and slam the phone down.

I can't breathe. I just picked a fight with Lyle. I just *invited* him to come and try to take us back. Something is seriously wrong with me. I stand in the hallway, frozen for a few moments before I hear the front door open and then close.

"Hello! Anybody up?"

It's Roxy, her voice light and cake-sweet.

"No one's awake yet." She's talking to someone. I'm ready to storm down and tell her about Lyle's call, to demand answers about what she did or did not say to him, and to tell her that he may or may not be driving here right now in a psychotic rage, when I hear a male voice rumble back.

I inch down the stairs far enough to see that Roxy is in the doorway with Boner, the cop from the police station. He's got on a T-shirt and jeans and looks mildly less annoying than when he was in cop mode. His hair is still way too short and his pecs are still way too big. Roxy stands on her tiptoes to give him a quick peck on the lips, but he holds on to her and dips her, kissing her more deeply.

I try to click in to Boner, to see what secrets he's got hanging on him, but nothing happens. It's like trying to make fire with a wet match. I make a noise of effort and frustration, and Roxy glances up and blanches. "Oh May . . . hey."

I wave. "Well hello there, Mother."

"You remember Boner?"

I descend and Roxy moves away from him until we form a triangle.

"May." He comes forward to shake my hand. I hold it limply and search again, but there's nothing. No icicles or honeycombs. He's a cop who has lived a whole life. How can he have no regrets, nothing hanging off of him? He regards me curiously and takes his hand back, then checks his Timex watch.

"Time for me to get to the station and I need to go home first and change." He nods to me. "Now that we know that Sand Snatcher thing is real, all hands are on deck."

"Sure, of course." Roxy leans into him. Her blouse is open one button too many, and her hair is a mess. She might as well be wearing a neon sign that says I HAVE RECENTLY HAD SEX. I want to set my eyes on fire. "They found body parts." She glances up the staircase at me as Millie steps down gingerly, trying to get to her. "It hasn't even been announced yet."

"They're calling a press conference. Shouldn't be long now." Boner leans down to pet the cat, then waves awkwardly. "Hope to see you soon, May, and stay off the beach. After the press conference it's going to be shut down until this is over."

I cross my arms and stare at him until he leaves. He needs to understand right now no one is going to start telling me what to do.

Once he's gone, after having given Roxy a tame kiss on the cheek that is nothing like the other one I witnessed, Roxy turns on me, the smile dropped from her face. "You could be nice to him, you know."

"I thought you were going to Marcy's. That's what your note said."

"I thought I was, too. Plans changed." The smile is back, pasted on, desperate. "But guess what?" She reaches her arms wide.

"What now?" I say. Even though Roxy doesn't know anything about Lyle's phone call, I'm still mad at her for it.

"I got a job! You are looking at the brand-new employee of VHYes Video Rentals!" She shimmies her shoulders, laughing, then looks at me disappointed when I don't hurl myself into her arms with joy. "Oh come on, May! Be happy for me! There's side benefits and everything. I get free movies!" She glances up the stairs. "We used to have a TV. I'll bet it's in the attic somewhere. We can bring it down. We'll rent a VCR, maybe even buy one."

I remain expressionless. "So, let me get this straight. Since yesterday, you have gotten a job at a video store and have a new boyfriend?"

"Oh," she says, waving me off, "I've known Boner my whole life. We clicked! It was just a date."

"I guess that *is* what professionals call it."

"Mayhem!" Roxy says.

Elle is at the top of the stairs in a long T-shirt, hair in a bun on her head, eyes thick with sleep. "What's going on here? What's all the yelling? Did I hear the phone?"

"Oh, May is mad," Roxy says. "Gearing up for throwing a good old-fashioned tantrum, looks like. She's forgetting I'm a person and I deserve dignity no matter what I've been through in the past. I deserve the opportunity to start over fresh."

"She was out with Boner," I say. "She came in *kissing* him."

Elle bursts out laughing.

"Shut up, Ellie." Roxy turns to me. "You need to understand something. I may have things to work on, but I am here for you, and I am in this town which is scary on a million levels, and I am lucky to have a friend like Boner."

Elle laughs again. "This is wonderful."

"It's not funny," I say.

"Oh, sure it is. It's hilarious, actually. He's been pining for her since he was in diapers. Boy, Rox, I bet you made his life worth living last night. His eleven-year-old self is throwing a party right now. Hey, maybe now he'll do his job instead of ignoring everything so he can spend more time lifting weights."

Roxy says, "Maybe he will. Maybe we just had a really good time. We'll see."

"Come on, sis. Let's go make some coffee," Elle says. "You can tell me alllll about it. I didn't sleep well." She winks at me over Roxy's shoulder, and it's a lighthearted gesture, but all it does is remind me that the secrets between my mother and me are multiplying by the second, that Roxy's losing sight of who I am and she doesn't even know it. Maybe she doesn't even care.

"You coming, May?" My mother extends both hands, her palms scooped, head tilted, so she looks like a statue of a saint.

But she is not a saint and neither am I, and if I go with them it will be a morning of heavy conversation, of anger and regret. As soon as I say Lyle's name everything will go dark. More than that, I don't think I'll be able to keep from unleashing all my rage at Roxy for being so stupid, for calling a monster back into our lives.

So I leave her hands empty.

"Going back to bed," I say. "I didn't sleep much."

She nods as though she knew this would be my answer and her arms drop to her sides. I know Lyle's call is not a secret I should keep, but she's already in the other room, and she seems a sloppy kind of happy, like when we walked into the house from the movies before we left Taylor, totally unaware of what was coming. Let her be there a while longer.

It's only when I'm back in bed, folded around Kidd, who hasn't moved an inch, that I let Lyle's words come back.

I'm going to see you soon. Real soon. And I'm bringing a bar of soap for your dirty, ugly mouth.

In the silent dark punctuated only by the flutter of wings, it's impossible to pretend it's any different.

Lyle is coming.

He's coming.

PART THREE

Brayburn lady knows your sins
Reads your mind and kills your friends

TWENTY-SIX
SHIFT CHANGE

The boardwalk is filled with so many tourists I can hardly move at all. Neve and I have been sent down by Elle to try to identify the Sand Snatcher, based on my now-faded certainty that he's a lifeguard. It seems just as plausible that everything I experienced last night was made up. Meanwhile, Roxy is at Marcy's store. She was gone when I woke up after my nap, having left me a note that she'd be at VHYes, so I haven't told her about Lyle yet, and I haven't told Elle either because she's been totally preoccupied with this. I know avoiding it won't stop Lyle from coming, but I try to concentrate on what Neve is saying.

"The shift change happens in about thirty minutes, where the night guards come on and the guys who have been here since morning step down." She points to the lifeguard hut and the tall chairs lined along the beach, visible from here. "That's where they all converge before they go on duty."

I head through the break in the fence, toward the hut. Ever since the phone call with Lyle this morning and Roxy coming in giddy with possibility, I want to kick someone, bite someone hard, and this Sand Snatcher seems as good a place to start as any. Even though I may have been wrong about who he is and where he'll be now, I feel a pull to this place and to him that tells me different, that's almost like someone standing behind me, physically pushing me onto the beach, over to the little white hut filled with surfboards and lockers and a time clock I can see from here.

"Whoa, tiger." Neve yanks me back and speaks low. "What are you going to do? Walk right in and demand his identity? You still have a lot to learn and you're having to learn it too fast, so let's get everything oiled up before we go after the big boy. We have time, okay? Look." The chairs are still occupied by the daytime lifeguards. "You said he's a night guard so he's not on yet. He might not even be on the beach. Hey, hey look at me."

I do, but my breathing is coming short and my fists are clenched. I feel him nearby. He's somewhere close and the magnetic pull is almost too much for me to handle.

"You need to take a major chill pill, and I can't believe I'm saying that to you. This doesn't work if you're off your trolley." Neve clutches her hand to her heart. "I have to admit it's cute, though, like watching a baby birdy fly from the nest and turn into a man-eating pterodactyl."

"Gee, thanks," I say. She has broken the spell though and whatever had its grip on me has backed off. I take a few deep breaths.

"So let's get you warmed up, because even though you did some odd and impressive things last night, this takes precision. You have to be able to look and *see*, not just have your feelings or whatever, and you don't want that part taking you by surprise. Come, Grasshopper, I will teach you."

She pulls on me, and I force myself to follow her. We climb up to the boardwalk, back to the blinking lights and street performers and the zinging, screaming rides. It's swarming with people, and though I'm electric with possibility and what might come with the dark tonight, I settle as soon as we're away from the lifeguard station.

"Okay, so there are a lot of things in life that people make a big deal about that are actually not at all a big deal." She takes me by the shoulders. "This is not one of those times."

"I get it."

"You really don't. But you will."

A shiver barrels up my spine.

"Look there, one at a time." Neve points to the people on the boardwalk walking together, apart, laughing, hustling, slumped forlornly against walls. "Separate them out from each other. See them as individuals. We're all connected, right, and that's what we're using to see. Essential energy. But we also have our own lives and our own problems and memories and plans. That's what you're hooking in to. You're using the connection we all have to each other to find out what's happening with the people you want to know about. So look. First see the web. Then see the person. Then see the truth."

She stands behind me as I try to do what she says. "They're all little humans trying to live their lives. You only have to watch for so long before you find out whether they're guppies or sharks."

A woman in jean shorts tries to hustle a small child out of the store that sells all the cheap, neon, plastic toys. The little girl shrieks and slaps at her mother's thigh. The woman drags her a few paces and then the girl walks on her own and they disappear into the crowd.

"And what are we?" I ask Neve, who's pulled herself up onto the wooden fencing that runs along the beach. "Guppies or sharks?"

"We eat the sharks." Neve pats her belly. "Yum."

"And how do you know which is which?" I hoist myself up beside her. "How do you not make a mistake?"

"You make demands. You *make* them show you the truth."

"Them who?"

She furrows her brow. "You talk right to their inner selves. Bypass the skin they hide under. You make it happen because you can see. And here's the most important thing to remember: People want to be seen. They want their secrets to be shared."

I think of this morning with Boner, of how when I asked to see, nothing happened. I didn't get good or bad from him. There was just nothing at all, but I know there's no such thing as a person with no history, no pain. "You know how I told you my mom hooked up with that neighbor cop?"

"Right. The Boner guy Elle hates," Neve says distractedly as she watches the boardwalk from her perch.

"I tried to check him out."

"Good girl." She's still not paying attention, and I can feel her digging into these people one by one, checking them for distortions.

"There was nothing. Just a blank. Did I do it wrong?"

Neve seems to have given up and finally turns her attention my way. "What time was it?"

"I don't know. The phone woke me up. It was right after that."

Neve nods, the sky going pink behind her, hair fluttering in a salty breeze.

No matter the time of day or night, no matter what we're talking about, Neve always looks epic. She's a piece of art, beach-waved hair blowing as dusk gathers, tide rising behind us. Her waist is thin, torso long, and her brown, tanned legs kick out in front of her. She's the picture of what everyone wishes to be, down to the tiny mole at the upper left corner of her mouth and the large silver hoops in her ears.

"You had just woken up," she says. "Takes a minute to get everything up and running, know what I mean? Morning is the weakest time. Plus that Boner guy doesn't have anything to hide. I already checked the first time he gave us grief when he found us on Brayburn Road and he didn't know who we were."

"Oh." I don't know if I'm disappointed or not. Maybe I wanted an excuse to keep Roxy from hurling herself into yet another relationship.

"Can we please focus? We've got more to think about than your mom and her romantic habits. Besides, everyone has the right to get laid."

"Neve!"

"What? Stop being a prude. Your mom's a babe and Officer Biceps is a babe. Leave them alone. You have other things to think about. Like that . . ." Neve looks up and out again. "Can you hear yet? The air crackles and fizzes. You have to listen for it, but it's there, and that's when you know to ask. That's how you know the water has something to tell you."

Crackles and fizzes like when you first open a can of soda, only instead of burning out it gets louder.

Her head tilts to the side and her eyes narrow. "Over there," she says. "Check out that guy."

There's a boy maybe a little older than me, walking along the boardwalk. He has a little girl by the hand. I know right away it's his sister. They have a similar shape to their faces and the same skin, but that's not what tells me. I just know. And I know something else, too. This isn't the Sand Snatcher, but something about him isn't right.

"Yeah, that's the one." Neve hops off the fence and signals for me to follow. "He's perfect for practice."

Now that we're following him, threading through people to keep him in view, the crackling starts up, and then it gets so loud I can't hear anything else. Neve's lips move, but she's been overruled by fizzing and snapping.

"Stop." I say it as I think it. "Stop," I say again. "Show me."

Neve smiles and her teeth are pink from her Icee. They look like they're covered in blood.

The air whines and then whooshes, crystallizing the boy in his memories, ice all around him, but ice made of air instead of water. It's thick and has facets, and inside each one, a story plays out. I can't see anything specific because I'm too far away. These are the honeycombs.

I'm so excited I jump up and down so my bracelets jingle against each other, and the lady across from us with the MOM sailor tattoo and the pink hair stares at me.

"I see it! I see it!"

"That's my Mayhem." Neve pats my back. "Now look closer."

I'm almost distracted as a girl steps past us, whirring with her own crackle and her own stories.

"Eyes on the prize," Neve says, pushing at my cheek. "Shut it down from everyone but him. One at a time. That's the key. The longer you do it, the easier it will be to control. Now. Him. Only him. Everything about him. Ask."

Tell me, I think. *Tell me everything.*

The ice around the boy fills the space and blurs everyone around him so they are erased. There is only me and Neve and the boy and the invisible monster he carries with him, brought to clicking life, a prehistoric, giant locustlike insect.

Neve is a bird again, pale, her eyes gone hard and beady, head angled. "After a while, you can tell it to stay hidden. You can order it to show itself. It's the click you have to listen for. That's what tells you there's more. But it kind of depends on your mood, right? Like, if you're out on a date maybe you don't want every sicko Tom, Dick, and Harry ruining your good time, but if you're in the mood for a feast, you accept the invitation and find out what there is to see."

The guy mounts the carousel. Sunglasses on even though

the light is dim, mirrors reflecting a warped world. He's one of those preppie guys you see in the movies with his collar turned up. There's nothing about him that would make you suspect him of evil. Nothing but the ice whirring and ticking, playing out scene after scene, each scene changing, unfolding. It's alive and it buzzes.

"My mama always told me never to trust a boy who won't let you see his eyes." Neve winks.

I try not to watch what's happening in the honeycombs too closely, while also trying to understand, because it's not just that I'm seeing, I'm feeling, too. I'm *knowing*. "He would never hurt his sister."

"No," Neve agrees. "You can see it."

"The girls have to be drunk or high. That's how he justifies it."

Neve knits her eyebrows. "Yeah? You can see that?"

I shake my head. "Not *see* it. Feel it."

"Hunh," she says.

We get tickets, hand them to the bearded guy manning the gate, and jump on the carousel after Preppie and the little girl. We choose stationary horses a couple behind them.

A dull thud starts up in the center of my forehead, like a headache is coming on. My throat constricts and my mouth moistens. More than that, a rolling in my chest, restless, like I've got nothing in me but feathers and need more inside to hold me down, like I need his stories to fill me up. I want him to give them to me. I shiver and shake but the yearning hunger only grows. I'm holding on to the gilded pole in front of me, so hard my fingers are purple and white.

"Doin' okay, cowgirl?" Neve says.

"Fine." I grit the words against my closed jaw, lean my cheek against the ridges and push until it hurts. It helps me stop wanting.

"Okay, then," Neve pulls a pack of gum from her pocket and offers me one. "Sometimes having something to chew on can bring you down."

I shake my head, but she shoves the gum into my hand.

"Put it in your mouth and chew. You'll like it. Cinnamon."

I take the gum and the spicy sweetness rushes my mouth.

Up, down, up, down, I think as I chew. But it's almost impossible to focus on anything other than what's in front of me. Because now I do see. Clearly. Scenes play out on repeat, slivers, moments. Girls, not moving, eyes closed, not even awake enough to fight. And I hate him worse than I ever hated anyone, maybe even Lyle.

The carousel stops and the boy helps his sister step off.

"What if what we're seeing isn't accurate?" I say. "What if it's just thoughts?"

"It's not just thoughts," Neve says. "When it's just thoughts the honeycombs are blurry."

The guy meanders for a minute, then gets in line for cotton candy or peanuts. Now that I'm not looking into it anymore, his honeycomb shrinks down to a shimmering aura. The line for cotton candy is long, so Neve drops her Icee into the trash and we stand off to the side.

NO ONE GETS OUT ALIVE is scrawled on the wall across the way, outside Dark Side of the Spoon, where everyone gets their yogurt.

The seagulls squawk from the trash can, picking at scraps. "It's about karma, the great wheel of cause and effect. There's no escaping it, right, except sometimes people do. They get away with things. Terrible, awful things. We're just cleaning up where the law can't, in corners the universe has forgotten."

I wish I could see Neve's past, because she's heating up, the air around her charged.

"It's about doing bad things and getting exactly what you

deserve," she goes on. "It's about dirty little secrets that would go undiscovered if we weren't here. It's about people paying for what they've done and not just getting away with it all the time." Neve is near hysteria, like she's not talking in theory anymore, but speaking from experience.

I put my arm around her shoulder, and she leans her head onto mine, so silky strands of hair tickle at my skin. She lets her breath settle.

"He's looking at me," Neve whispers. "Isn't he?"

He's almost to the front of the line, staring at us and for a brief second of insanity I'm afraid he knows what we're doing, that somehow he has sight, too, but then I realize what's happening. The guy is ogling Neve, checking her out, running his eyes up and down over her form.

"Yep." I try to look casual, like we're talking about lipstick and eye shadow instead of good and evil and secrets we want to keep but that leak out of us anyway.

"Good." She gathers herself, pushing back whatever emotions had surfaced. "He'll be dessert. Now for the main course."

My stomach coils.

"Let's go." She skips a few steps toward the water. "That's all the training you're going to get. Now it's time for the shift change."

We leap onto the beach, the two of us, hand in hand. The sunset is love as a color, the smell of suntan lotion and salt rising up as the heat dies down. The lifeguards aren't the only thing changing right now. The daytime beach bodies are being traded in for the night crew, bikinis replaced by leather jackets, a now familiar transition. We plant ourselves about thirty feet from the lifeguard hut, up on the small sandhill where a bunch of people are gathered to watch the sky change.

"This will probably be harder than usual," Neve says. "These kinds of psychos, they believe their own stories. When they're playing normal, they can even hide from themselves."

But I can hear him coming.

"No," I say, chest tightening. "He's right there."

Neve scans the beach.

"Straight ahead."

"Where?" Neve clutches her own arms and squints hard. "I got nothin'. You sure?"

"I'm sure." I can barely get the words out now, because he's headed straight for us. This isn't a joke or a game we're playing. This is real and as he saunters my way I feel myself slip under the cave water and choke on it.

"May, are you okay? Say something." Neve nudges me hard, but I'm hypnotized and still trying to catch my breath, my hand at my own throat.

The whirs and clicks, the ice so massive. His sickness cuts through everyone he passes. When I feel stable enough, I look into one of the honeycombs and then away, bury my forehead in Neve's shoulder.

I don't need to see that.

No one does.

She shrugs me off, seems annoyed. "Come on, don't be a baby. Where is he?" she says.

"There."

"Him?"

I nod.

He has brown hair, blue eyes, a blinding smile, a shell necklace at his throat. He stands out because he blends in so well. He's practically flawless. He's loping toward us in a wetsuit, a board under his arm, taking his time, owning the whole wide world. He pauses between us and the hut.

"This is where I leave you, babe. Out of the water and into the grind," he tells a pretty girl who is keeping pace next to him.

"For sure." She adjusts her board, tosses her wet hair. "At least there will be waves again tomorrow."

I can tell by the way Neve is looking at him that she still can't see. If she could, not even she would be able to keep her cool. I focus on the gum again. Up and down. Up and down. It works, keeps me calm.

"Come over after work?" the girl says.

"I think I'm going to my place. I don't get off until three a.m. Got to protect the beach. Beware the Sand Snatcher!" He curls his free hand into a claw, then drops it back at his side. "Anyway, you wore me out last night."

"Yeah, I did." She grins. "See you tomorrow, then?"

"For sure, for sure." He gives her a quick peck on the lips and a squeeze around the waist.

The ice shivers like it's trying to shake off something gross.

He disappears inside the hut, then a minute later steps out in a red bathing suit and heads over to the chair to relieve the lifeguard on duty. I watch them chat, like everything is normal. No one knows. This prick is walking around every day, living his life and then doing *that*, and there's not one person who's figured it out. Except me. I know. And that means something.

"Are you one hundred percent sure?" Neve says. "Because that's the guy who was on the beach the other night. Remember? With the flashlight?"

That seems like ten lifetimes ago, but Neve is right. He's the surfer lifeguard who told us to be careful.

"That is *extra* twisted," I say. It's true. Sometimes the patterns are too much to bear.

"I didn't see it at all," she says. "Nothing." She seems perplexed.

"Maybe he believes himself like you said."

"Didn't stop you from spotting him in five seconds," she

says. "He was standing right next to us the other night, and there was nothing."

"So what do we do now?" I try to change the subject, to put her back in the driver's seat where she likes to be.

Neve folds her arms. "We go home, I guess. We tell Elle. We await instructions. That's how this gig works."

This trip to the beach has been way too intense and strange to walk home the regular way. "Can we run?"

Neve is still staring at the lifeguard chair like it's a riddle.

"Neve, pleeeease! Can we run? Can we run up the hill?" Part of me knows this is what I do with Roxy, try to cajole the self-doubt off her. But part of me just wants to see Neve smile, and for her to stop worrying about the power she does or does not carry. "I bet I can beat you!"

The shadows peel away from her and she brightens. "You're so dumb," she says, but through a smile. "Fine, when we get to the base of the hill." She pulls me to my feet. "Then hell yeah, we can run. Victory!" she yells, so the lifeguards still milling around the hut stop to look over at us. One guy shakes his head. Neve gives him the finger. "Sayonara, suckers," she says, and I'm nothing but relieved she's recovered.

But I also know I can't protect Roxy and protect Neve and keep everyone from being sad all the time. I know that's not actually helping anyone when it's a lie.

"Wait," I tell Neve, looking to the boardwalk. "I have one more thing to do."

TWENTY-SEVEN
CURFEW

When Neve and I step into VHYes, my mother's hand is wrapped around Boner's. She drops it as soon as she sees me. Everyone exchanges hellos, but their focus is on something else. Marcy, her red hair teased to its greatest heights yet, watches the TV over the cooler and waves at me, but she's transfixed.

As I try to make sense of what's happening on the screen, I feel like I'm being vacuum sealed.

Neve puts an arm around me. "No way," she says.

"They're announcing it," Boner says. "About five weeks too late, if you ask me, which no one does."

Roxy pats his shoulder.

A woman at a news desk with feathered bangs and too much blush as well as giant shoulder pads in her suit jacket says, "We are joining the press conference live. Please stand by."

A tall Hispanic man stands in front of a mic with a slew of men in suits at his side, several of them in uniform.

"Good evening," he says. "It is with great sadness that I must report to you that, with the help of an unsuspecting hitchhiker who shall remain anonymous at this time, we have located the skeletal remains of the first two girls to have disappeared from Santa Maria in the last months, Tina Chaput and Karen Delano, on Redwood Hill. Though the details are continuing to unfold and more information will be forthcoming, we can confirm that a femur belonging to a third female has also been located. We fear that it belongs to another victim. As a result, we have reason to believe the other girls may also have been taken by the same perpetrator, and that we may be dealing with a serial killer."

"No shit," Boner says.

"Shhhh," Marcy says.

I am faint with the images I only glimpsed; of what happened to those girls, how afraid they must have been, so many unanswered prayers, so much pain.

"As a result, the council has voted to place a curfew in effect beginning tonight. No one is to be out past nine p.m., and the beach will be entirely off-limits. Citizens of Santa Maria are urged to keep windows and doors locked and to exercise extreme caution while out and about. All victims have been between the ages of thirteen and sixteen, so families with children of those ages are also asked to take whatever extra precautions necessary. We hope to have this case solved and everything back to normal as soon as possible, but in the meantime, it's simply not worth the risk of any more loss of life, so please take this seriously. We will be patrolling to ensure our streets are safe. In order to protect the integrity of the investigation, I will not be taking any questions at this time. Your extreme vigilance is appreciated. I urge citizens of Santa Maria to contact law enforcement should you see *anything* suspicious. Thank you for your cooperation." He steps away as cameras flash and reporters begin shouting out questions, ignoring his attempt to end the press conference. A man in uniform approaches the mic, his forehead sweating, and Marcy mutes the TV.

"I can't believe they let Lonnie do the closing," Boner says, still watching. "Guy's a doofus."

"Jesus have mercy," Marcy says, picking at her press-on

nails. She looks at Boner. "You know what this is going to do to me? It's going to kill the tourist business, and no one is going to be out after dark."

"What are you talking about? No one is going to have anything to do except watch movies. You're going to be rich!" Roxy says, lighting a cigarette.

Everything is surreal, and I know Neve is thinking the same thing as me: that we could solve this right now. I could say, "Boner, the Sand Snatcher is a quarter mile away." Sure, he will have an alibi. And that smile. But if they go digging, they'll find out who he is.

"Don't you dare," Neve whispers. "The Sand Snatcher is ours."

"Hopefully there won't be a curfew for long, Marcy," Boner says, the three adults oblivious to anything other than their own immediate problems. "I'll let you know what's going on. Meanwhile, make sure you get Elle to batten down the hatches. I know she thinks she's invincible, but even she should take some precautions here."

"No one's going to go all the way up there," Roxy says uncertainly. "Who would bother to attack the house? Who would *dare*?"

Lyle. Lyle would dare. That phone call seems so long ago.

"Roxy, can I talk to you?"

She comes over to me, arms crossed, then glances at my necklace. My hand goes to cover it automatically, but not fast enough. She didn't notice it this morning because it was under my clothes but she sure has noticed it now, and she grabs it and glares at me.

I am so stupid.

"Where did you get this?" she says.

"Elle gave it to me."

"Why? Why would she do that?"

"Ow!" I pull the necklace from her grip. "You're hurting me."

"We all have them," Neve says smoothly, pulling hers from under her shirt.

Roxy looks from me to Neve.

"Elle said something about your grandma having them made?" Neve says. Damn, she should be a politician. "She wanted us to feel like family, so she passed them out. You should have one, too, Roxy."

That's going too far. I want to drive my elbow into her side.

"I *did* have one." Roxy's voice is cold. "I gave it back. And so should you." She looks up again, eyes filled with regret, sucks on her smoke. "Oh, Mayhem. I should never have come back here. Look what's happening to us. Look what's happening to Santa Maria."

"Lyle's coming," I blurt to stop her from saying what probably comes next, that we should have stayed in Taylor, where we were safe. I can't hear that lie even one more time. I have to shock it out of her head for good.

She lets out a little laugh before her face falls flat. "What? Are you serious? Mayhem, this isn't funny."

"I'm not kidding. Why would I joke about that?"

"What do you mean, then? Tell me what you mean!" She's stammering, stumbling like she's looking for solid ground and not finding any, but I can't catch her now. I need her to understand.

"I'm telling you because I'm not going back to Taylor and neither are you. And we aren't running away. We are never running away again." My voice is so strong I'm scaring myself. "I can't leave Santa Maria anymore."

"You *can't*?" Roxy's words are a warning. "What do you mean, you can't?"

"I mean I *won't*."

"Well, this is just ridiculous." She throws off her seriousness with a sharp laugh. That laugh is one of Roxy's favorite ways to shut down, to den. "I mean, why do you think he's coming all the way here? Because I know Lyle St. James and he is far too proud."

"Roxy, you're an object," I say, trying to maintain my calm, but also not letting her blow this off like it's nothing. "He thinks you belong to him. When you lose an object that's yours, what do you do?"

"He said that? When? When did you find out all this valuable information?"

She's going to be mad. So mad.

"He called. This morning."

Roxy blanches but I go on.

"First he asked for you, and then when I told him you weren't there, he said he wants to come and get you because he wants you to go back to Taylor."

She crosses her arms in front of her. "And did he say he was coming? I mean, did those actual words come out of his mouth?"

"What he said, *Mother*, is that he was coming with a bar of soap to wash out my filthy little mouth." I feel that rush of hatred again. "He threatened me. He bashed the phone. He is really, really angry. Do you even *care*, Mother?"

"Harsh," Neve says, under her breath.

"Easy, honey," Marcy says from the corner, where she's stopped straightening a shelf. "Go easy on your mama."

Roxy's face drops, then clamps up again as I'm flooded with guilt I have no room to carry. I know Roxy could only leave him when she could, and I know all the reasons she stayed. I want to go to her and comfort her, take back everything I said. I take a step toward her.

"No no, don't. I'm okay." She stubs out her cigarette, which is at its bitter end, probably burning through the filter. "Now, I know you're afraid, probably of everything, but Lyle is not coming here. I'm sure of it."

There's not going to be any getting through to her. Not now and probably not ever. "Yeah, Roxy—I'm sure you're right." I grab Neve and we head for the exit.

"Good night, Miss Brayburn," Neve says.

"Oh by the way," Roxy trills, ignoring Neve and stopping me before I reach the door. "I'm not coming home tonight. Nobody wants me there anyway."

I consider doing what I used to, making a joke, reassuring her, throwing her a Twinkie, hugging her into smiling.

But the truth is, I plain don't want to.

"Good," I say. "Go have another night of passion with Officer Whatshisface. I'll be just fine."

"Fine!" she says.

"Fine!" I say back.

"You two need to calm down," Marcy says.

"Shut up, Marcy. You don't know anything about it," Roxy snaps.

"Well that was rude," Marcy says. "I was just trying to be helpful."

"Don't be helpful, Marcy. Mayhem and I don't need anyone in our business," Roxy says, keeping her flinty eyes trained on mine. "Just remember, I could make you leave here, Mayhem." Roxy's voice trembles now, her words slow and deliberate. "You're not eighteen. You have to come with me if I say."

I fix Roxy with a glare hot enough to start a fire. "You try it," I dare her as she stumbles backward, her face empty of everything but shock. "Just try."

TWENTY-EIGHT
MURDER MURDER KILL KILL

It is a much simpler plan than I thought it would be. Two phone calls by Elle and we have the lifeguard's name and license plate. Kurt Selinger of Wild Wood, Wisconsin, moved to Santa Maria a little over a year ago, after graduating from college, which he attended in Milwaukee, and from which he graduated with honors. That deep surfer accent must be fake. He has a record for a minor assault, but other than that he's clean. He drives a white Toyota Camry and has been working as a lifeguard since he got here.

"Why does Rebecca tell you so much?" I ask Elle as she goes over everything with us.

"Oh, I took care of something for her years ago. She's very generous." She goes back to giving us what we'll need to get this done. Sand Snatcher makes the guy sound big and powerful, but as far as I can tell his only advantage is that no one knows who he is and he can hide.

"Are you ready?" Elle asks me. She's taken me into the orchard, and we're under such a peaceful sky. It's hard to believe what we're planning to do just a few hours from now. There should be a storm, dark foreboding clouds, maybe some turkey buzzards swooping around overhead; not this smell of peaches and blossoming bougainvillea, this utterly dreamy weather, the valley below us in glorious greens and our crows nattering by our sides. Even though everything around me is ideal, I'm still smarting from my fight with Roxy, still worried about Lyle showing up, and of course the fact that soon I'll be hunting the Sand Snatcher. It's gotten hard to make sense of anything.

"I'm proud of you," Elle says, and she hugs me to her with her powerful but bony arms. "I hope this isn't too much. But you know what I think?"

"What?"

"I think it's no coincidence that you came when you did. In fact, I don't believe in coincidences at all. The human race might be a wreck, but the grand plan is perfect."

Neve comes out to meet us with Jason and Kidd at her side. I have a hard time knowing what to do with my eyes with Jason so close. My fingers ache to touch him, my legs want to wrap around him, and mostly I want to lay my head against his chest. It seems like a person would have to be blind not to know it just from looking at me, at the way I don't know how to be, but no one seems to notice my flush.

"So what's the plan, my captain?" Neve says, plopping herself at Elle's feet.

Jason sits next to me, lets his fingers graze my thigh then weave through mine, briefly, before retracting, leaving enough of a trace that I heat even more.

Kidd puts her hands on her hips and looks from me to Elle defiantly, which brings a smile to Elle's lips.

"And why are you here, little miss?" Elle says to Kidd.

"She thinks she's going tonight," Jason says, more than a little miserably.

"I *am* going. I'm big enough and I hate psycho killers so much." Kidd scowls, screwing her mouth into a tight O to demonstrate her hatred.

"Oh no, Kiddo," Elle says, smiling. "You are staying right here at home with me."

"What?" Kidd is just about stomping her foot. "That's ageism."

"How do you even know that word?" Neve says.

"I know lots of things!" Kidd says. "That's what I'm talking about. You guys don't even know what I know."

"Kidd," Elle says, "this is not something to play with. You are too young to be kept safe." She sighs. "To tell you the truth, you're all too young for this, but we have to get this man out of rotation in Santa Maria. He can't be allowed to go on doing these things or we're not doing our jobs."

Kidd pouts, staring at the ground in front of her pink lace-up shoes.

"Kidd," Elle says in the softest voice, "I promise we'll have a good time. We'll have hot chocolate and cake *and* we'll watch TV until everyone gets back."

Kidd looks up. "Seriously? That's all the things that are against the rules."

"I know. But it's a special night and you're my girl. We're going to have our own date. Let's run to town and get some movies, and Jason can bring the TV down." She gets up and takes Kidd by the hand. "You leave here at two a.m. You go on foot, you do it, you come back. Keep it clean and quick. No antics," she says, her voice hardening again.

"Yes, sir," Neve says.

When Elle doesn't smile, she says, "We *will*."

"You better."

We're all dressed in black. We don't need flashlights. The town is ghostly and empty and dank. Only the lifeguards are still on. As Elle explained, they're helping to enforce the first night of curfew, making sure no stragglers are loose on the beach. Jason has neatly used a tool to jimmy his way into the

Sand Snatcher's car before his shift ends at three, and Neve and I slip into the back seat without any problems, squeezing together on the upholstered interior.

There are still the remnants of a party on the beach, a bonfire close to burning out, but other than that, the whole town is silent. When I look up, Jason is watching from the tree above the car. To the naked eye, he would be completely camouflaged, but I can feel him there. Nothing, not even pitch-dark, can keep me blind.

"What if he checks the back seat?" I whisper after a few minutes, my anxiety getting the better of me.

"He won't," Neve says.

I wait a few beats, focus on the gray seat pocket directly in front of me. There's nothing in it. In fact, the car is pretty pristine.

"How do you know?" I say.

"Because he thinks he's invincible. Why would he think he has anything to worry about? And anyway, if he does, we'll still get him. Now shut up!"

A cop car shines its spot into the car and I hold my breath. The cop can't see us in here, but in the harsh light I can see even Neve is sucking in her breath, trying not to make a sound. Even Neve is trembling.

Maybe this is what it feels like to be the Sand Snatcher, stalking. Everything is a threat, and every near miss a sign you're fulfilling your destiny. We rearrange ourselves so my head is on Neve's hip, so we can both leap to action when it's time.

Nothing happens.

Nothing happens.

Nothing happens.

Time creeps.

I don't like waiting.

It gives me too much space for contemplating what I'm doing and how every decision I've made in my life has led me exactly to here.

"Your hip is so bony," I say. "You're going to pierce my skull."

"He couldn't get a bigger car?" Neve says. "It's practically a clown car."

We both laugh but then I feel a whoosh, pressure. I hear a tick.

"He's coming," I whisper.

The whirring starts up in earnest, a warning. The clicking and whirring get louder, just as Jason lets out the crow call we agreed on.

Neve says, "Hold it together."

"How do I do this?" I whisper.

"You'll know," she says. "Follow my lead."

I am not a baby bird.

Kurt the Sand Snatcher gets in, driver door still open, and the car fills with the stench of his misdeeds, and underneath them, a sweet beckoning. My throat thickens.

He gets the key in the ignition, checks the rearview mirror, and the sound of Phil Collins fills the car. When he closes the door, Neve sits up in one smooth motion and reaches over the front seat, locking him in with an arm around his throat. He tries to fight but she's got him pinned. She's so strong. He writhes, his eyes searching.

"Shhh." She looks at me. "Well, help!"

I climb over the seat, and Jason slides in the back. Kurt Sand Snatcher doesn't say anything because he can't because Neve has just shoved a sock she had in her pocket into his mouth. Jason slaps tape over the top of it and then sits back, expressionless, next to me.

"We can all see. You don't have any secrets anymore because

we can see them all," Jason says. "And man, you deserve what you get."

The car is filled with nightmares.

I grab hold of his arms and get right up close to him. It's easy to pin him. He smells like terror and the want clicks in. I will gobble his transgressions and they will satisfy me.

"You tortured those girls," Neve says. "They had lives and parents and people who loved them and you killed them. You took everything away."

He moans and tries to shake himself loose while I keep checking around for more cops. Elle said they were patrolling every thirty minutes but you never know.

Neve makes eye contact with him in the rearview mirror and forces his face still with her free arm. "God has sent a reckoning, Kurt Selinger. And it's us."

He squeezes his eyes shut and she pries one open. "I want you to look at me."

He stops fighting and is slack with confusion so palpable it's a reaching thing. Nausea bulldozes over everything else and I lose my grip for a second, let go of his arm. He immediately flails and knocks Neve back.

"Shit," Jason says, scrambling, reaching forward. Kurt reaches for the handle and flings the door open. He pulls the tape from his mouth, spits out the sock, and shouts. It all happens so fast and my reaction is so swift, I almost don't know how I got on top of him, knocked him to the ground. I have his foot first and use it as leverage to crawl over him, flip him over, and am now mouth to mouth with him, inhaling with new lungs that never end.

I am two Mayhems. One who can't believe what she is doing, and a second one who has discovered her purpose.

The Sand Snatcher watches me, as I breathe in. The honeycombs are losing their shape, deflating. I feel Jason settle on one side of me. I know he's talking and he's pulling but I can't hear him. Then Neve is beside me, inhaling, too. We breathe together, filling up. It's all Phil Collins and the clicks and whirs slowing, like clockwork going backward, straining against its own machinery.

And then, a beautiful silence. I stop, back away from his body lying in the street. A few seconds later Neve jumps off him and lands next to me, glowing like that first night on the boardwalk when they left me with Kidd.

"That was good." She hugs me. "You did a really good job."

"Good? That was amazing," Jason says.

His words don't match his tone. He doesn't sound like he thinks this is amazing. He's a few feet away from me, squatted down with his head in his hands. He won't look at me.

I'm breathing hard. I see the beach without any light at all, as though it's daylight. My lungs are infinite and my body buzzes, everything operating exactly as it should.

Jason finally lifts up. "Mayhem, that was crazy."

I try to take his hand, but he lets go and shakes his head. He looks down at Neve, at the Sand Snatcher's limp husk splayed out, and then at me.

"Jason?" I say.

He doesn't answer, but silently wipes down the car with a cloth he pulls from his pocket. I sit on the curb, holding on to my knees. And then it hits me, why Jason is skirting me like I'm a wild beast who might attack any second.

I killed someone.

But that's not what it is, at least I don't think so.

I did a really good job. I killed someone *well*.

Everything in life is hard.

But killing the Sand Snatcher was easy.

TWENTY-NINE
BILLIE BRAYBURN
DAUGHTER OF JULIANNA

1929

Karen Thisby has taken her own life and it's my fault.

I confess I was lonely in this mission of ours. I would never speak of it to Tommy. He is my husband and would never allow me to continue if he knew, especially with a baby on the way, and then I made a horrible mistake.

I showed Karen the cave. She seemed perfectly suited to it, having such character and physical prowess, and we get along so well. But after a few weeks she began acting quite mad. There'll be no point in sugarcoating it. She took off all her clothes and tried to tear off her own arm. She tried to walk on water. She murdered men with little reason. And I attempted to get her to stop taking the water, but she grew gravely ill. She sweated and shook and scratched at herself. She didn't want to stop. She couldn't. She took her own life rather than continue. For all the lives I have taken, this is the one that will haunt me. Poor, dear Karen. If I hadn't showed her, she would never have come to such an end. I will make sure to tell my child this news and see that she passes it on.

I will tell her:

Drink the water.

Find true love.

Embrace your fate.

Protect Santa Maria and you protect yourself.

And never, ever tell another about the spring.

We are none of us invincible. We are all of us made of flesh and bone.

It is for us alone to carry.

THIRTY
FATE

When the phone rings out into the house I'm still awake, in the room I should be sharing with my mother. I jump and the Brayburn book falls off my chest. I run to the hallway, but Jason is already there with the phone against his ear.

"Hello?" he says.

I don't move. Roxy wasn't here when we got back. I had assumed she was off screwing Boner, but now I am picturing that rickety old car she finally got gas for toppling off a mountainside. I'm picturing her wasted, careening or jumping or falling or drowning. I am wondering whether she even wants to be on this planet and whether I'm enough to keep her here. A person can have enough of it. Just look at my dad.

Obrigado.

Amor.

"Hello?" Jason says again.

He couldn't look at me, down at the beach when the Sand Snatcher was lying there dead. He *wouldn't.* But he's looking at me now.

After a few moments, he replaces the phone on its cradle. "Nobody there," he says, and shrugs.

It's five in the morning, and I don't think I'm ever going to be able to sleep again. I'm going to be awake, swirling in my own tornado until a house lands on me and puts me out of my misery.

"I just realized I have to start school in a month," I say. "High school." I drop my face into my hands. I'm really not sure I can come through all this in one piece. Really.

"You didn't come upstairs." Jason gets closer, so I can feel his body heat.

"I didn't think you wanted me to." I keep my face covered. I don't want to look up, not because I'm afraid, but because this way I can smell him, feel him inching in.

"I've never seen anything like that. The way you took him out . . ." He peels my hand away, so gently. "It was mastery. It was fierce. And it was terrifying. I just needed a minute. But I wanted you to come upstairs. I couldn't sleep. Like, at all."

"Me neither. I was reading. I'm . . ." I hesitate. "I'm trying to understand."

"Yeah," he says. "I bet you are."

Above us, the fairy lights blink out their soft rotation of color: pink, purple, blue, yellow, green, pink . . .

"It was different than when you did it?" I ask.

"Oh, I've never done it. It's part of the agreement I have with Elle. I can't, and Kidd isn't going to either."

"Then why did you drink the water in the first place? Why are you even here, Jason?"

There's a long pause.

Finally he says, "I wonder that all the time. I wonder if I did something so stupid I ruined everything."

I pull him to me, half expecting him to push me away, but he doesn't. He puts his arms around me and applies just enough pressure for me to feel safe. "I wanted Kidd to be able to protect herself," he says into the top of my head. "Neve knew. She understood. She told me we would be invincible. We would be heroes."

"Yeah, but—"

"But I don't think I really believed her. I thought it was

some hurt girl pretending she was a witch or something. And the part of me that did believe it was like, yeah, we could use some extra help, my sister and me. I think I fucked up real bad."

I pull back so I can see his expression. He's looking for me to reassure him, I think, but I can't, not after what I just read in the Brayburn book. Because he may be right. He may have fucked up real bad.

I watch him carefully for the signs of madness Billie wrote of in her diary entry, but he seems calm, just sad.

Elle must know the risks for people who aren't Brayburn blood. She must have felt like there was nothing to be done since they had already found the water by the time she got to them. She could only take them in and teach them, keep them as safe as possible, make them her own children.

They did need her.

"Speaking of fuckups, that was my stepfather on the phone," I say. "I'm almost positive. Sending a message."

"Whoever it was didn't say anything. There was just breathing. And you know people call Elle at all hours to help them."

"Yeah, except I know because I know. And time's running out." It's such a relief to speak what's been circling around in me. "If Lyle left right after he threatened to come here, stopping for some sleep at some point, he'll be here soon. I mean, he should be here now."

Jason seems to think about this. "How do you know he's coming? It's a long way to come for someone who doesn't want you."

"I made him mad. It's hard to explain. I just don't think he'll let my mom go. And if he comes, he could be dangerous. It depends where he is on the loop."

"Loop?"

I forget other people don't know about this. They don't have to watch for a cycle, a rounding of the horn from sweetness to violence. I know Jason has had other, worse things in his life, but it sounds like his parents loved each other the right way.

"Like, in order to know whether or not he would hurt us, you have to know if he's feeling repentant, or just pissed, and oh my God, my mom isn't here. She's with Boner, and if Lyle shows up, that's a whole other issue. I wish she would have left him alone, but she didn't. She called him. I know she was lonely but if she had just waited, she would have gotten better."

"Yeah, but it's hard not to reach for comfort when you're lonely, right?" Jason says.

I soften, understand the question he's really asking. "You think that's why I like you? Because it's not that. It's that you make me feel crazy but in the best way. You . . . your actual self . . . it's the better magic."

"The better magic," he murmurs, slipping an arm around my waist. I almost go limp. My throat swells. There is pain and there's hurt, and then there's this, an ache right into my marrow.

This isn't like with Roxy, where our bodies fit together and I know I came from her, that she made me. It's not the telepathic connection that's all filled up with tinny resistance and being too close to be healthy.

"Let's talk this through," Jason says, and we slide down the wall, hold hands. A lot has happened in this hallway, I realize. So much in between. Between rooms, lives, loves, locations. Between me and myself and me and Roxy and me and Jason and me and Neve.

"Take this a piece at a time," Jason is saying. "You think but you don't *know* that this Lyle idiot is coming, right?"

It's true, except I feel he's coming and lately that's accounted for a lot. But still.

"Right," I say.

"And if he does, you *think* but don't know that he *might* have left after he talked to you."

"True."

"And you think if he comes here that you won't be able to defend yourself?"

This stops me. Lyle is strong. He's wicked strong. But is he stronger than me? Now?

Maybe not.

Probably not.

"You think he'll be able to waltz in here and take you wherever he wants to and there's nothing else you'll be able to do about it?"

I let out a little snort.

"Exactly. Come *on*. Remember what you did a few hours ago. Remember who you are." It startles me to realize I haven't thought about the Sand Snatcher since we left the boardwalk. Because I truly feel no remorse. "You're not that girl anymore, Mayhem. You couldn't even pretend to be if you wanted to. Your body wouldn't let you."

The images of Lyle coming in here and dragging me out of bed, of being trapped in the truck and going back to Taylor, evaporate. Instead, I see I could undo him. I could literally suck the life out of him and he'd be gone forever.

"And anyway," Jason says, "even if you were a normal girl and couldn't defend yourself, I would do my best to make sure you were safe." He sniffs. "For what it's worth, which let me tell you, is not much."

And then I remember my father in this hallway, holding my mother, dipping her backward, telling me there is only one love like this. I hear my mother and my grandmother and her mother before her all saying Brayburns have one love and one love only that is the kind you don't recover from, the kind you risk everything for. And I remember a Brayburn can claim that love and it will be hers if she wants it.

"This is scary, Mayhem," Jason says. "You're scary, from your name on down the line. I don't want Kidd . . . I don't want this for her. She's so *into* it. She's only nine. What's going to happen a few years from now? And I don't want to do it either. I see the value, but I also see the problem. I feel like I'm trapped and I don't like to be trapped."

I let my hand rest on his shoulder. "You know what's funny? I've spent my whole life feeling wrong. Tonight is the first time I've ever felt totally, one hundred percent right."

"I get that," he says. "Who are we to let murderers roam around doing whatever they want either? I don't know how to get out of it or what I would do instead." He shakes his head. "Like I said, I'm trapped."

"Elle said there was a way to get the water out, to go back to normal, but it hurts. Would you do that if you could?"

"Yes," he says without hesitation. He shudders and then spritzes the water in his mouth. "But have you gone without the water? It hurts like your bones are trying to walk out of your skin. I can't put Kidd through that either. I don't know what to do."

I feel the trap, too. I could no more walk away from this than he could.

But I'm not like him.

I wouldn't. Ever.

"Mayhem," he says.

"Yeah?"

"I'm glad you came here. I'm gladder for that than anything. You changed things and now it's like there's hope. I don't know how or why, but there is."

I can't stand to be so close to him but not close enough for one more second. I pull him into my room and we fall onto the bed, kissing. Sometimes words are not the answer. Jason and I kiss, and now it isn't soft or gentle. All the troubles of the world are between our bodies. My chest hurts and my throat contracts and the closer he gets, the more I let everything out and onto him.

I am a monster.

I killed someone.

My mother is an addict.

My stepfather is coming.

I am an addict, too.

There is this boy. A hurt boy.

It's like my nerves have nerves and they're all exposed to the air.

"Mayhem," Jason whispers.

I'm on top of him. I kiss his cheeks, his neck, let my hair brush his chest.

I feel heat all up and down my legs.

"Stay with me. Stay with me, Jason," I say. "Stay." I kiss him again.

And then I take from him, a little at a time, breathing in as we kiss. He moans and it's almost a whimper. I take his pain, his memories, his stories, his regrets, his wishes, his desires, and I use them to fill me up.

He grunts, low, and for a second I think I'm hurting him.

I stop and look at him, all the way into his eyes, making sure it's what he wants.

"More," he pleads, and pulls me back down to him.

THIRTY-ONE
GRATITUDE

"May." Roxy is standing over me, and my first instinct is to feel around the bed for Jason, but I come up empty. I don't know when he left, but he's not here.

My second instinct is to cover my naked torso. Roxy is in sweatpants and an oversized T-shirt. She looks like she's swimming in it. The last conversation we had in the video store echoes, and I am flooded with guilt. I was cruel. I think I was cruel to her, and now she looks like she hasn't eaten or slept.

I point to the shirt on the floor. "Please."

She throws it to me, looks away as I slip it on.

I check the clock. Lyle still isn't here. Maybe I was wrong. Maybe Lyle isn't coming after all.

"Are you okay, Cookie?" Roxy's voice is steady enough to stop me. She looks tired but like herself. I mean her actual self. No extra jitters. No slurs or droopy eyes.

"I'm fine," I say.

"Anything you want to tell me?"

So much.

I shake my head no.

I wouldn't know where to begin.

Murder? Love? The fate of my everlasting immortal soul?

"Okay, why don't I start?" she says.

"Go ahead."

"It's all over the news," she says, settling down next to me.

"Boner had to leave this morning at the crack of dawn to get to the crime scene. When the lifeguard crew came on at six, they found him. The Sand Snatcher."

Last night comes flooding back in a sickening cascade of desire and guilt, and I bring my knees to my chest. So much happened. I lived ten lives.

Roxy strokes my head. "So are you all right? It was you, wasn't it? Who did that to him?"

"Yes." A little heaviness lifts.

"And how was it?" Her eyes search mine. I wonder if she's looking for permanent changes, for signs of damage.

"I liked it." My voice trembles at the edge of tears. "A lot."

Roxy pulls me against her. I wind my fingers into the fabric of her shirt like I used to when I was little and for the first time in so long.

"After my first time I felt like a superhero," she says. "I felt like I was on a mission, like I understood my purpose. Elle was the reasonable one, the one with all the moral quandaries. I didn't want to hear about any of it. I wish I had listened."

Roxy is actually talking to me. She isn't mumbling or whispering or laughing it off or speaking in code.

Maybe she can listen, too.

"I don't want to hate what I am," I venture, "but how can I be okay with it? How is it okay to make a decision about whether someone lives or dies? I mean, that guy, he was doing such terrible things, but still . . . how do you know if it's right?"

"I don't know. I only know you have to stay close to your heart and your own truth. It's okay to learn from other people with more experience, but in the end, you have to build trust with yourself."

I lean back so I can see her.

"I know what you're thinking," she says. "I betrayed myself by leaving. Smothered myself. You, Mayhem. I smothered you. I haven't listened for years. I think it might have cost your dad his life." She makes a sipping sound, like some pain has taken her by surprise. "I . . . I don't want you to hate who you are. You shouldn't. We're warriors, and that's a good thing."

"Crows," I say, because I can feel my wings spreading out behind me. "We're crows."

"Yeah," she says. "We're that, too. Not far from it, anyway. Just pay attention and you'll be fine. You've always been fine in spite of me. But promise me, if you find yourself not knowing what to do, promise you'll follow your gut and not the water. You know better than *it*, because it is a thing with a desire. Understand?"

"Not really," I say, and we both laugh.

"May." My mother takes both my hands in hers. "I am so sorry. About everything. You're right about me not listening. You were always right about Lyle. I'm so sorry I called him. I just thought of him worrying about us, and for some crazy reason I thought maybe if I told him my decision was final, he would leave us alone. If I hadn't been so buzzed I would have known that wasn't right. I'm sorry you had to talk to him. You shouldn't ever have to talk to him again."

"I'm sorry I've been making you feel bad," I say.

"No, that's normal. Of course you're mad at me. I would be mad at me, too." She takes a deep breath and exhales shakily. "Listen, sweetheart, I'm taking a couple days off work. I need your help. I've made a decision, and I talked to Elle and Marcy about it. You were right about what you said at Marcy's. I'm going to detox from my pain pills and the Valium and the booze. It's going to take me a couple days just for the first part, and it's going to hurt, but it's time. I've been weaning myself this week, but it's still going to be brutal and ugly. I have all these decisions to make and I can't get my head clear." She rubs my back. "I can't even properly talk to you about what's going on until I do. I know we've been having a real hard time lately, and I've been so out of it I haven't even been there for you." She fingers my necklace, letting the silver hang heavy in her palm. "I know what this means. But I've got you, and I've got a brand-new job and someone I might actually like. We've got to get you ready for your junior year." She inhales heavily. "And mostly, I have to wake up. I've been asleep a long time. Too long." She pauses. "I took my last pill this morning." She leans over to fish three empty prescription bottles from her bag, clear brown with the letters *Rx* in brown across the top right-hand corner. "It's a little tricky. I've been trying to take it slow so it won't be dangerous. I don't want to go to the hospital. I want to be here, where it started. That probably doesn't make sense to you . . ."

"It does," I say.

"I would have had to find a new doc here anyway, one who wasn't Lyle's best buddy, and it would have been hard to justify. And the booze . . . just makes me feel terrible." She scoots closer to me, and I lean my head on her shoulder. "And then there's you, May. You deserve a mother. I'm scared, but I know I have to do it, even if it means seeing again."

I tap her toes with mine. "You seem fine right now."

"Well, you know what they say. A junkie's okay until she runs out."

Junkie. I'd never heard her say the word.

"I'll take care of you." I curl my toes around hers. I can hardly tell whose feet are whose. "You won't be alone."

"You're right," she says. "I won't be alone. Elle will do it. I've been through something like this before, and trust me when I tell you it gets awful. I'm proud of you and I'm worried about you. It's my responsibility to educate you. That shouldn't be all Elle. I do know some things, and nothing is going to change until I do this."

I feel how afraid she is, but she's also sturdier than I've ever seen her. Almost like I could be the one going to her for comfort.

Neve bounds into the room in a leather skirt and lace shirt. "Come downstairs," she says. Then she stops. "Oh, did I interrupt a mother-daughter moment?"

"We were done," Roxy says, tightening.

She doesn't like Neve, I realize.

"No, no, it's cute!" Neve says. "Keep on loving each other."

"What's going on, Neve? Just tell us," I say.

"If you really want to know, you're going to have to come down!"

Roxy follows behind as we head for the living room, where Elle, Jason, and Kidd are gathered around the old brown radio. I can tell something is really wrong. Elle's face is pale and stern.

The man's voice booms from the speaker by the table. "The sometime lifeguard was found on his chair with the word 'murderer' scrawled across his naked chest in his own blood. A search of his home has revealed belongings missing from each of the victims, trophies. Based on evidence, it is believed that all five of the missing girls are deceased and that he may be responsible for cold cases in his home state of Wisconsin. It is a sad day for the families and friends of these victims, and our thoughts and prayers are with them. In the meantime, the question remains, who is the vigilante who took it upon himself to rid Santa Maria of its Sand Snatcher? For now, the town is preparing for the next steps as its citizens attempt to recover from a truly unusual summer."

"Kidd, I'd like you to go upstairs," Elle says, muting the radio. She's in a pair of overalls and a sun hat and is still holding a trowel.

Kidd frowns. "But I don't—"

"Kidd," Jason says.

"Oh my gosh! Fine!" She stomps off, stopping only to glare at us from the top of the stairs.

When Kidd's gone, Elle says, "Who did it?" She searches the room for an answer.

I personally don't know. Jason shrugs. When we left Kurt Sand Snatcher, he was on the sidewalk. His body would have shown he had died of a heart attack if someone hadn't defiled his corpse.

"We didn't," I say, "I swear. We came right back here like you said."

I took a shower and tried to go to bed. I read the journal. Then, Jason. I wasn't drawing on a dead man's body in blood, that's for sure.

"All of you?" she says. "All of you came back here?"

The room freezes. I feel guilty even though I didn't do anything.

Well.

I didn't do anything I wasn't supposed to do.

"Fine." Neve is sprawled on the chaise lounge, her knee-high boots kicked up. "I did it, okay."

"When?" I say. She's keeping secrets?

"More importantly, why?" Elle lurches toward Neve. "Why would you ever do something like that? Why would you put us in that position, expose us?"

"She's not a Brayburn, Elle," Roxy says. "You know damn well what's coming. She's not right in the head."

"Oh, you mean that dumb shit about non-Brayburns going crazy when they drink the water?" Neve says. "That's just a bunch of bullshit your family has spread so you can control this town. But it's not true."

"Watch the way you talk to my sister," Elle says. "And mind your manners in my house."

"Watch the way you talk to *me*," Neve counters. "And mind

your manners. I'm getting sick of everything being under the surface, of hiding and keeping up appearances and getting fruit baskets at the gate in return. Don't you get how pathetic that is? Don't you think it would be a lot more effective if these pieces of garbage knew they weren't going to get away with this shit, for them to know someone's watching them?"

"Neve, this isn't how we do things," Elle says softly. "We do them neatly."

Neve bristles. Elle has made a mistake trying to calm her this way. Even I know Neve well enough to know she's not going to respond to someone trying to take her in hand.

"No, Elle, it's not," Neve says, imitating Elle's measured tone. "It's justice served warm instead of after thirty years on death row. And California doesn't even have the death penalty. That guy got exactly what he deserved."

"Be that as it may, I want you to stop. You can stay home from now on, or at least until you can get yourself under control."

"Wait . . . you're *grounding* me from murdering people?"

Elle flinches.

"Oh, I see. You don't like to think of it that way." Neve steps on a footstool. "Well, what if I told you I've figured out a way to make this little system of yours better? I've improved."

"What do you mean?" Elle's gone pale. She steadies herself on a chair.

"I'm not telling you yet, if I ever do. You're going to have to stop treating me like I'm an inferior moron just because I'm not a Brayburn," Neve says.

"Oh, Neve. That is not where I'm coming from at all," Elle says. "I appreciate the job you've done, but you're putting yourself and all of us in danger. I just hope you didn't leave any evidence behind. This is how we've survived so many generations here with almost no incident. We don't need you to improve our system. It works fine as it is."

"If you don't count Lucas and everything that happened with Marcy and Boner," Roxy says. "Or Granny's friend Karen."

"The curfew is going to be lifted now, because they know who he is," Neve says. "Everyone can get back to regular business. How long would that have taken if I hadn't made it easy for them? And what about the families? Maybe they wouldn't have found the secret compartment in his place if they hadn't been searching for evidence. Maybe the families of the two girls they haven't found yet would always have been wondering. Don't you see this was the right thing to do?"

"You didn't ask," Jason says, finally speaking up. "You didn't tell anyone else. You didn't make sure we were all okay with your decision. You acted unilaterally. You did what you wanted to do."

"Well, it wasn't like I could consult you while you were rolling in the sheets with Mayhem, right?"

"Hey," Jason says, taking a step toward her.

She steps back and folds her arms.

"It's time for you to take a break. We never know how the water will react to a person. It's not doing well with your system." Elle reaches for Neve, but she shoves Elle's arm away.

"Well, maybe this isn't the place for me anymore, then," Neve says. "Maybe I don't want to follow those rules."

The room is suddenly quiet.

"Neve," Elle says, "it's possible the water is affecting your ability to process clearly. I just want you to take a minute to let us think about what we want to do moving forward. You might be fine if you stop now."

"Yeah, right," Neve says. "Your family may have started this, but you are all a bunch of nerds at heart." She glares at me. "You can keep your precious fucking Brayburns. I don't want them anymore."

There's a whoosh, and then she's gone so silently and decidedly, it's as though she was never there.

"It's not her," I say to the room, trying to fill the void. "It's the water. It's making her crazy, making her do things. The journal said—"

"I know what it says. I'm sorry. I think I need to go lie down. You did a great job, all of you, really. The town is safer for it." Jason helps Elle up the stairs. She stops and looks back. "I didn't know you would ever come back," Elle says to Roxy. "I wanted a family. They had already had the water. They had already found the cave. Did I do the wrong thing?"

Jason slumps miserably, still holding her by the elbow like she's an old woman.

"Shit," Roxy says, fishing in her pack for a smoke. "I don't know a thing about right and wrong, honey. I wish Mama was here now."

"Me, too," Elle says. "She would know just what to do."

"I know. She would, Ellie. She would."

Elle disappears up the stairs, Jason supporting her.

"I'm going to stop taking it." I lift the necklace from around my neck and put it in Roxy's hand, fold my own over hers. "Take the necklace. It's okay. I can be sick and get through it. We can do it together. I'll get off the water and you'll get off your pills and then we can figure out what we're going to do."

Roxy touches the side of my face and looks at me mournfully. "Oh, Cookie, I wish I had done better. I wish I had explained it all to you instead of trying to pretend it wasn't there. Elle promised to leave you out of it, and I believed her."

"It wasn't her. It was me. Now I'm going to make another choice."

She squeezes my hand. "It's too late. It's not going to go away. Quite the opposite, baby. When a Brayburn stops taking the water, that's when things really get cooking." She leans her head against the wall. "Mayhem, the water likes the Brayburn cells. It will never leave you now. I didn't have water for thirteen years, and it never stopped trying to get me back here. It never stopped twisting my guts to get its way. I stopped seeing because I was away from Santa Maria. I was almost normal, but I was sick, always. I was weak. I don't want that for you."

"And what about my friends? Jason? Kidd? Neve? Elle made a journal. It says how people who aren't Brayburns go crazy when they have the water. What happens to them now?"

"The water will kill them if they keep taking it," Roxy says. "Most probably, anyway. I suppose there's always a chance it will go another way, but it doesn't seem likely, not the way Neve is acting."

"Is that what happened to my father?"

She grimaces and sits in the golden velvet chair, so she appears even smaller than usual.

"Roxy. Mom, just tell me. I know he didn't fall. I know he jumped. Elle kept your letter to your mom."

She massages her temple for a second, then nods.

"I should never have told him about it, but we shared everything. I didn't want to keep a secret that big from him. I felt like I was lying to him. My mother, my grandmother, they were able to keep everything separate from their husbands, but not me. I'm too *romantic* for that. In my mind, marriage meant sharing everything. So I showed him." She seems so tired from holding it in. "He was fine for a while. He liked being able to see who was made up of more good than bad. But then it started to make him crazy. I knew. I knew that he couldn't. He wouldn't be able to do the job. The ugly part of the job. He was a lover, you know? He loved birds and cats and women and standing outside on a warm night just to listen to the world hum along. He was not one to look under rocks." She sniffles.

"That's why we left, May. Your dad thought he was immortal. At the end he thought a lot of things. He thought he could survive that fall. After he was gone, I couldn't be here anymore. I didn't want that for you, and it was only a matter of time even if I did everything I could to keep you from it. Elle was furious, of course. Taking the heir when she couldn't have babies. I was selfish, unfair. Keeping you from the rest of the family."

"Has anyone survived not having the water anymore? Anyone not Brayburn, I mean?"

"At least two," Roxy says. "That's enough to know it can work."

My heart twists.

She tells me how when Boner and Marcy decided to detox, my grandmother and great-grandmother worked together to keep them hydrated and fed and distracted, how they played cards and made necklaces and how they slept. When it was over, they seemed to remember things, but as though they were things that had happened to someone else, long ago. Marcy became a psychic in her spare time, and Boner became a cop, continuing on in the same work in their own ways.

She goes on, but I'm not listening much anymore, because I'm planning how I'm going to help my friends.

THIRTY-TWO
GIFTS

The birds shuffle from side to side, squawk their greetings. Under them, gifts in bright wrapping with golden ribbons, so many the whole driveway looks alive: a cheese plate covered in cellophane, being feasted on by several of the crows, a tapestry of a rich red draped across the wood, cards in embossed pastel envelopes, and flowers everywhere, some in bunches, some single roses laid on the ground. There are always gifts to be picked up each morning and carefully catalogued, but this is different. There is so much.

Roxy and I are out walking. She has a sheen of sweat building across her forehead and doesn't want to stay still.

"This is what thank-you looks like, Cookie," she says. "The people in town know what's what."

Everything takes on color. The house waits for us, and the birds, and Millie on the chair on the front porch, and Kidd and Jason on the swing sipping on lemonade.

The phone rings, clanging into the peaceful early afternoon, and I twitch upward, eyes on the second-story window.

Before Jason can even stand up I'm in the house with the phone in my hand.

"Where are you, Lyle? What do you want?" I say.

"Oh, hey there, Mayhem," Neve's languid voice returns.

"Oh, hi," I say. "Neve?"

"I was just calling because there's going to be a party tonight on the beach and I thought you might want to come."

I look behind me, hoping Jason will appear, but the hall is empty. "Do you want me to get Elle? I think she would really like to talk to you."

Truth is, I don't know if Elle would talk to her. She seems pretty mad, said something about how Neve might be sick, but what's underneath is still a different kind of sick.

"Elle knows exactly how to find me if she wants to," Neve snaps, then smooths again. "You guys should come down and help me celebrate. The Sand Snatcher is gone, the town is grateful."

"I know, they left presents—"

"Of course they did."

"Neve, come home," I say, "please."

"I don't think so," she says. "I don't actually think that place is home for me anymore. But that doesn't mean we can't be friends, May. *Best* friends."

"Right," I say, "of course."

"Pier Four, the beach, from nine till whenever," she says. "*Arrivederci*."

The line goes dead.

THIRTY-THREE
STITCHER BRAYBURN
DAUGHTER OF BILLIE

1949

I drank from the well the first day they tested the tsunami siren in Santa Maria. They had them all up and down the coast. I didn't know whether bombs were going to descend on us and blow us all to shreds like we did to Hiroshima and Nagasaki, or if we were going to die from not finding higher ground fast enough. Up on the hill I would have been safe from a wave. But I wasn't on the hill. I was at the cave with my mother. She told me the water would make me shine. It was a shine that never left her, and it never leaves me either. It's a shine that deflects, that makes people look at you instead of into you.

She didn't give me a choice about the water. I wish she had. I might have chosen no.

That siren wailed after I took my first sip.

<u>It's a test,</u> Mom said. <u>There's no danger.</u>

And yet, as far as symbols go, as far as warnings, the timing of that siren wailing into the foggy air—well, it was a reminder that you can't win against nature, and nature is in charge here.

The spring is nature.

We are servants of the spring.

Mom doesn't see it that way. She tells me the cave called to her, and to her mother before her. She says we are Brayburns, and Brayburns and the spring are one thing.

After the first time I drank the water was when I started making everything. I made doll clothes and wove tapestries. I made the most elaborate dresses in pink silk. I took picture after picture. I couldn't stop. My fingers can produce anything, and Mom never fails to remind me it is that extra shine. It took what was in me and magnified it.

They call me the stitcher.

And so I am.

<u>Most people never live at all,</u> Mom says.

There is a chant now. The town tells stories about the Brayburns, about what we do, poems recited by firelight. They don't know if we are evil or protecting them from it. But they know something, all right.

I have decided. I have made a decision to accept myself. I have decided that although this wasn't my choice, I can choose it now. When I have a child, I will teach her as Mother taught me. I will not allow her to fall into it alone. We need our stories, to pass our traditions from one generation to the next.

Meantime there are sock hops, and Peggy Lee.

Life goes on.

Let them whisper.

THIRTY-FOUR
MAYHEM BRAYBURN
DAUGHTER OF ROXY BRAYBURN
PARTY MONSTERS

1987

"No. No. No." Kidd holds up a yellow polo I brought with me from Taylor, one of the few things I threw in a bag as we left. We're in Roxy's room. Roxy's in Elle's. Kidd and Elle did find the TV upstairs in the attic and dragged it down the other night, so Roxy's watching *Tootsie* with the lights out and has forbidden me to come in. I can hear her pacing around in there. She won't hear of me going in there with her so unstable going through withdrawals and everything, so now we're all going to the celebration on the beach, where I hope I'll find Neve so we can talk.

"Oh God," Kidd says, holding the polo as though she's in physical pain. "What *is* this?"

"I know," I say. "It's bad, right? My grandmother who wasn't really my grandmother bought it for me. I don't know why I brought it."

"I don't have a grandma," Kidd says, pulling a handful of jelly beans from her pocket. "I really like the black ones. Some people don't. What do you think?"

"Love them," I say.

Kidd amazes me all the time, and all I can do is squeeze her more than she probably likes.

"Hey, uh." Jason peers in from the hallway and then averts his eyes like we're naked, which we're not. The makeup is out, though. "Holler when you're good to go. I'll be upstairs."

Kidd is busily picking through my things with a disgusted scowl. "Wear this," she says, and hands me a red dress with lace at the bodice.

"This isn't prom," I say. "It's a beach party."

"It's a party to celebrate what you guys did," Kidd says. "You should look pretty. When it's my first time doing something good for Santa Maria and there's a party for me, I'm totally going to wear a pretty dress."

I kneel down. "You know," I say, "maybe we should talk about that. It's good that guy can't hurt people anymore, but I don't know if . . . *that* . . . is the answer either."

I've been thinking about it more. Maybe there's a way we can work with the cops, Boner for instance, or something like that. There has to be something better than this. Eye for an eye is so Old Testament. We don't know if a person is born broken or what they can even control. It can't be right to kill them for being who they are, although having them loose isn't right either. And if I can't get rid of the water, I can at least work with it in a different way. When my mother is done detoxing, we can figure it out. Still, it's hard to feel bad about the Sand Snatcher. He had to go.

"Your light is swirling," Kidd says, then pats me on the head as if I'm too young and innocent to understand the complexities of the situation. "You should relax."

I can only imagine what it would be like to talk to someone from Taylor right now.

So, *whatcha been doing since you left Taylor, hon? How's your summer been?*

Oh, you know, I been murdering serial killers, doing drugs, as you do. I've also done some heavy petting. Oh, and my best friend is possibly an unhinged psychopath. How's church?

I might be missing that little town right now, just for a second.

Kidd is at my feet with Millie in her lap and takes a spritz of the water. "Put on the dress, please!"

When I have it on, Kidd whistles. I've glossed my lips and given myself shiny cheeks and mascara. It seems wrong to get dressed up and everything with Roxy in the other room. But I tell myself if I can get Neve to come home it will be worth it. When everything is falling apart, you have to put it back together, step by step.

Punk blares from the speakers that have been set up on the beach. The bonfire looms above everyone like a drunk, bobbing and weaving. Boys with hair dyed blond from the sun, skin crisped to an unnatural brown, girls still in their bathing suits, colorful dots, eyes dancing; a Chicano crew, fully dressed, hangs together away from the fire. Some people clutch bottles in brown paper bags while others pass joints around. One guy has a bowler hat on his face. The Gecko brothers, in full fatigues, pace around the fire. The pinging of the rides, the slow circle of the Ferris wheel, the screams like sirens as the roller coaster flings its passengers into the night, are a reminder that though the curfew was short-lived, it's not anything anyone wants to see happen again.

Santa Maria is safe.

As we approach, people part, making room for us. Jason and I hold hands as we walk through the crowd with Kidd a few steps ahead.

"Good job," one girl says.

"You rocked it," a surfer tells us.

Jason gets several high-fives.

Finally they break into cheers and whoops until they're all standing around us. I don't know what I was expecting, but it wasn't this.

"Well, hello," Neve says, emerging from the middle. "Welcome."

"Thanks," I say.

Kidd runs to her. "Neve!" she says, and jumps into her arms.

Jason stays next to me, but I feel him watching Neve, wanting to say something to her, wanting to pull Kidd back.

"Jay, sexy as usual," she says. "You look good in red, Mayhem."

She looks good, too. Blackberry lipstick, eyeliner winged out, black fingernails.

"Full moon," I say.

Neve looks feverish. I notice there's nothing around her neck. She looks up, then back down, disinterested. "Yeah, well, I wish I could stay and chat, but I have things to do. Enjoy all the gratitude. I have to go deal with something. Talk later?" She kisses both my cheeks and then both of Jason's and gives Kidd a big hug. "I'm so glad you came," she yells, "really!"

"This is not good," Jason says, when she's gone.

"No. Something bad is happening. I wish I could read her so I could know what."

Then I spot the guy with his stupid sunglasses, even at night, and swoopy hair, the one we saw the other day on the boardwalk who had taken his sister on the rides. He's in a pink polo, grinning at everyone, no mirrored sunglasses on now, and Neve is headed straight for him. I wouldn't want to take out another guy so soon, but Neve and I are different.

"You okay?" Jason says.

"I'm fine," I drawl. "That guy over there isn't going to be for very long, though."

Kidd comes over and hugs my waist. "It's a party over there! Don't you want to celebrate?"

I wonder how much water Neve has had, how many times she has fed and how many is too many. I wish I knew more about how all this works.

Kidd is breathing hard next to me.

"Take some water, Kiddo," I say, but she's focused on the boy at the fire with Neve, the one whose air is crystallizing around him as he dances.

She hides her head against my leg. "He's not good," she says.

"Stop looking, Kidd," I say. "You can make it go away if you want to. Tell it you don't want to talk to it right now."

She shakes her head. "I can't. It doesn't work anymore. I can always only see."

"Hey," Jason says. He taps on her cheek, and she drops her jaw long enough for him to spray inside. Her breaths come a little further apart, her chest rising and falling more normally. We wait a few moments until she smiles up at us looking like herself again.

Still, Jason looks at me worriedly.

A girl with glitter in her hair comes over and takes Kidd to dance. "Can I?" Kidd says. "Can I go dance?"

"Sure," Jason says. "I'll be watching you." When she's gone he says, "What's going to happen to her if she doesn't have it? The water, I mean."

"I don't know," I say. "I'm working on figuring that out."

"How else am I going to keep her protected? What about when she's grown and she doesn't want her big brother trailing after her everywhere she goes? You think anyone's going to mess with her now?" He shakes his head. "No. No one is going to ever be able to mess with her, and if they do, she can defend herself. She's stronger than all of them, right?" He nods toward the guys our age and older, dancing around the fire. It's true, with the water, Kidd is more powerful than all of them. For now.

"The water is dangerous to people who aren't Brayburns," I say.

Jason looks at me, sharply enough that I want to recoil.

"I read it in that journal Elle put together. That's what Neve was talking about this morning. She didn't tell you?"

He shakes his head.

"I wasn't sure what to say. I don't even really know what it means for you guys, except you shouldn't have the water anymore, just in case."

"Elle knows about this?" he says.

"Well, yeah, but I think she was hoping since you found the cave on your own you would be immune."

He's frowning hard.

"She really loves you guys. She wouldn't do anything to hurt you on purpose. Anyway, you got to the water before she could stop you. It was already too late."

"She should have told us, though. What else do you have to drop on me?" He comes closer. He's really asking. "What are you hiding in there?"

"Nothing." I pull him close. He only resists for a second.

Kidd has stopped dancing and is scanning the crowd, eyes widening. She starts walking toward Neve and the boy like she's being pulled by an invisible rope.

"Kidd!" Jason says.

Kidd stops like she's dazed, then lurches back in our direction.

"Oh man, this is not working out. She can't be in public right now. I'm going to take her home," Jason says, pulling on me.

I pull back and he drops my hand. Neve is dancing with that boy, and I don't want to leave her here.

"I'll be back up there soon."

"I don't like it," he says, watching Neve and the boy.

"It's okay for you not to like it," I say. "I'm going to stay anyway. I'll be safe. I just want her to hear me out. If she decides not to come home with me, I'll run up the hill. No big deal."

"Okay," he says.

He kisses me before getting Kidd and heading toward the van.

I approach Neve as the boy takes her in, his eyes lingering on Neve's butt and legs. He's chiseled, with rock-solid pecs like he's an athlete. He's also obviously wrecked, unable to stay focused on anything.

Apparently he's the only person in Santa Maria who doesn't know who Neve is and exactly what this party is about.

"Hey." I sidle up to the guy. "Did you drive here?"

He raises his eyebrows smugly. "Why? You need a ride?"

"Actually, I was thinking you should get out of here," I say. "Like now."

"I don't remember inviting you over here." Neve is clearly annoyed.

"I need to talk to my friend here, and I think you should get out," I say, with even more force.

He grabs Neve's waist. "What's wrong with her?"

"Oh," Neve says, "she's a total bummer. Don't pay attention." Neve runs a finger along his cheekbone.

In a honeycomb a girl is sleeping and he is on top of her. I look away, because if I get drawn in I won't be able to stop myself from sucking the life out of him.

"So I'm here," Neve says. "What are you going to do about it?"

Neve eyes him seductively, and he dances in her direction, looking like a complete moron.

"Neve!" I'm desperate for her to hear me, but she only has eyes for him. I can tell she's not just going to walk away from this one.

I look away. He does smell good, like he would melt in your arms, like he would be so satisfying. I bite the inside of my cheek.

Neve checks the party. One guy swings a girl over his shoulder and everyone pours beer on her and shrieks. Neve is standing now. She's heart to heart with this guy, taking a sip from his beer, smiling so her teeth glisten in the night.

"You should go home," I say to him again, and it's like throwing the fruit bowl at Lyle, the way it bounces off, like it's nothing. I take the boy by his arm. "You go home," I say to him.

"Heyyy," he says sloppily, "wait a minute. I know who you are. My friends told me there's a new freaky Brayburn chick in town."

So he does know who we are. Who *I* am.

Neve smirks.

"*Brayburn lady coming for you.*" He lolls about in an imitation of jumping rope. "Everyone knows who you are. Everyone says you and your friends are baaaaad."

"Maybe you should pay attention to the rhyme and get as far away from me as you can," I say, desperate for him to go before I can't control myself anymore either.

"Nope," he says, "I'm not scared of you."

At that, Neve, who's been sucking on one nail looking bored, rolls her eyes. "I've had enough of this. Mayhem, are you coming?"

"I . . ."

"I don't know why people are scared of you," he says, leaning in confidentially. "You seem like a really nice girl."

"Oh man, that does it," Neve says. "*Nice*?"

"Neve." I try to keep my voice calm. "Let him go. We can take care of this another way."

"What?" She grimaces. "Are you kidding me?"

"Neve, if you don't let him go . . ." I take a deep breath. "I'm not going to be . . ."

"My best friend? My *sister*?" She pouts. "Really? No more reindeer games?"

"I was going to say I'm not going to be able to think about anything else or do anything else. I love you, remember? We're *family*, remember? Come on, Neve. Come home."

"Beat it," the boy says. "She doesn't care if you hang out with her or not."

"Dude, shut up," I say.

"No, you shut up," Neve says, then turns back to me. "You know what? You don't know anything. I've taken all the Brayburn ways and turned them into a *system*. So how about you and your whole family go fuck yourselves nice and hard?"

"Neve—"

In less than the blink of an eye, Neve hooks her arm around the boy's neck and disappears down the beach. I search for them in the dark.

"Neve!" I theater-whisper. "Neve, please."

But she's gone.

And so is he.

THIRTY-FIVE
TUNNEL

I only stand there for a few seconds searching into the darkness before I remember I can find her even if she's hiding. I try to think of her personality and who she is, and nothing happens. All around me people are dancing and picking each other up and chanting that the Sand Snatcher is dead and no one even knows the boy who was talking to Neve is gone because no one ever notices anything. I'm disturbed by the oblivion around me and disturbed by Neve's new unbridled glimmer and—

It's Neve's words that come back to me and keep me standing in the sand instead of collapsing into it and through it. That I need to be as strong as I am and that I am not demure or weak. But I'm running out of time to stand here and think. It goes so fast once there's someone in your grip; a matter of minutes at most. She dragged him away like a mountain lion with its prey.

The crowd around the fire begins to chant:

Brayburn lady coming for you
Brayburn lady coming for you

Delirious and frenzied, they hold hands and skip around the fire, and they don't even see me. They don't need to. I don't even need to exist. I step out of the light and breathe and imagine. Neve holding my hand, stroking my shoulder, telling me the truth, being my friend. Neve, who is disturbed from the water and disturbed by life and who is angry and jealous and also needs someone to stand by her.

I have her.

She's close but not too close, and she knows I'm coming but she doesn't care. She wants me to see. In an instant I'm running toward her, zipping over the sand toward the boardwalk, the rides, the people screaming as they rise and fall, and then I stop.

All I see is darkness. If I didn't know she was in there, I wouldn't think there was anything at all. I'm in front of a tunnel that leads directly under the boardwalk next to the roller coaster. The tunnel is made of gray concrete and is big enough to stand in. There's graffiti everywhere.

WARNING

KEEP OUT

Murder house

It's like a clubhouse slapped together by twelve-year-olds. There's so much noise coming from the rides and another bonfire party behind me that I can't hear anything until I go in, ducking down and holding on to the sides. It's smelly, like old seaweed and sweat, and a dripping noise comes from somewhere, invisible to me.

Beyond the concrete, the tunnel widens and the walls turn to dirt. Maybe this is the old system that runs under Santa Maria.

Then there's a moan. A male voice.

I creep along the wall as quickly as I can, careful not to cast a shadow as a flickering light guides me to the sound. I expect to find Neve over the preppie boy and to step between them, but he is not what I find when I round the corner into the dirt room, or at least not just him.

Nine boys are lined up against the tunnel wall. Neve is moving over their bodies, one by one, straddling them, bringing her lips close to theirs, then releasing them. Each one moans, then sinks back in a daze.

The world loosens its grip on me as I try to understand what I'm seeing. And then I remember the boy from the Ferris wheel on the first day and how he loved when my lips came close to his. He said I could do it again.

Neve releases one boy and goes to the next. She breathes him in until his honeycombs are flat and there is only a thin layer of ice, then lets him go.

"Thank you," he whispers.

Even from my vantage point it's obvious they're malnourished. They're too thin, veins popped out, heads against dirt.

She doesn't look like a bird anymore. She looks like a bug. A roach.

Neve lifts up, wipes at her mouth and then bends down again, cocking her head to the side.

"Come on, Mayhem," she says. "Don't you want to join me?"

I step out of the shadows.

"Doesn't this solve your moral quandary? It's symbiosis, my friend," she says as a red-haired boy reaches for her.

"Please," he says.

"Shhh," she returns. Then to me, "It doesn't hurt them, just makes them forget everything they've done. They like it, and for us it's better than the water." She puts her hand out to me. "We take care of each other, right? This is the wave of the future. Nobody dies and nobody has to remember if they don't want to. Nobody disappears, either; they come and go."

"Neve." I squat down beside her. "Please come home with me. We will take care of you." I look around. "Let these people go."

She grins. "They can go anytime they want. They come to me. I have a waiting list, practically. Soon I'm going to need muscle at the door." She claps her hands together. "Ooo, or maybe some kind of secret knock like at a speakeasy. Want to be my bouncer?"

I can't even begin to think about how to deal with this.

"How are you any different than the Sand Snatcher, Neve?"

"I'm insulted." Her face flattens. "I'll tell you how I'm different. I don't kill them, they come back of their own free will, and they're begging me to give and take." She stands. "That's three ways. This keeps me from needing the water. I'm not going to go crazy and lose it like those other people the Brayburns wrote about. Anyway, it's the perfect solution. Keeps potential problems out of the general population and could keep us from needing anything else. So stop trying to get me to go back to the farm. I'm not going back there. Elle will never listen to me about any of this, and it's the only way shit isn't going to go totally wrong for me. I'm trying to survive, just like everyone else. I have a right to do that, don't I?" Her eyes plead for me to understand, and beyond that, to agree. "Stay with me, Mayhem."

Right then, I want to. We could be powerful, independent, and I could shuck the feeling I have, like I'm carrying generations of tradition on my back. But then one of the boys moans and when he turns his head his cheeks are covered in sores.

"I can't."

She waits, as though hoping I'll change my mind, then flicks her hand dismissively. "Bye, then," she says, dropping to her knees again, this time over a boy with black hair and cheeks pulled tight over his skull, like she's sucked all the fat out of him. It takes me several seconds of waiting for reality to take a reasonable shape before I recognize Jake, the boy from the Ferris wheel. His head swivels on his neck as he smiles. "Thank you," he says to Neve. "Thank you."

THIRTY-SIX
ROXY BRAYBURN
DAUGHTER OF STITCHER BRAYBURN
1974

The people come to us thinking they're bees and we're flowers, but they have it wrong because we're jellyfish. We sting while they stare at our lights going, "Oh, pretty."

Marcy and Boner are sick because they can't handle being jellyfish, and Lucas doesn't want to sting.

I always have. Never minded it a minute. Mama says it's the Brayburn nature to be calm and certain, and to wait, but it hasn't been that way for all of us. I was born on fire like my great-grandmother Julianna. Explain that.

Last night I woke up and Lucas was at the foot of the bed. He was babbling about how nothing can hurt him anymore.

He went outside and I had a lost feeling like he was going to leave me and he wouldn't be coming back. The way he went seemed so permanent and decided. Before I heard him talking to Daddy outside, I glanced around the room at our things and the little life we've squeezed into this space, and I thought, Of course this can't go on forever. It's too perfect.

I tried to picture myself without Lucas and the simple idea had me doubled over so hard I swear to God it woke Mayhem up out of a peaceful sleep without me making a sound. I was only sitting on the bed, clutching at a pillow, tensing up my belly as though by doing so I could push away the thought that I am losing my husband.

Thank goodness Daddy was down there messing in the rosebushes like he does when he can't sleep. I saw from the window, Lucas sinking to his knees with the car keys in hand, Daddy hugging him until he calmed down. I couldn't hear what he said, but it was something about Brayburn women and how to live with them, I'm sure.

Mayhem caught sight of her dad and banged her little hands against the window. Lucas looked up and he had sadness all over him, bits of light that were jagged and stabbing at him, but he still smiled for Mayhem.

I've decided to leave Santa Maria for good. I've asked Mother before and she says we can't, that we have to stay and do our jobs, but if we go, maybe the water will loosen its grip on Lucas. When I think of the greater world outside Santa Maria, it's like there's the ocean and the boardwalk and my friends and all the green and blue and yellow, and then everything else is one big desert, like in those movies where people get lost and end up crawling around on sand dunes.

I hope we don't get lost.

THIRTY-SEVEN
MAYHEM BRAYBURN
DAUGHTER OF ROXY BRAYBURN
DRY

1987

I walk back to the house instead of running. I need everything to slow down and it's whirring in a way I don't like, an invisible machine picking up speed. So I take my time. I stop at a wall of honeysuckle on the way up, lean into it to remind myself that the earth is good and that life can be beautiful. I need that reminder or that discovery because things are getting harder to see. While I get high on honeysuckle smells, I catch sight of a family through windows like peeled-back eyelids. A woman with brown hair holds a baby, and another woman on the first floor works dough in the kitchen.

It must be nice just to live. As I am watching, the woman upstairs calls down, and the woman kneading the dough carefully places it into a bowl and covers it with a checkered towel she dampens in the sink. Briefly she stares ahead, and I think she has seen me skulking in her bushes, but she hasn't. She's looking at herself and there's gray in her hair at her temples and I don't have to ask for her secrets or see them to know she's thinking about her life right then and she's maybe wishing she could just live, too. And we meet in the middle between her window and my watching, and we linger there until she remembers herself and dashes away to where I can't see her.

I had a dream of coming here and drifting through my days, of going to the beach and having friends and fawning over Rob Lowe, on my belly in a white nightgown with a blue face mask on and writing letters to River Phoenix at the address you can get from *Tiger Beat* magazine. We don't shuck layers in life. We add onto them. And then we carry them.

Elle meets me in the driveway.

"Thank goodness you're back," she says. She has a look on her I've never seen before. It's far past worry. She is terrified. "I was going to send Jason for you . . ." She clutches at her own hair as though trying to pull right answers out of her skull. "Think, think."

"What is it?" I say, ready to run in, ready to pee my pants, too. Something must be wrong with Roxy.

A sickly glow emanates from the second-floor window as though the whole house is in ill health.

"Okay," Elle says, sniffing herself straight. "Your mom needs you right now. She's burning up. I should never have let her send you away tonight, because as soon as you left she started asking for you." She opens the door to her old Mercedes, and calls into the house for Jason and Kidd. "I have a friend at the hospital, Joan, and I helped her with a . . . that doesn't matter! She says she can give me something. Jason's been trying to feed Roxy, but she actually threw broth at him, so . . ."

I can definitely picture that.

"I'm going to get some supplies," Elle says. "Joan said to keep Roxy hydrated, and I'm going to get the stuff so she can be more comfortable. She's going to be okay, but she took some sleeping pills, so can you just check on her?"

"Of course." I have wasted a lot of days being mad at Roxy.

Jason and Kidd come outside, and Jason questions me silently and I give him the slightest shake of the head because Neve. He tightens his lips and they go into Elle's car and they say something about how Kidd is hungry and they're going to stop and Elle is really almost crying and then they're gone and the driveway is silent except for the crickets and the crows.

"Don't you ever sleep?" I ask them, and the crow with a little brown dot on his beak swoops down and lands on my shoulder. I just about get to the door before he hops off and back to the trees, but he has helped me just by being there anyway. I wish he could come into the house with me. He fits so well on my shoulder. But he seems to think his place is outside, right here.

I climb the stairs and there is no sound. This house always creaks and buzzes. Sometimes there's Fleetwood Mac playing and sometimes it's tribal flute music, and it always smells like flowers and incense, and there is always noise and stomping around upstairs. Even when there isn't that, there is Millie meowing and the house itself, stretching and settling. And so this non-noise buries itself in my belly.

The house smells empty now except for a slight note of sickness, of bathroom visits and throw-up and cleaning up after both those things with bleach.

When I get into the room, Millie is on top of Elle's bed next to Roxy, peering at her worriedly, paws tucked under her chin.

"Roxy, are you okay?"

Roxy doesn't answer, but seeing Millie the way she is, I think she probably is okay, because I have a feeling Millie would not be sitting so calmly if something were seriously wrong.

"Good kitty." I chuck her under the chin, and she makes a noise that is clearly asking me if Roxy's okay. "She'll be fine, Millie."

"She's magic," Roxy slurs.

"Who, Mom?"

"Millie. She's a magic cat. Just like the birds are. Look on the wall. My mother took that picture when she was little. Millie's going to live forever," she whispers. "The animals protect us."

I smooth back her hair.

"Millie drank the water," she croaks. "And we put it in the bird feeders. *Shhhhh*," she says. "Don't tell Grandma."

She snores for a second. I slap lightly at her cheek. "Roxy?"

"I took some sleeping stuff," Roxy says, voice thick.

"Elle said. How many?"

She puts up two fingers and her eyes flutter and she half-smiles. "Three," she says. She's messing with me.

"Are you sure? Only three?"

"Promise," she says. "I'm not going to lose you now. Or me either. It just hurt too much."

I flop onto the side of the bed. "Mama," I say, "I'm really proud of you."

Her breathing is uneven, and a tear slips quietly down her cheek. I get a washcloth and wet it down and then bring it back and pat her forehead and her neck with it. She is so hot.

"I know this is hard," I say. "And I know why you did it. I know you had to. And I know you thought you were doing good leaving here when you did."

"I'm sorry I brought you back," she says. "Santa Maria is such a bitch."

"No," I say. "Don't be sorry about that. Even with everything that's happened I wouldn't change any of it. I found . . . I found myself, or a piece of myself or something." I search for words. "I found the truth of me."

Roxy grabs my wrist with surprising strength that reminds me when she comes out of this, she's going to be a whole different Roxy, one with sight and intuition and vision. She's going to be a mother I've never seen before.

"Your dad," she says, eyes still closed, "he wanted to be with me. There was this guy who was taking out hitchhikers, girls trying to get to San Francisco, and *I* took *him* out." She laughs. "You're a lover like your daddy, I bet. Not me." She shakes her head against the pillow and peels her eyes open. Millie begins to purr. "He was for world peace and adventure and surfing. He wasn't for murder. He wasn't for even knowing people had thoughts like those, did things like that."

Tears slip down Roxy's temple again, and I feel wetness on my own cheeks.

"While I was doing my thing with my sister, having my baby, hanging out with my family, your dad was slowly dying. He was nothing but light. He was *good*. He was better than all the rest of us."

Like Jason is.

I should let her rest and sleep now, but I need to know one more thing. "Why were you so mad at Elle before? When you left?"

Roxy wipes sloppily at her cheeks. She can hardly hold up her own hand. "She told me to get over it when Lucas died. She told me that we had a job to do that was more important than him or even you." She shakes her head. "Nothing is more important than you. You know that, right? I wanted it to be different between us than all the Brayburn mothers and daughters. I wanted to know you."

I nod as she tries to wipe my cheeks. If only she had let me know her, too. Maybe I don't have to take care of her anymore. Maybe we can take care of each other.

She is snoring again.

I tuck her arms under the blanket, turn on the fan.

"There's a puke bowl right here if you need one," I say, knowing she can't hear me.

She is completely still, and for a moment I'm afraid that three pills is too many and that she will die in her sleep. But Millie has crawled onto her chest, watching carefully. I need her to live. I want to tell her that I'm okay with being part of this fight and that I'm okay being covered in dirt. This is my life and it's the life she gave me and that all the other Brayburns inherited before her ever since Julianna, and it's the life I want.

THIRTY-EIGHT
FINALLY

In spite of circumstance, it's nice to be here in the quiet in the low light. I used to be the loneliest person there was, but now I'm content to make some tea from the loose leaves in the pantry and eat a couple chocolates. Roxy is finally asleep, and Elle and Jason and Kidd should be back soon. I contemplate a bath, or adding my own entry to the journal. Finally I settle for a book on tinctures and the couch and a blanket. The sky has stormed over, and last time I checked it seemed there might actually be rain.

I must have fallen asleep, because when there's a thud upstairs, I startle awake. I am halfway to the landing when I hear the whirs and clicks coming from the bedroom. This could be the sound of Roxy coming to. This could be her story starting up around her, but as I have the thought I know that's not it, because we don't see into each other like that. The doors to the house were open. Hell, the windows were open.

And that's how Lyle must have gotten in.

I can smell him, feel him as I push the door back from where it's sitting open a foot.

Lyle is on the bed, hugging my mother so the tips of his fingers whiten against her black T-shirt. The smell of sick and sweat almost makes me gag. Roxy's eyes are open and pleading over his shoulder; the bowl I gave her to throw up in if she needed sits a few feet away, upside down, vomit sprayed across the floor. It must have made the thudding noise I heard. She doesn't speak or move, so I scan her quickly to see if she is hurt in some way. She shakes her head the slightest bit, and I remember this secret language of barely twitching fingers and head signals between us, one we developed to keep ourselves safe.

Millie is watching Lyle with her back up from the bottom of the bed, but she isn't hissing and she isn't moving. When Lyle hears me, he turns around so Roxy is next to him, though he doesn't let go of her, keeps one arm around her shoulders.

My eyes have to adjust to Lyle, like he's the sun. I haven't seen him in so long, I don't know if he's actually thinner. His carefully kept five o'clock shadow has grown into a beard, and he is now ruggedly handsome in a way I hadn't noticed before, as though the pain of losing his wife has made him fit for the pages of a magazine. His wiry body is what I do remember, his sandy hair falling across his forehead, his polo pulled across his chest. The smell of Listerine freezes me right into place, and as he stares at me, unreadable, I remember.

No, I don't remember. I'm there, the night we left, my head whacking into that wall. Right in the middle of my body being hurt, I thought about the crow that had been dancing outside my window that morning; about the sun rising up over the trees sending dappled light across my arm; about my mother always being a little hidden but me knowing her anyway; about the water covering me so I was safe. And I thought, *Not yet. Please, not yet.* It was the first time I'd ever wanted to live, that I'd even thought about it as a choice. Lyle was still over me, still yelling and shaking, and I went limp and I knew that whatever he did on the outside, inside I would be free. Then I looked him in the eye and I decided that I *was* free, that he couldn't keep me locked up for one second more.

And it was like Roxy heard me. It was like she saw.

Because that's when Roxy got between us.

"Stop it!" she yelled. "Stop! It's my fault! It's because of me!"

He punched her. He jammed his knee into her wherever he could. I screamed, but no sound came out. I couldn't move. He wasn't stopping. I looked for something to hit him with, but the only thing I could find was a fruit bowl, and when I aimed to slap it against his head, it hit his back and rolled to the floor. It didn't hurt him, but it did break the spell. For a moment I thought he would redouble his efforts and kill us both, but instead he smirked, grabbed his wallet and keys, and left us both there.

"Stay put," he said, as though he knew we would simply because he had ordered it so, and he closed the door behind him.

Now he's only considering me, his head slightly to one side, while I make calculations of how long it will take Elle to find her friend at the hospital and bring back whatever she was going to get, and about how sick Roxy actually is and about how long I was asleep.

"I didn't mean to scare you," he says. "You were sleeping on the couch."

Roxy is green again. She gags, and I reach for the bowl. I see how Lyle tenses when I flip it over and hand it to Roxy.

"She's sick," I say.

"I can see that," he says.

I want to pounce on him, to yell at him about coming in the house without knocking, because surely I would have heard that, but we're circling each other carefully.

"Elle went to get her something for Roxy's stomach." I hope this will put some fear into him, but instead he only looks at Roxy, concerned. "I don't know how many people she's bringing back with her."

"Why're you not feeling good?" he says, shaking Roxy awake.

Roxy moans.

"She's off all that stuff she's taking ever since she met you."

"It helped her," he says.

Helped her deal with living with you.

Roxy looks at me, then at Lyle beside her. She pats his chest. "Lyle, you can go home now. I'm fine."

He blanches, holds her tighter. "We can go now. We can go together."

"She's sick. Even if she wasn't—" I begin.

"Now." He sits up. "I don't want to hear this. I'm not going to listen. You're sixteen years old, and this is my wife. We've been married for thirteen years. I'm going to take her home. You stay here," he says reasonably. "You do whatever you want, but Roxy comes back with me."

"You're going to stick her in the truck and drive her away and that's going to be the end of it?"

"I can take care of her." It's like he's a little boy who wants his toy truck back even though he broke off all the wheels and slammed it into pieces.

"Did you ask her?" I say.

"What?" He scrunches his nose like I've said something that smells funny.

"Did you ask Roxy what she wants to do?"

Lyle looks at her in her boxer shorts and T-shirt, no makeup, hair in two short pigtails, ten pounds lighter than she was when we got here. He crouches down in front of her, cups her cheeks with his hands, and peers deeply into her glassy eyes. "What have you done to her?" Lyle says to me. "You and that sister of hers she never liked anyway. You ever think about anyone but yourself, Mayhem?"

"She's dope sick," I say. "She'll be okay in the morning, but you can't move her now."

"Roxy and I have something special. Our love is good. She

knows she can't handle things on her own. She'll burn herself right up. She needs someone to cool her down. Look at her. I don't know why you can't see that." He shakes his head as though he feels sorry about my ignorance.

I want him to let her go so I can get him out. But as he is before me, I see he won't take his hands off her until he has her in the truck, and he cannot be allowed to do that.

Roxy moans. "Lyle," she says, "no." She pushes at him feebly and he holds her yet more firmly, albeit as gently as he can while not letting her go. He wipes at her forehead with his free hand and then dries his palm against his jeans.

"She doesn't know what she wants." He says this more to her than to me. "She needs to come home."

Roxy pukes white pasty oatmeal that dribbles down her shirt. I rush forward to get the towel from the side of the bed, and Lyle yanks her toward him.

"Give it to me," he says. "I'll do it."

I hand him the towel and he wipes the sick from Roxy's chest. Her eyes flutter open, and for a moment they are clear. She strokes at his cheek and his eyes well up.

"Lyle," she says again, "no."

The fear leaks from my body until it is gone.

All around Lyle, honeycombs are beginning to form, and the click click clicking is getting louder, picking up its volume to a deafening wail.

THIRTY-NINE
A MURDER OF CROWS

"Put her down." I know I say it, but I can't hear my own voice.

I'm waiting for Lyle to let go of Roxy so I can get him out of there. I have to try real hard not to put my hands over my ears. This has not happened before. Lyle's mouth is moving and I can't hear him and I don't care, because what's in the honeycombs is me all over. There are some with Roxy, but mostly it's me with hands over my face, around my throat, being slapped, kicked, pummeled. The honeycombs chatter at me. They warn me. His face may be placid, but inside him, murder lies in wait.

"Stop," I shout, and the room goes silent, the honeycombs shrink, and Lyle narrows his eyes to lupine slits.

"What'd you say?"

"I said, put her down." I can hear myself now, and without the whirring, the room comes back into proper focus.

He smiles and clutches Roxy more tightly. "See, honey," he says to her as she groans and rests her head on his shoulder again, "I told you to stick with me. I told you Mayhem needs a firm hand. Now look at her. All sass."

He takes his time putting his attention back on me. I am steeling myself. I know that curl of his lip and the way his muscles tense. Lyle is gearing up for a fight. Thing is, I know something he doesn't know. I can see his secrets, but he can't see mine. So I smile, too.

He stands and wraps Roxy's arm around his neck, then scoops her up before I can get to him. "I'll be back."

He moves so quickly and with so much grace that he is past me in a shot, hauling Roxy down the stairs, not looking back. By the time I get outside, Roxy is sitting up in the truck, shaking her head, looking more awake though with some effort. He is kneeling down beside her, holding on to her legs as she squirms. The trees rustle with birds, their leaves nearly black with feathers.

"Hey!" I shout.

Lyle and Roxy both turn to me. Lyle swipes a hand through his hair. "Little bitch," he says, "would you shut the fuck up? I'm trying to have a conversation with my wife, and you keep on interrupting." He is walking smoothly toward me, face reddening, veins beginning to pop.

Ah, there he is. There's the Lyle I know and hate.

"You just *never* know when to say when. Always getting into my business. Always something to say. Like you have the *least* idea what your mother needs. You don't know. You don't know a thing."

I back into the house, through the doorway. Spittle pools in the corners of his mouth in a frothy white, the Listerine smell not covering the sepsis beneath it.

Lyle places a hand on his hip and looks upward. "Lord," he says, "please help me to assist Mayhem in seeing her wicked ways." He nods as though he's heard something and then shakes his head just a bit and inches in a couple steps more. "Spare the rod and spoil the child."

He reaches for me, and I think maybe I'll still be meek and fearful, that he'll still be able to petrify me into submission. The bowl will still bounce off of him. I will have no effect. But then I feel it. The pull. Though I cannot bear him, I want to hold him. I hug him.

"What—" he says.

I clutch tightly. He struggles, but he can't escape me. He can't move his arms. He yelps, then swiftly backs me into the wall, slamming me the way he did before, my spine colliding over and over again. It doesn't hurt. Nothing hurts. The slamming grows weaker, and his mouth hangs open and his eyes are full of questions because I am not doing this the nice gentle way. I am doing this to hurt. And then hands are prying my arms away from him. Voices are whispering in my ear.

No, May. No, honey. Not this. Not now.

I come to, as if from a dream. My mother is there. Elle is there. Jason and Kidd are close behind. Only Elle and my mother speak. Elle is sparking. My mother is pushing to be here from a great distance, but some of the dullness has been purged and parts of her shine.

They are between Lyle and me. My mother leans into Elle. Jason and Kidd are to the side now.

"What in hellfire was that?" Lyle says incredulously. He tries to stand up tall, but he's wounded somewhere, everywhere maybe.

"Get out, Lyle," Roxy says. She clears her throat. She struggles to stand upright, to keep her eyes open. "Get out."

"You want me here."

"I don't."

"You love me."

"I *don't*," she says, and she shoves him in the chest. Hard.

He stumbles back a few steps.

"Stop telling me what I want," Roxy says.

He tries to grab for her.

Elle gives him another shove. "She said get out."

He lunges at her, and she easily casts him aside so he falls on his hip.

"Shit," he says, "that hurt."

"And that's as good as it's going to get, bully," Elle says.

Lyle stands and wipes himself off, takes one step toward the three of us, then reconsiders. The squawking from the trees gets louder.

"What is this place?" he says, dazed.

Elle smiles. "Why, Lyle," she says, "this is Brayburn Farm."

She makes a slight gesture with her hand, and that's when the birds come. They descend in a great cloud. I didn't realize just how many there were until they swarm Lyle, pecking, wings beating. Crows hold a grudge, and they know a piece of garbage when they see one.

"And stay the fuck out!" Roxy screams, before falling to the floor.

We shut the door and leave him to the birds in favor of tending to Roxy. She is crying. I haven't ever heard her cry like that before, great sobs from her dark place. Millie hops into her lap and licks at Roxy's hands while Elle strokes her hair.

Jason puts his arms around me. "You okay?" he says.

"Okay is overrated," I say.

We open the door a little while later. Lyle and his truck are gone. He's left a trail of blood behind him. Maybe he will drive himself to a hospital. Maybe to the police. It won't matter around here. We do things the Santa Maria way. He's better off driving himself right on out of town.

FORTY
AND THEN CAME THE RAIN

I don't know why people always want to put a blanket on a person after trauma, but they do. That's how I end up on the bench overlooking the valley, sitting between my mom and Elle, blanket on our heads while the rain drizzles over us, the first rain since we've been here, a welcome break from the sun. We have been overheating for weeks, so we don't put on sweaters or anything. We let the rain fall around us and the wind whip at us a little and all we say is yes and I stick my tongue out to catch some. And the birds sit around us and everything is especially green, and when the crow with the brown on his beak perches on my shoulder again, which is his habit now, I say, *I think I'll name you George.* I don't know why except it sounds royal, like a king, and in the light George is deep purple, and since purple is a royal color, it suits him.

When I say it he makes a series of cooing noises and bobbles back and forth on his feet, so I am almost sure he likes it.

Roxy is gorgeously worn, and light is beginning to show around her, in weak wisps. But they are there. Her fever is gone, sleep meds worn off, and she, like Elle and me, is wiped out, wiped clean. She won't stop fussing at me, rubbing my back, squeezing my shoulders, checking my face for expression, then settling her head onto her sister's shoulder and going quiet again, knees tucked up under her chin.

The air feels good up here on the hill. Clean. Like the rain is washing everything away and we are all at bare bones.

Footsteps crunch behind us. "Ladies," Boner says.

Roxy untangles herself from us and wraps her arms around his waist. She called him, of course, after Lyle left and she had taken a long shower and gotten some more, less feverish rest. She won't be completely herself for days, and I can't wait to see her for the very first time.

"Hey, Bone."

"Hey, Rox." He kisses her on the forehead and then looks to me reflexively.

It doesn't make me angry.

He hugs Roxy close. "I'm sorry I wasn't here."

"No," she says. "We handled it."

He turns his mouth up on one side. "I'm sure you did." He hesitates.

"Bone," Elle says, "please spit it out."

"I have news," he says.

"Duh," Elle says.

"Lyle showed up at the hospital. He's got a couple broken ribs, about a million cuts on him, and he's . . . uh . . ."

"What?" we all say.

". . . missing an ear."

Elle lets out a joyful laugh.

"He's been babbling about murderous birds."

George does his little dance on my shoulder again, and Boner looks at him nervously.

"He would like to press charges."

"Good luck with that," Elle says. "He came here and attacked—"

Boner clears his throat. "Not against you. Against the birds."

"Really?" Roxy says. "Shit. He's lost his mind."

"One can only hope," Elle says.

"He's going to be okay. He called his mother, so . . . ah . . . she'll be here soon to get him. I think we'll leave it at that. It's been years since animals have been put on trial."

"Can you imagine Grandmother in Santa Maria?" Roxy says. "She's going to burst into flames at the county line."

"Your lips to God's ear," I say, repeating something Grandmother used to say often.

"Amen," Roxy says.

Elle wraps the blanket around her shoulders. "I might just have to sneak down to the hospital and take a peek."

"I'm going to strongly suggest you all keep your distance," Boner says. "Unless you want to press charges yourselves, but, uh, frankly, I met Lyle."

"Met?"

"Well, actually I went down there to let him know if he ever comes back here what will be waiting for him, but it turns out he's an incoherent mess."

Elle nods, satisfied.

Boner takes a step closer to me. "Mayhem?"

"Yes?"

"I want you to know that I would never hurt you or your mother, ever, no matter the circumstances. I was a real prick about that report when you first got here, and I am sorry."

I look up at Boner, his cargo shorts and button-down shirt, his socks pulled up midcalf, rain dripping down his nose and chin. He's a dumbass with poor fashion sense, and that makes me like him.

I ask for his secrets again, and this time they rise. All he has in his beckoning honeycombs are pictures of his unwavering, lifelong love for my mother.

"I know," I say.

"Oh, and, uh, looks like a dead end with the Sand Snatcher thing. No clues anywhere. No sign of who put him in that chair. Nasty business. Good riddance to bad rubbish, right?"

He puts his hands in his pockets and leans back on his heels and Roxy kisses him on the cheek and Elle makes a disgusted sound and George caws and that is enough.

FORTY-ONE
NEVE

I find Neve in the tunnel under the boardwalk like I knew I would. She doesn't have anywhere else to go, except maybe the hideout, but that is Brayburn territory. She's in her bikini lying right against the curve, hair splayed out around her, so skinny I can see her ribs with that stupid dagger I thought was so cool running down her arm. She's shaking. I sit down next to her and put my hand on her shoulder. She comes awake feral and ready to fight, scoots herself into a corner so I put my hands up until her eyes clear and settle. Around her, holes in light, a halo like Swiss cheese.

Her chest rises and falls.

"Where did the boys go?" I ask.

"I kicked them out," she says. "They're gone."

"Why?"

"Because I'm sick of them," she says, and it echoes all around us. "I'm sick of everything."

She collapses down again and stares at me. Her lips are cracked and bleeding. Because no water and no boys.

"I came to tell you I'm sorry," I try. I'm half-braced for her to attack me, but I'm not sure she could even if she wanted to.

"The way you looked at me." She shakes her head. "I'm not a monster. I'm not."

"I know," I say.

She waits, arms around her legs, still breathing hard.

"I took Elle away from you," I say. "I didn't mean to, but it doesn't matter. I know I took Jason, too."

Her eyes fill up.

"I should have asked you if it was okay."

She shakes her head like she doesn't want to hear what I have to say.

"Take me," she says, and puts her arms out to me.

"Home?"

She shakes her head. "I have to get out of here. I want to go. I have to leave Santa Maria."

"Come back to the farm."

She shakes her head again, more vigorously. "I'm done. I can't go back there. I have to be done."

"Where do you want me to take you, then?"

What Jason told me. About her dumpster diving. She can't go back to that.

"I'm going to die," she says. "I don't want to."

"You won't. That's what I was trying to tell you last night." I think for a second, and then it comes to me. "I know what to do."

FORTY-TWO
THE WEIGHT OF US

Jason and Kidd are on a bench outside We've Got Issues, the comic-book store, just before dark, chewing on granola bars, hanging with the Gecko brothers. It's been almost twenty-four hours since Lyle, and the storm has cleared up and it honestly feels more like one thousand years and that's how old I feel, too, but also like a baby. Also like all my skin is new.

"Hi, Gecko brothers," I say.

"What happened to you?" Jason says. "You left the house." He colors up. "I worried."

"He was freaking out," Kidd says, showing me her hands wide apart. "This much!"

"Thanks, Kidd," Jason says.

"I had to take care of something," I say.

Jason nods, and I love him for accepting things.

Neve is with Marcy now. Marcy has been through this. She can help Neve. And then she will help Neve get out of town, too. She made a lot of phone calls to friends in Oregon, and it looks like Neve has somewhere to stay if she wants. For right now, Neve wants to be away from all of us, and that's okay. She still managed to give me a short lecture about being true to myself before I left her at VHYes.

"'What happened to you' is right," the Gecko brother wearing the beret says. "You have bruises all over. Look like shit."

The smell of Joop and Drakkar Noir rises from around them.

"Fighting the good fight," I say.

"I think you look all right," Jason says.

"You seen any vampires around tonight?" Beret asks. "They're out in full force, man. Must be the moon."

"Vampires aren't real." I smile at Jason, who shakes his head, and sit beside them.

"Oh, really?" Beret opens his jacket to reveal a huge strand of garlic.

Bandana pulls a cross from under his shirt. "You of all people should know better," he says.

"What's that supposed to mean?" I ask.

"It means what it means."

"Cool," I say.

Bandana hands me a comic with murderous bloodsuckers on the cover.

"One thing I never could stomach about Santa Maria," Beret says, "all the goddamn vampires."

They fold their arms across their chests.

"We'll keep on keeping this boardwalk shithead-free," Beret says, saluting. "As we must."

"Conspiracy," Bandana adds. "Man, do you know about MK-Ultra? It's vast, bro, vast."

"You two take care," Jason says, shaking their hands, "and thanks for the snacks."

He puts out his elbow and I hook in my arm. There's so much we have to talk about. If he wants to be free and wants to take Kidd with him, maybe he should go with Neve. Or he could go somewhere else. Or he could stay and get off the water.

But for now Kidd runs down the boardwalk, fast but not so fast that she'll scare people, and then Jason and I look at each other and we are running, too, cutting out toward the water, where my father died and I was reborn and where every Brayburn woman has ended up. We break sand with our feet and we are laughing and worshiping with our laughter and light peels off of us and we strip down to our underwear and we leap into the water.

And we are weightless.

Dear Reader,

Like Mayhem, I experienced a period of time when my life was extremely unstable. I can still remember what it was like to be shaken so hard I thought my head would come off, to watch the room vibrate, to feel unsafe in my own home, to never know what was coming around the next corner. I wanted to run. I *always* wanted to run.

I ran to friends, but also movies and books, and although girls were more passively portrayed in movies like *The Lost Boys* back then, that feeling of teenagers prowling the night, taking out bad people, being unbeatable . . . that got me through it.

I guess that's what I tried to do here. I wanted girls who feel powerless to be able to imagine themselves invincible. And yes, I used a rape as the seed for that fierce lineage, not without thought. For me, there is nothing worse, and I like to think great power can rise up as a result of a devastating trespass.

Please know I took none of this lightly. Writing this now, my heart is beating hard and my throat is dry. This is the first time I not only really looked at my own past, the pain of loss, the pain of the loss of trust that comes when someone puts hands on you without permission, the pain of people dying, the shock of suicide, and put all of it to paper in a way that made me feel victorious, strong, and warrior-like. It is also terrifying.

I know I'm not the only one who had a scary childhood, and I know I'm not the only one who clings to stories as salve to smooth over burnt skin. I am so sick of girls and women being hurt. This was my way of taking my own vengeance and trying to access forgiveness.

Thank you for reading and for those of you who can relate, I see you and you are not alone.

Estelle Laure

ACKNOWLEDGMENTS

First, my husband, Chris, and my children, Bodhi and Lilu, for not loving me because of books, but in spite of them. You are all my feathers.

Emily van Beek, dearest and most beloved human and agent, you are the *only* voice I can hear through my own fear sometimes, and it is clear and beautiful and certain. For that, for your friendship, and for the fight you are in on my behalf, eternal gratitude.

As always, Folio Literary Management and everyone in it, thank you, but especially Melissa Sarver White.

Without my editor, Sara Goodman, this story would never have been. Thank you for the spark and the shared memories of California in a time that smells like coconuts and cherries, but also a little bit like a serial killer. I will never forget that first call; the crackle and spark. And thank you for loving Sax Man as much as I do.

Beyond Sara to the entire team at Wednesday Books: Jennie Conway, Sarah Bonamino, Alexis Neuville, India Cooper, Kerri Resnick, Elizabeth Catalano, Joy Gannon, and Nicole Rifkin. You have made me feel truly special and that my story is in the best of hands.

Anais Rumfelt, for all the birds and the friendship and your Anais spice. Your art was my special sauce.

Joy, and Tanya Who is Missed, for giving me the basis for a tight, breathless love. Laine, Shandra, and Sunny, for being sources of unending light. Sonya, Bonnie, Sam, Yvette, Jessie, Elisa, for being all the fire and reason and for making me laugh. Mindy, because you are my Mindy and there is only one. Cory, because kids and life and it all goes on. My students: I'm grateful to be your teacher as you are mine. My writer friends, thank you, especially the great Jeff Zentner, who has given me hope when I had none, more than once. Awesomeness, thanks for the awesomeness. NCW, you rule. We need community and you all give me one.

Booksellers, teachers, readers, and all lovers of books, my continued gratitude.

My nearest brother, Christophe, for roaming California with me when we were kids. This one's for you, and for the California of our childhood, a place that was certainly not without magic, both dark and light in equal measure.